# RAGE IN THE WILDERNESS

### KATHRYN LANE

Rage in the Wilderness is a work of fiction. Any references to historical events, business establishments, real people, or real places are used fictionally. Other names, characters, organizations, incidents, events, and locations are the product of the author's imagination, and any resemblance to actual events or locations or persons, living or dead, is entirely coincidental.

Copyright © 2024 by Kathryn Lane

All rights reserved. No part of this book may be used or reproduced in any manner, including electronic storage and retrieval systems, except by explicit written permission from the publisher. Brief passages excerpted for review purposes are excepted.

Paperback ISBN: 978-1-7354638-5-8

eBook ISBN: ISBN: 978-1-7354638-6-5

Printed and bound in the USA

Copyright fuels creativity, encourages diverse voices, and promotes free speech—creating a vibrant culture. Thank you for buying an authorized copy of this book. By supporting authors, you are making it possible for writers to continue publishing their works.

Tortuga Publishing, LLC

The Woodlands, Texas

bobhurt@tortuga-llc.com

Editor: Sandra A. Spicher

Cover Design: Tim Barber, Dissect Designs, tim@dissectdesigns.com

Interior Design: Danielle Hartman Acee, authorsassistant.com

Expert Readers: Pattie Hogan, David R. Stafseth, and Jorge Lane Terrazas

*For my husband, Bob*
*My son, Philip*
*And in loving memory of my mother, Frances*

# LIST OF CHARACTERS

(This list is provided for the reader's benefit. Characters are loosely listed in order of appearance. A few minor characters are omitted.)

**Nikki Garcia**—private investigator at Security Source, a firm in Miami, Florida
**Eduardo Duarte**—Nikki's husband, a Colombian citizen and medical doctor
**Floyd Webber**—Nikki's boss and owner of Security Source, a firm in Miami, Florida
**Charlotte**—office manager and computer geek at Security Source
**Andy Garcia**—Nikki's brother
**Cindy**—Andy's wife
**Olivia**—Andy and Cindy's one-year-old daughter
**Samuel Amaya**—Andy's friend who breeds and sells mules
**Domingo**—local Peñasco deputy
**Martin Oliveros**—helicopter pilot from Raton, New Mexico
**Ramón**—a mercenary
**Bembe**—leader of the mercenaries
**Celso**—a mercenary
**Fausto**—a mercenary

**Macario**—an injured mercenary
**Clive Underwood**—possibly an undercover CIA operative
**Daniel**—CIA pilot
**Steven**—CIA agent
**Frank**—FBI agent
**Apollo**—FBI driver
**Cougar**—NORAD employee
**Matt**—FBI agent
**Stan**—FBI pilot
**Neptune**—Sammy's German shepherd dog
**Jackpot, Gus, Sassy, and Galaxy**—a few of Sammy's mules

Teams

**Clive's team:** pilots Daniel and Stan, Steven, Frank, Matt, Apollo, plus other agents
**Bembe's team:** pilot, Celso, Ramon, Faus

# GLOSSARY

**ay, jijos**—colloquial phrase in Spanish used to show surprise.
**cabrón**—Spanish slang that loosely means *bastard* in English.
**caramba**—expresses surprise or anger in Spanish, depending on the context.
**chiquita**—endearing term.
**comemierda**—shit-eater.
**comepinga**—Cuban slang insult meaning that someone is "sucking dick."
**coño**—slang that refers to female genitalia. Cubans use it in the context of shit or damn.
**está muerto**—he's dead.
**están fritos si no se escapan**—you guys are toast unless you escape.
**hermano**—brother.
**levántate**—get up.
**mi amigo**—my friend.
**mira, que milagro**—look, what a miracle.
**mierda**—shit.
**ristra**—a garland of sun-dried chile peppers used either for cooking or to decorate doorways of private homes.
**vámonos**—let's go.

# PROLOGUE

Calculating that they had less than twenty-four hours to leave Mexico, he blew through caution lights and ignored the residential speed limits. Dodged potholes. He needed Ana and the twins out of the house in the next thirty minutes.

Skidding around the corner to catch sight of their home, he frowned. All the lights were on, including the ones in the boys' bedrooms. Ana did that when she was angry with him. He had no idea why she would be upset tonight, other than the late hour. But that would soon change. He was about to shock her with the news that they had to leave everything behind, even their names, if they were to escape with their lives.

He left the engine running and dashed up the few steps to the front door. It gaped open, crooked, its mangled deadbolt glinting in the light from the hall.

# ONE

## NIKKI

Nikki scanned her emails. Andy, her brother, planned to pick her and her husband up from the Taos airport the next morning. But wasn't a wildfire burning nearby? Should she and Eduardo still visit New Mexico?

She dialed Andy to ask about the wildfire.

"Did you know there's a fire northeast of Santa Fe?" she asked.

"Just a controlled burn," he explained. "Don't worry, the rangers will have it out in no time."

"If you say so," Nikki said.

"You're not going to let a little brush fire scare you away, are you?"

She laughed. "You work with hibernating bears. In dark caves, no less. Not sure I can trust your judgment. But Eduardo is eager to explore archaeological sites near you, so I don't dare cancel."

"Great," he said, "we're looking forward to our first family reunion."

After the call, Nikki shook her head and leaned back in her chair. A family reunion? Is that what Andy called it? It would just be Andy, his wife Cindy, and their one-year-old daughter, plus Nikki and Eduardo. Their only other family lived in Barcelona.

Maybe Andy had a point. Their parents had been killed in an auto accident when Nikki and Andy were teens. After that, they lived with their grandparents, who were gone now too. In high school, Andy and Nikki were very close. But when Nikki's son Robbie died at age twelve, Andy made himself scarce.

She sighed. His being there would not have changed anything, but Nikki missed having his shoulder to cry on. Losing Robbie put a strain on her marriage to Robbie's father, and the marriage did not survive. Nikki hoped this reunion would ease her resentment at Andy for failing to support her when she needed him.

To stop her sad thoughts, she walked down the hall to speak with Floyd, her boss. A former CIA operative, Floyd founded Security Source after he left the Agency. It now numbered ten investigators. Bright and geeky office manager Charlotte kept the operation running smoothly.

As usual, Floyd had a cup of coffee on his desk next to a short stack of paper files. A toothpick dispenser was a recent addition to his workspace. Since giving up cigarettes, Floyd had taken to chewing on a toothpick, sticking it between his lips.

He swiveled a computer monitor out of the way to look at Nikki as she took a chair in front of his desk. "What time do you leave tomorrow?"

"At seven a.m."

Floyd took a sip of coffee. "You're due for a good vacation. Take as much time as you want."

She fidgeted with her Mayan world tree pendant, a gift from Eduardo. "Eduardo starts his new job in two weeks, so we can't stay forever."

"Okay, but no work on this trip. Understand? Unless it's helping your brother with all those critters around the house."

Nikki laughed and explained the animals were in a barn.

"Including the bears?" Floyd raised his eyebrows.

"No, no! They're in caves. He only works with them during the winter to study their hibernation."

"Really?" Floyd took another sip of coffee. "Wouldn't they wake up when he prods them?"

"He claims it's safe. They wake up groggy. But his wife Cindy maintains they can be dangerous if aroused unexpectedly. Especially the females."

"Is his research for the Sleep Foundation?"

She shook her head. "The European Space Agency. Part of the funding comes from the Canadian government. In a few years, they hope to use hibernating astronauts to cross vast amounts of space, like from Earth to Mars. And beyond."

"Sounds complicated. You and Eduardo stay safe, you hear. And don't be calling the office to check in."

# TWO

## NIKKI

The commuter plane descended toward Taos Regional Airport, where Andy and his wife, Cindy, would pick Nikki and Eduardo up. She hoped this visit would rekindle her relationship with Andy after the distance that had developed between them in the last few years.

Nikki gazed out the window to the topography below. A deep and jagged gash cut through the desert. Ochre and crimson canyon walls glistened in the sunlight. A narrow ribbon of blue snaked along the canyon floor, following the tectonic chasm that runs from southern Colorado through the Taos Plateau. The gorge was carved by erosion, over millions of years, from basalt flows originating from the plateau's volcanic field. Each new basalt flow covered the area, creating colorful layers.

She touched Eduardo's hand. "Take a look at the Rio Grande Gorge below us."

He leaned toward the window. "Wow! It's a baby Grand Canyon."

The pilot banked for final approach, giving the passengers on Nikki's side of the plane a gorgeous view of the distant Colorado mountains.

Once they landed, two airport workers secured portable steps against the plane. When the pilot announced that passengers could disembark, she and Eduardo stepped into the aisle and followed fellow travelers ahead of them to the tarmac. The Sangre de Cristo mountains to the east of Taos were majestic, and the Taos Plateau stretched out for miles in the other direction.

Entering the small terminal, Nikki saw her sister-in-law waving at them. She took Eduardo's hand as they walked toward Cindy. A petite woman with short curly hair, Cindy had expressive blue eyes. She was working with patients suffering from sleep disorders when she met Andy in graduate school in California.

"Where's Andy?" Nikki asked, hugging her sister-in-law.

"At home taking care of Olivia."

Eduardo greeted Cindy and stepped away to grab the suitcase from baggage claim. He doubled back and followed the two women to the gray GMC crew cab.

Driving through Ranchos de Taos, Cindy pointed out the St. Francis of Assisi Mission Church. She explained it was one of the most photographed churches in New Mexico. "Georgia O'Keeffe painted it several times," she said.

"It looks like an adobe pyramid." Eduardo sounded unimpressed.

Miffed that Andy had failed to meet them, Nikki distracted herself in the back seat by texting Charlotte, the office manager, that after a long layover at the Dallas airport, they had arrived safely. She texted back, telling them to enjoy their vacation. Nikki turned her phone off and stared out the window at the desert landscape. It lacked the orange splashes of ocotillo flowers she'd expected this time of year.

The road climbed and spiraled into the mountains. The juniper, oak, spruce, and aspen at the higher elevations looked tinder dry.

Cindy drove through Peñasco, a tiny village nestled in a valley of the Sangre de Cristo mountains and turned onto a small road toward an adobe structure and nearby weather-beaten barn. "Here's paradise," Cindy said. "We've arrived." Another pickup, a spotless white Ford F-150 crew cab, was parked in front of the house.

"Dry chile ristras," Nikki said, admiring bright hanging peppers at the front door. A wooden rocking chair near the door looked inviting. "You've become New Mexican."

"Native born," Cindy said, joking, and then added, "I don't miss California at all. I hope we can stay here forever."

She parked near an old Chevy Silverado crew cab that was partially backed into the wide barn door. It seemed a crew cab was the only vehicle to own if you lived in New Mexico.

Andy, with little Olivia in his arms, welcomed his guests. Nikki gave them a hug and tried to take Olivia. The child pulled away and clung to her father's neck. Olivia looked a little like Robbie had when he was a toddler. A jolt of pain ran through her, missing her son, followed by anticipation of happy hours while getting to know her niece.

"She's shy of people," Andy said, stretching to embrace Eduardo. "It's a stage, and she gets over it. In a couple of hours, she'll follow you around like a puppy."

Behind Andy stood a tall, muscular man, a German shepherd at his side.

Andy introduced the man as his friend Sammy Amaya. "Ever since we found out Cindy was pregnant with Olivia," he said, "Sammy's been helping me check on the hibernating bears." Andy admitted it was dangerous work, especially dealing with the females and their cubs in late spring. No place for a pregnant woman.

"Now I only help with the sleep studies on hibernating chipmunks and kangaroo rats," Cindy said. "Honestly, I'm happy to be done with bears."

Andy handed Olivia to her mother and invited Nikki and Eduardo to the barn.

The dog approached Nikki.

"Wait, Neptune," Sammy ordered. "Down." The dog obeyed.

Inside the barn, Andy grabbed a large wooden case off a work bench and handed it to Nikki with a grin.

"Ay, jijos!" Nikki screamed. It was full of spiders. She almost dropped it but saw that the top was tightly sealed with a plastic mesh. "I thought you researched mammals. Why do you have these?"

"To prove spiders also experience the REM stages of sleep. Those are the jumping variety."

"If spiders go through REM, they must also have dreams," Eduardo said. "I wonder what Freud would think of that?"

Sammy laughed. "They must experience their repressed desires by dreaming."

"You guys are nuts." Nikki placed the crate back on the bench. "Sex is all you think about."

"Look who has the dirty mind," Eduardo said, winking at Nikki.

Andy showed them around the barn. The chipmunks, in plastic mezzanine cages, scurried up one floor and down another. Andy called each chipmunk by name, reading them off collars that included bar codes. The kangaroo rats hid in spaces provided for that purpose.

"What's that 'chuck, chuck, chuck' sound they're making?" Eduardo asked.

"That's how they communicate," Andy said. "When they feel threatened, they make a high-pitched 'wee' sound."

"They must be relaxed now. At least they won't be working out their fears in their dreams tonight," Eduardo said.

Nikki playfully punched his arm. "You'll be the one with nightmares if you keep this up."

From the back door of the house, Cindy called them to dinner. The bright lights inside the house made it look like a typical postcard of an adobe home in the scant evening light.

"Release," Sammy said to Neptune. The dog got up and walked with them toward the house.

"I'll show you the chips and 'roo rats in hibernation tomorrow," Andy said, pointing to what looked like a commercial refrigerator along the back wall.

# THREE
## NIKKI

Nikki admired the family-style dinner arranged on the rustic wood table. A vegetable casserole and an oven-proof dish of macaroni and cheese sat in the middle. A basket of bread and a large platter of pulled pork were at one end.

Sammy sat next to Nikki and ordered the dog to lie down. Facing them, Eduardo took a seat next to Cindy. Olivia sat on her father's knee at the head of the table, but before long, she climbed down to play with the German shepherd.

After everyone filled their plates, Nikki asked Sammy what he did when he was not helping with the bears.

"I raise mules at a nearby farm."

"How did you meet my brother?"

"I'd gone mule riding in Hermit Peak after reading about an Italian monk who used to live in one of its caves. I spotted a man, in a black overcoat, walk right out of the cave. Scared me to death. I thought he was a ghost." Sammy laughed. He served himself more pork and a slice of bread. "Andy stopped to talk with me. Told me about his bear research. Said he'd been checking on one of his sleeping subjects."

Eduardo suggested they find time to visit the peak and hike to the hermit's cave.

"As long as we won't encounter mama bears with cubs," Nikki said. Sammy laughed again. "It's not the season for hibernation."

"Do you sell your mules?" Eduardo asked.

"Of course. Want to buy one?" Sammy chuckled. "I'll deliver it to Florida."

"I'd like to learn more about mule sleep," Andy said, breaking in, "but Sammy sells them before I can set up a study. Ships most of them to Spain. They must be a status symbol over there."

"My husband is so passionate about sleep that he married me," Cindy said, glancing at Eduardo. "I'm his guinea pig. So far, he hasn't cured my sleepwalking, but we've been doing breathing exercises and I'm much better."

"Except when she's nervous," Andy added.

"You must be your husband's best subject," Eduardo said. "I'd be interested in those results."

"Your brother believes sleep cures whatever ails you," Sammy said to Nikki.

"You know Andy grew up on Star Trek reruns," Nikki said. "I don't remember hibernation on the Starship Enterprise, but he'd quote Spock regularly."

Andy scoffed. "I'm a Trekkie, all right. In this case, though, I'm working on the theory that our prehistoric ancestors, Neanderthals and early *Homo sapiens*, survived the Ice Age by hibernating in caves the way bears do today."

"That's an original idea," Eduardo said.

"Not really. Other scientists have reported similarities between the growth pattern found in bear skeletons to the bones of our ancient ancestors."

"I thought you were doing research for the future of space travel," Nikki said.

"Exactly," Andy said with a playful smile. "If early hominids relied on torpor to survive food scarcity, maybe astronauts can sleep their way to other galaxies."

"And avoid boredom," Sammy added.

"I wonder if a bear's unconscious mind works through the winter's repressed desires," Eduardo said with a wink at Nikki.

She balled up a little piece of bread and threw it at her husband, who caught it in midair.

Olivia crawled to her father and stretched her arms out, begging to be picked up. He took her and set her on his knee again. She slapped the table. Andy placed his hand momentarily on top of hers. She burst into giggles.

"What kind of mules do you breed?" Nikki asked, steering the conversation back to Sammy.

"I use Percheron and Belgian draft horse blood lines. Which makes for big mules. About seventeen hands."

"Why mules and not horses?"

"When the conquistadores explored the American mainland in the 1500s, they preferred mules. More sure-footed than horses. The males make for good cargo animals and the females are best for riding."

"Did you grow up on a mule ranch?" she asked.

Sammy looked down and shook his head. "I grew up in poverty in northern Mexico. I worked on a horse farm when I was a teen."

"You should see him," Andy said. "He rides like a rodeo champ."

Nikki asked when he moved to the US.

Nine years ago, crossing illegally, he told her. "Now I'm a citizen." He smiled broadly. "First, I was a gardener and worked as a handyman on the weekends. After saving money for a couple of years, I rented some land near here, bought a jack and five mares and started breeding them."

Andy interrupted to add that Sammy was a real success story. "He now owns the farm and uses top-quality mares to breed with his jacks."

"I don't own the mares, but I've found a fellow who has very docile female horses that we use to breed. He gets sixty percent of the baby mules."

"Why does he get more?"

"The babies stay with the mother for six months."

"You speak excellent English for someone who has only been here nine years," Nikki said.

Sammy laughed and thanked her, saying he had a natural ability with languages, though he still had an accent when he spoke English.

Cindy served dessert and Andy waved a spoonful of ice cream in front of Olivia. She puckered her mouth and turned away.

"I can load three mules and my dog into a trailer tomorrow and take you for a ride near Hermit Peak," Sammy offered. "It's in the piñon and juniper woodlands. Beautiful country. We'll unload the mules at Montezuma Hot Springs."

Eduardo glanced at Nikki.

She nodded. "That sounds fine."

"I hate to rain on your parade, but my sister is afraid of fires. They still haven't put that blaze out," Andy said, "but you can ride around Montezuma and see the peak."

"Montezuma," Nikki repeated. "Shouldn't it be Moctezuma?"

"Right," Andy said, "but here it's called Montezuma."

Sammy asked if they wanted to ride despite the fire.

Eduardo glanced at Nikki again. She gave him a thumbs-up.

"I'll bring you my book on the Italian monk," Sammy said.

Olivia grabbed her father's empty spoon and banged it against the table. Nikki glanced at her niece and waved. To her surprise, Olivia waved back. The child slid off her father's knee, crawled to Nikki, and pulled herself up by holding onto Nikki's leg. She made baby sounds and repeated one that sounded like *up*. Delighted that the curly-headed child was warming up to her, Nikki helped Olivia into her lap.

Sammy thanked Cindy for dinner. She handed him a container with leftover pork to make sandwiches for their excursion the next day. He called Neptune, but Cindy asked him to leave the dog with them overnight.

"You know how much Olivia loves him."

He nodded and told everyone he'd arrive at nine the next morning. "We'll hit the road by nine-fifteen."

# FOUR

## NIKKI

In the guest quarters, Nikki showered and put on a skimpy black negligee. Eduardo was in bed, leaning against the headboard, reading a novel.

"Ahh, my darling has interesting sleep gear on," he said, putting the book on the nightstand. "No torpor for us tonight."

She crawled in next to him, resting her head on his shoulder. "Something about Sammy's personal story doesn't make sense to me. For a presumably uneducated man who came from poverty in Mexico, entered the US illegally, and worked as a gardener and handyman, he's very well read."

"I love it when you talk sexy," Eduardo teased.

The investigator in her could not shake off her skepticism. She suspected the man harbored deep secrets. She only hoped it would not endanger her brother and his family. She resolved to find out more about Sammy's background, but that could wait until tomorrow. Nikki would ask Charlotte to investigate him. After all, that was Charlotte's specialty—uncovering secrets online. What would the firm do without her research skills?

"You just wait and see," she murmured, snuggling closer and touching her husband.

Eduardo moaned with pleasure.

# FIVE

## EDUARDO

Eduardo woke to total darkness when the alarm in the next room went off. He glanced at the clock on the nightstand. *We're on vacation. Who the hell would wake us up at four in the morning?* Recalling that he was a guest at his brother-in-law's home, he got up, dressed without waking Nikki, and joined Andy in the kitchen.

"You can help me in the barn if you want to see the animals in our refrigerated incubator."

"Refrigerated incubator?" Eduardo repeated.

"Follow me."

Intrigued, he trailed his brother-in-law to the barn.

"We've adapted it for our purposes. It's equipped with air, and we put in food for the chipmunks." Andy opened a large compartment that was set up with dirt, rocks, dry leaves, and a section that resembled frozen snow. He pointed at the ice. "That's where they get the water they need when they wake up for brief spurts."

Eduardo glanced inside. "What if something goes wrong, like a power outage?"

"A generator comes on automatically. Trust me, we take good care of our laboratory animals. A veterinarian specializing in small mammals comes by once a month to check on them."

Eduardo watched Andy work quietly with three sleeping chipmunks. Without touching them, he scanned the codes and temperature readings from their collars with a handheld scanner and uploaded the information to a computer. He swept up the feces inside the cages with a small brush like the ones Eduardo had seen archaeologists use at excavation sites. Andy checked the settings on the refrigerated unit and closed it. He stepped to the cages of the non-hibernating rodents and refilled their food and water. Finished, he used a generous amount of hand sanitizer and Eduardo did the same.

The men returned to the kitchen and refilled their coffee cups. Eduardo sat at the table and watched Cindy comb Olivia's hair. Nikki was preparing breakfast. Andy popped bread into the toaster and got plates and utensils ready.

Eduardo glanced at his watch. "It took almost three hours to work with the chips and 'roos, as you call them. Is that your normal routine?"

Andy nodded. "Yep, seven days a week."

"We have chipmunks and kangaroo rats and the odd specimens, like spiders," Cindy said, putting her daughter down. "We work the barn critters together, except when Andy works with the bears, and then I handle everything here. I love it."

Olivia walked toward the sleeping Neptune, falling on her way across the room. Her cries awakened the dog, who went to the next room.

"Who takes care of the animals when you go on vacation?" Eduardo asked.

"This is paradise," Cindy said, smiling. "Why would we want to leave home?"

"So that's why you didn't come to our wedding. Barcelona couldn't compete with Peñasco." Nikki couldn't help the hint of sarcasm in her tone.

"That was shortly before Olivia was born," Andy said, buttering the toast. "Don't you remember?"

"Of course, I'm only teasing."

Eduardo glanced at Nikki. Her lips tightened and her brow furrowed. She must be feeling that stab of pain again.

Andy asked Eduardo when his job in Miami would start.

"In two weeks. They're installing equipment and office furniture in a new wing of the hospital where my office will be. I've been working from home."

Cindy wanted to know how a doctor could do that.

"Reviewing case files for special-needs patients, verifying that their treatments are appropriate and cost effective."

"Makes sense," she said, refilling coffee cups.

Andy helped Nikki serve, and they all sat down to a breakfast of scrambled eggs, sausage, and toast.

# SIX

## EDUARDO

From the kitchen window, Eduardo saw Sammy climb out of his crew cab at precisely nine o'clock. Neptune barked and ran for the door, tail wagging.

Sammy, wearing a cowboy hat, bounced into the kitchen. "Your tour guide is here," he said, tipping his hat in greeting. He patted Neptune's head.

He handed Eduardo a book about Giovanni Maria de Agostini, the Hermit Peak monk. Turning to Cindy, he laid a bag of cucumbers, zucchini, and kale on the table. "For you. Picked from my greenhouse this morning."

Eduardo flipped through the book. "I see the hermit was a world traveler. Isn't that a paradox?"

Sammy laughed. "Yeah, I guess. He loved to explore, help people, and yet he was apparently very devout. He'd hang out in the cave to meditate."

At the index, Eduardo whistled. "Looks like Brother Giovanni traveled all over the Americas, from Argentina to Canada. In the nineteenth century, no less." Putting the book down, he put his fedora on. He and Nikki had bought matching hats for this trip.

Sammy led them to the trailer hitched to his immaculate white crew cab. He called for Neptune to follow.

The wind ripped Nikki's fedora off and tousled her hair. She ran after the hat and put it firmly back on.

The trailer had six diagonal stalls. A seventh one could be set up down the middle. Three stalls held the mules they would use today. Sammy named the main parts of the trailer, pointing to the loading door at the rear and the escape doors at the front, which served to protect the caretaker from angry mules. "It can save a person's life."

"They're gorgeous. Their coats are so shiny," Nikki said, keeping her hand on her hat to prevent it from blowing off again. "Which one am I riding?"

"Jackpot in the middle compartment. Eduardo will get Gus, the one up front. I'm kind of fond of Sassy, so she'll be mine."

"Male mules for us?" Nikki asked, raising an eyebrow. "You said last night that females make better mounts."

Eduardo laughed.

Sammy looked at them sheepishly. "I only have one female. You guys decide who will ride Sassy."

"Thanks, but I'll keep Jackpot," she said.

Eduardo nodded. "Gus looks like a great mule for me."

# SEVEN

## SAMMY

On the drive to Montezuma, Sammy pointed out facts about the terrain and vegetation. Eduardo listened and asked questions.

In the backseat, Neptune's head rested in Nikki's lap. Sammy could see her in the rearview mirror poking away at her phone. Probably writing an email.

Over an hour later, Sammy followed an almost impassable back road to the thermal springs. "This place is full of legends."

"Like the monk?" Nikki asked.

"He was for real," Sammy said, "but the local people believe a legend that the infant Montezuma was raised at the springs. When the time came for him to lead his people, a flock of eagles carried him to Tenochtitlán in the historic center of today's Mexico City."

Neptune sat up, looking out the window. He must have sensed they were stopping.

"We'll park here, saddle up, and take a nice, easy ride before stopping for lunch. The cave where the monk lived isn't far. Then we'll double back to see the springs."

Nikki helped unload the mules and tie their bridles to a cross bar on the trailer. She and Eduardo helped themselves to pads and saddles stored in a covered compartment at the front of the trailer, between the escape doors on each side. Its top and sides had dime-sized holes drilled in them.

"I've carried some of your brother's lab animals in that compartment. Those holes let them breathe."

The wind ripped Nikki's fedora off again and Sammy ran after it. Then he rifled through the glovebox to find a rubber band behind his Smith & Wesson. He took it to her. "If you put your hair up, maybe it'll keep your hat on."

Nikki gathered her hair into a bun and put the fedora back on. Then she put a saddle blanket on Jackpot. Sammy helped her with the saddle. Jackpot moved away, rebelling. Sammy positioned a strap over the mule's hindquarters and finished cinching him.

Nikki stepped aside and snapped a couple of pictures. Sammy covered his face.

"Coño, don't take photos of me," he said. "I hate to see how old I'm getting."

"You guys are only in the background," she said. "I wanted to catch Jackpot."

The three of them mounted their mules and took off, Sammy in the lead and Neptune walking beside Sassy. The cawing of crows and the chirps and trills of other birds sounded over the wind.

After riding for some time, they smelled smoke.

"Should we turn back?" Nikki sounded worried.

Sammy turned in the saddle to face her. "It's the wind. I won't lead us into danger." He led them through the woods and stopped, dismounting after they crossed a creek carrying a trickle of water. Eduardo and Nikki followed his lead and got off their mules. "We'll eat lunch here so the mules can drink."

"Really?" Eduardo eyed the almost dry creek bed.

"When they're thirsty, they'll manage some." Sammy pulled a sack from a saddle bag near Sassy's rump. He handed sandwiches and a plastic bag full of celery and carrot sticks to Eduardo. "I grow the veggies in my greenhouse."

He pulled a pair of binoculars from another saddlebag and handed them to Nikki.

"I'm starving," Nikki said. She hung the field glasses around Eduardo's neck and reached for the food instead. She took a big bite of a sandwich made with last night's leftover pork. "Aww, this is delicious."

Sammy was in no hurry to eat. Instead, he told them about the trail they could take to get a better view of the peak. "If you think that's too long, we can cut out the Porvenir Loop. That takes us halfway up the side of Hermit Peak. It's the best part of the trip, but if you'd feel safer, we can stay in the valley and find a clearing for visibility."

"The valley sounds good to me. Let's keep away from the fire." Nikki looked nervous.

She offered a stick of gum to Sammy when they were done. Then she gave the packet to Eduardo, telling him to keep it.

They remounted the mules and continued their journey. Sassy had a mind of her own and turned back toward the trailer.

Sammy pulled on the reins harder until she headed in the direction he wanted. Just down the road, Neptune started barking. Sassy balked and Sammy could not get her to budge.

Six coyotes appeared on the road in front of them.

# EIGHT

## NIKKI

The coyotes halted and stared back at the mules and riders. Neptune whimpered, but Sammy quieted him. Nikki snapped photos of the reddish-gray animals, managing to include the men in the frame. When she saw that Sammy noticed, she tucked the phone away.

After the coyotes ran into the woods, Sammy had to coax Sassy to move again. She seemed reluctant to walk the trail.

The dry, howling wind chapped Nikki's face. They were all getting windburn. Feeling a more urgent concern, she asked the guys to wait while she ducked behind some bushes.

Once she had privacy, she pulled down her jeans and squatted. Catching sight of movement in the bushes next to her, she saw that Neptune had followed her. She shooed him away.

He took off, barking. She stood and zipped her pants. The mules brayed and Sammy yelled at them. Next he hollered for Neptune to come back.

"Nikki, get back here," Eduardo cried out.

Gripped with fear, she rushed back. Sammy had dismounted and was holding the reins to Sassy and Jackpot. Clearly panicked, they were thrusting and swinging their heads.

Eduardo was also dismounted, keeping the reins short and tight. His mule's nostrils flared, and he jerked his head and tail into the air.

"A mother bear and her cubs," Eduardo said.

Trembling, Nikki looked around. She saw nothing but knew that a mother bear would fight off any threat to her cubs.

Neptune returned. He sniffed the ground and looked up into the woods. Sammy ordered his dog to sit.

The mules settled down.

Nikki inhaled and exhaled slowly as she watched Sammy study the terrain.

"With this wind, the fire will spread faster," he said. "The clearing is about ten minutes from here. Then we'll head back."

Nikki looked around nervously. She straightened her hat and glanced at her husband.

"It's your call, my love," Eduardo said.

The trees blocked her view. "If it's safe to see the peak from the clearing, let's do that. It's what we came for. Then we can go back."

Sammy mounted Sassy.

As Eduardo helped her get back on Jackpot, Nikki caught sight of something strapped on Sammy's boot, protruding from under his pant leg. A knife, perhaps. Or a gun?

They followed Sammy through the forested area. The smoke smelled stronger, and Nikki imagined the fire racing toward them. Her hand gripped the bridle and her legs tightened. Jackpot's ears flared back, and his head rose higher. He must be detecting her unease. She tried to relax. Then she saw a small meadow through the few remaining trees.

Sammy stopped at the edge of the clearing and pointed at Hermit Peak.

"The whole mountain is on fire!" Eduardo's voice sounded higher than usual.

Sammy took his hat off. "Holy shit! The fire's going straight up the mountainside!"

"Mountainside, hell!" Nikki was already turning her mule. "This wind is blowing it right at us."

Eduardo gripped the reins. "Let's get out of here."

# NINE

## SAMMY

Sammy broke into a sweat, worried about the fire's direction and the swiftness of its spread. The mules seemed as anxious to get back to the truck as their riders. The wind howled and the smoke grew more intense. Sassy, in the lead, veered right and broke into a gallop with Neptune at her heels. The other two mounts followed her. Sammy slowed Sassy to a trot, knowing the two males would follow.

Sassy's ears bent close to the side of her head. On their left, flames leaped from one burning tree to the next one as if propelled by an invisible flamethrower. A red glow reflected in the smoke above the tree line. White light from the fire spread along the ground, broken only by the trunks of intact trees.

Sammy could feel the fire's heat. It matched his shame for putting his guests in danger. He stopped Sassy, swiveled around in his saddle to face them, and yelled instructions to gallop again. "Watch for low tree limbs and stay with me. If the fire encircles us, we'll get down and dig a pit to hunker down in." He sat straight in the saddle again and urged his mount to pick up the pace.

As they fled, Sammy slowed Sassy to a trot for brief periods. Then he loosened the reins and let her take off again. After a hair-raising half hour, the fire was behind them, and he slowed her again.

Riding their mules right up to the trailer, the three riders dismounted. Eduardo and Nikki followed Sammy's lead and tied their mules' reins to a metal bar. Sammy jumped onto the bed of the trailer and opened the compartment behind the cab. He filled two buckets of water from a plastic barrel and took out three feed bags.

Nikki and Eduardo wasted no time removing the saddles.

When Nikki lifted the saddle pad, she gasped at how badly her mule was sweating. "Oh, Jackpot, I'm so sorry." She used her hand to rub his back. "Water is on the way. And maybe oats too."

The mules closed in on the water. Sassy established her status by side-kicking Gus away from one of the buckets, and he, in turn, pushed Jackpot's head out of the way to get a drink. When Sammy considered they had drunk enough water, he took the buckets away, getting a side kick from Sassy, still intent on slaking her thirst. Sammy slapped Sassy to remind her he was the one in charge.

With Eduardo's help, Sammy loaded them into their stalls and strapped on feed bags, which immediately calmed the animals.

The three people and the dog jumped in the crew cab and Sammy drove fast, bumping over the road back to State Highway 518.

Sammy apologized that they never made it to the hot springs. "I'll bring you next time you visit."

Eduardo whistled when he saw a patrol car. "Looks like the wildfire has brought out the law."

"Guess you're right." Sammy stopped at the entrance to the state road.

A sheriff's deputy walked over. He requested Sammy's driver's license and pickup registration in a gruff voice. "Are you aware this area is under evacuation orders?"

Sammy, noticing the man's name tag, replied that he would not have driven in if he'd known.

"What were you doing in there?"

"We were on our way to see the cave where the hermit lived. But the fire was moving so quickly, we turned back."

"When did you go in?"

"Around ten this morning."

"If you'd used the road, the one that goes to Montezuma, you would have been stopped. Evacuation is in effect since ten today." The deputy told them they were free to leave but to check the state's online evacuation system. "Areas around Peñasco are safe. Be cautious, Mr. San—"

Interrupting the deputy, Sammy thanked him and drove onto the highway.

# TEN

## NIKKI

Nikki used her phone to search for the website the deputy suggested. She read aloud. "As of ten a.m., the governor's office has declared the Hermit Peak and Calf Canyon fires in the Pecos Wilderness of the Santa Fe National Forest a state of emergency. The fires have merged. The current dry conditions and high winds are forcing the evacuation of surrounding areas."

She scrolled through more websites and news reports, reading snippets. She also texted her photos of Sammy to Charlotte.

"Call your brother," Eduardo suggested, "and see what news he has. Is he planning to evacuate?"

"Peñasco should be fine," Sammy said, repeating the deputy's claim.

Cindy answered and Nikki told her she was on speaker.

"I was just about to text you. We're not on evacuation notice, but we've decided to leave. Even rushing, it'll take time to get all the laboratory animals ready. Andy is awakening the hibernating ones since we can't move the incubator."

"Where will you go?"

Cindy responded that she was searching for houses with barns or warehouses. "You and Eduardo should still visit Chaco Canyon. It's far from the fire."

Eduardo suggested that he and Nikki could help them pack, but Cindy did not want to hear about any changes to their vacation plans.

"We'll talk about it when we get there," Nikki said. "After we drop off the mules at Sammy's place."

# ELEVEN

## EDUARDO

"Be reasonable," Eduardo told Andy. "Just how much do you think Nikki and I will enjoy Chaco Canyon knowing that fires are threatening you? We're staying to help you. No arguments."

"Plus, he can put his medical training to use and pack the scientific equipment," Nikki said, smiling at her husband.

Sammy laughed out loud.

"You haven't laughed all day," Nikki said, glancing at Sammy.

"The wind took it all out of me," he responded.

Andy thanked Eduardo. "With your help, we can get out of here early tomorrow morning. The place Cindy found is a few miles from Taos Ski Valley. It should put enough distance between us and the fires. Being so close to a world-class resort will have its advantages. The state will do everything it can to protect it."

Turning to Sammy, Andy pointed out that his ranch was closer to the fire. "The place Cindy rented has enough room for you and the mules."

"I can't impose like that. No way."

"You are family to us," Andy said.

Cindy poured coffee for everyone. "You're going with us, Sammy.

No arguments. Why don't we talk over the logistics while Nikki helps me fix sandwiches?"

They discussed packing the equipment, which Eduardo suggested would be time-consuming. "The lab animals in cages should be the easiest."

Everyone ate hastily, propelled by stress.

As they finished with ice cream, they assigned drivers to each vehicle. Eduardo volunteered to drive one of Sammy's trucks with a trailer of mules attached. Sammy would pull the other trailer with the second truck. Nikki would drive Sammy's white crew cab.

Andy would drive the old Silverado. Cindy would have the GMC. Olivia would travel with her mother.

Cindy asked if Neptune could stay overnight with them again. "He's good company for Olivia. And you'll only need to get the mules ready."

Nikki and Sammy stood. She would drop Sammy off at his place, then come back with the crew cab and help pack.

# TWELVE

## NIKKI

Nikki eased out of the driveway and followed Sammy's instructions to the narrow highway winding through Peñasco. Glancing in the rearview mirror, she noticed another vehicle following them. The hair on her neck bristled as it continued to tailgate. When it passed before the turnoff to Sammy's mule farm, she dismissed her concern as part of the overall tension she felt from the wildfires.

She dropped him off at his cabin. He would load up his mules and be ready to join them at Andy's house early the next morning.

On the return drive, she rolled down the window, hoping to smell pine despite the nearby fires. The dry air stung, but there was no hint of smoke.

She arrived back at her brother's place and helped get the animals and equipment packed and loaded on the trucks. They finished by midnight.

# THIRTEEN

## SAMMY

Sammy's trucks were gassed up and ready for the trip the next morning. He fed and watered the mules and loaded them on the trailers. When he finished, he was wide awake. Instead of tossing and turning in bed, he opted to spend an hour or so on the drums. He had a brand-new bass drum whose deep and resonant sound relaxed him.

He played solo these days. He never liked to think about the band he had formed in Mexico. Those thoughts depressed him, so he concentrated on jazz and rock, totally different music. He might never perform before a live audience again. His small ranch house had no nearby neighbors to bother when he practiced. A recent remodel, the room off the kitchen had carpeting and floating wood panels on the walls and rubber flooring for good acoustics. A side benefit was that his new studio was soundproof. His next project, which he hoped to start soon, was to put in a secure door and make the whole room impenetrable, safe from intruders.

He loved the booming resonance when he played his new bass drum. The vibrations running through his body made him feel powerful. He could also play with a speed that had eluded him years ago.

And he was in complete command of the process, starting with mallets to set the flavor before going to sticks, then combining his kicks into the rumbling boom of the double bass drum, syncopating his rolls with crashes. By mixing his playing with band recordings, it felt like a real performance with a solo interlude.

He wiped the sweat from his forehead. He sorted through the recorded music on his laptop to select another piece. Picking up the sticks to play again, he thought of grabbing a can of Sprite first. That's when he heard a sharp noise, followed by a tinkling that confirmed someone had broken a pane of glass. He stopped and turned the dim lights off. Careful to maintain silence, he closed the door to his studio, leaving only a crack to peek through.

Muffled footsteps went up the dark stairs. His heart pumped faster. How had they found him?

Neptune, trained precisely for this type of situation, was not here. Sammy was alone. His heart weighed him down. He closed and latched the door.

The intruders would not find him asleep upstairs.

But the latched door was insufficient protection. He looked around, assessing how he could barricade the door, but none of the drums were heavy enough to secure the room against anyone attempting to break in. The wood panels were secured too tightly to remove soon enough to reinforce the door. His Smith & Wesson was in the glove box of his crew cab, the truck at Andy's house. He had a rifle upstairs. Useless. His only defense was the knife always strapped to his boot. He was livid with himself for letting his guard down.

Footsteps, no longer trying to remain quiet, stomped down the stairs. He pulled his knife out. The boom, boom, boom of his heart scrambled his thoughts.

The intruders would see the rickety door to the music room when they reached the main floor. They would bash it in. Escape was impossible. He struggled to breathe. If only he had made the room secure before making it soundproof, as his gut had told him all along.

He heard the dull sound of muscular bodies ramming against the door. It came crashing into the room, falling off its hinges.

"Grab him," an angry voice bellowed.

Two men knocked him to the floor. His knife flew out of reach.

The man with the angry voice laughed and pushed the muzzle of his rifle into Sammy's face. "You thought a knife could keep you safe?"

# FOURTEEN

## EDUARDO

The odor of smoke penetrated the house, adding to a mood in the kitchen as somber as the darkness outside the window. No one spoke over a meager breakfast. Eduardo noticed Andy nervously glancing outside, perhaps hoping to catch a glimpse of Sammy arriving. They had agreed he would come over with a trailer already hitched to a truck. That way, Sammy could give Eduardo driving tips on the way back to the mule farm to get the second truck and trailer.

By five, an orange glow outlined the mountains to the east of the village. It reminded him of a fire he once saw in a wooded area of his native Colombia. *Smoke pollutes, but it makes for gorgeous sunsets and sunrises.* He chastised himself for the thought.

Sammy had not yet arrived. Andy had called him twice, leaving messages each time.

Olivia was awake and crying. "Quiet her down," Andy muttered to his wife.

"Can't you talk to her? Use a nicer tone of voice," Cindy said. "No need to take your stress out on your daughter. Or me. Besides, she only wants attention."

Nikki picked up Olivia and took her to the bedroom, leaving Cindy to reprimand Andy.

By five-fifteen, Eduardo suggested they drive to Sammy's place.

Andy agreed. The twenty-minute drive took them through the tiny town of Vadito, where they turned onto an unmarked dirt road leading to a clearing with a greenhouse, corrals, and a barn. Eduardo sensed Andy tensing as they approached the log cabin a few hundred feet beyond the corrals. A US flag hanging near the front door flapped in the wind.

"Something's wrong," Andy said. He circled back to the barn, near the greenhouse.

Eduardo pointed out tire tracks around the barn, headed toward the paved road.

"The mules are gone. That worries me. He couldn't drive both trailers," Andy said. He circled back to the cabin and parked. He unlocked the glove compartment and grabbed a handgun. Stepping out of the pickup, he tucked the gun into the back of his pants before heading to the cabin.

He signaled for Eduardo to follow.

The front door was unlocked. Andy drew his gun before entering.

Eduardo stared at the overturned table and chairs. A bright ceiling light shone on glass fragments that glistened across the kitchen floor. Outside, the flag snapped in the wind creating the solitary sound penetrating the cabin. He assessed the damage and took pictures with his camera app.

Andy checked the whole cabin. He flipped a switch to turn on a light in the adjoining room near the stairs. He stuck the gun back into his waistline. "Come see this."

Eduardo tentatively moved to the doorway, expecting a horrible scene, maybe even Sammy's dead body sprawled out on the floor.

Instead, an assortment of drums filled the space, their shiny edges reflecting the light Andy had turned on. They were set up as if waiting for fans to arrive for the concert. Whoever caused the chaos in the main room had not been interested in the drums. They were by far the most expensive items in the cabin, yet they were untouched. Close inspection of the doorway revealed a broken latch. The door, off its hinges, was on the floor.

It confirmed his first thought—the intruders were after Sammy. But why? Nikki had been suspicious of him from the beginning. Perhaps there was something shady about the man after all.

Andy dialed home to ask if Sammy had shown up there. He ended the call and kicked one of the overturned chairs.

The men walked outside.

"Something's wrong," Andy repeated. His voice choked up. "Sammy's like a brother to me."

"What about the drums? The set looks professional."

"Sammy can play like a pro." Andy sounded nostalgic.

"Is he part of a band?"

Andy shook his head.

Eduardo thought that was odd. Most accomplished musicians want to practice with other people and perform concerts—the social aspect of music.

"How long have you known him?"

"Seven years. Why?"

"Just wondering what brought him to the US."

"Looking for a better life, like most immigrants." Andy gripped the steering wheel and drove home in brooding silence.

# FIFTEEN

## NIKKI

Nikki was outside, holding Olivia while Cindy finished last-minute packing. Smoke curled over the mountain facing the village of Peñasco. Flames hidden by the mountain were reflected in the smoke, creating a beautiful sunrise. She checked her watch and stared down the road.

Crows cawed nearby. Nikki turned toward them. A couple of dozen gathered on the ground beneath a tall, pale aspen, some screaming and others clawing and pecking at the ground, and still more watching from the tree. She told Olivia that the birds were crows, repeating the word several times. Those in the tree descended to join the ones already jabbing the dry earth. Entranced, the child watched them and waved her hands.

Preoccupied for Andy and Eduardo, Nikki paced back and forth. Olivia looked at Nikki's world tree pendant and tugged it. Then she squirmed to be released and toddled, flapping her arms, toward the crows. She stumbled and they flew away in a noisy flurry of wings and feathers. Nikki picked a tearful Olivia up and soothed her little ego by telling her that's what birds do—they fly away. "You will too, someday, sweet child."

A vehicle roared onto the property and stopped abruptly. "Here comes your daddy. Wave at him." Glancing at Andy behind the steering wheel, Nikki sensed something was wrong.

Eduardo climbed out of the Silverado. "With this wind, the fire will move quickly. We must leave."

"Where's Sammy?" she asked.

"Don't know." Eduardo shrugged. "Seems he's missing."

Calling everyone for last-minute instructions, Andy told them the plan had changed.

When Olivia saw Cindy, she cried "Mama!" and stretched toward her.

"Someone's stolen the trailers with the mules, and they've probably taken Sammy too," Andy said. He instructed Eduardo to drive his Silverado. He would take Sammy's crew cab.

Nikki immediately objected. Who knew where Sammy was, or why he had left so abruptly?

"The least I can do is take his pickup in case he needs it."

"You don't know where Sammy is. If you drive his vehicle, the police could stop you."

"Me? Why?"

"You said he's missing. And his mules too. If you think someone has stolen them and kidnapped him, you could be considered a suspect if you're using his crew cab."

"Let me handle this," Andy said with determination.

Nikki scoffed. She headed inside, followed by Cindy carrying Olivia.

In the kitchen, Nikki heard an approaching vehicle. She looked out the window. A sheriff's department Tahoe pulled in beside Sammy's pickup. The deputy—it looked like the man who'd stopped Sammy the day before—got out and spoke to Andy.

Cindy came to the window and watched the men outside. Nikki held her breath, saying nothing. They saw Andy pull his wallet out and hand something to the deputy.

Nikki exhaled as she watched the Tahoe drive away.

Eduardo came in. "Time to lock up and leave," he told them.

"I hope Andy wasn't bribing that deputy," Nikki whispered.

He shook his head. "Andy gave him a donation. He asked for help setting up an evacuation shelter in Peñasco. They're bringing people here from the Mora area, including Montezuma, where we were yesterday."

"Here?" Nikki gasped. "We can see the glow of the fire, smell the smoke, and they're setting up a shelter? That's crazy."

# SIXTEEN

## NIKKI

Nikki rode with Cindy. Olivia was in a safety seat in the back with the German shepherd, who was trying to sleep despite Olivia's pulling on his ears.

They were leaving Peñasco when Olivia started babbling.

"You recognized our theater, baby girl," Cindy cooed to her daughter.

"A theater," Nikki said, reading the sign on a salmon-colored building. "In Peñasco? You mean for shows like Broadway?"

Her sister-in-law laughed, breaking the tension they felt. "Better than Broadway."

They waited in traffic backed up at the intersection with the state road. Deputies directed traffic ahead of them. As Cindy eased up to the stop sign, two trucks pulling trailers drove past on the highway.

"Look! The trailers." Nikki felt a jolt of nervous excitement. "Are those Sammy's trucks?"

"My god, they are!"

A female deputy waved Cindy on, signaling her to enter the evacuation traffic on the state road. Two cars were between them and the trailers.

Nikki dialed her brother and asked if he had seen the trailers.

"Yeah. I'll catch up with them after I get on the highway."

She cautioned him to be careful. She cut the call and dialed her husband. Further back in the queue, Eduardo had also noticed them. He asked if Sammy was driving one of the trucks.

"Not driving, but there were passengers in both cabs. I couldn't see anyone's face."

"Why would he leave without letting us know? Where would he find drivers?" Eduardo asked.

"Something's wrong. Or the man has a dark secret."

He reasoned with Nikki that it seemed illogical for thieves to steal a couple of truckloads of mules when sheriff's deputies were posted at every street corner.

"Hiding in plain sight might be their game. There's something sinister going on." She ended the call. Turning to Cindy, she asked about Sammy's background.

"He never talks about it. It's almost like his life started when he came to the US."

That made Nikki even more suspicious. *What was he hiding?* While investigating a corrupt executive in Colombia two years earlier, she uncovered a horse business used to launder money. She hoped the mules were not serving a similar purpose. Sammy seemed very serious yesterday. Was it the wind, as he told her, or anxiety about the wildfire that had kept him quiet? Or had he been distracted for another reason?

"Here comes Andy," Cindy said. The stress in her voice interrupted Nikki's thoughts. "God, I wish he'd slow down. He's carrying the cages of lab animals. They'll be scattered all over the road."

Nikki gasped as her brother passed them on the narrow highway.

"Geez!" Cindy cried, watching her husband swerve around the truck in front of them.

"Shit," Nikki said. "He's crazy." Her body tensed as she watched her brother accelerate even more as he approached a blind curve. An oncoming vehicle veered onto the unpaved shoulder to avoid hitting Andy's pickup. The driver honked furiously and weaved for a few seconds before regaining control. Andy was out of sight.

Cindy slowed down, as if that might calm her own nerves. She took the curve with caution. Once the road ahead was straight again, they saw Andy had been pulled over. Flashing lights on a sheriff's Tahoe made Cindy inch past.

Both women rubbernecked in disbelief. Nikki recognized the deputy Andy had donated to and hoped he would let her brother off with a warning. Cindy picked up speed and passed the lagging mule trailer.

Fifteen minutes later, Andy passed them. The deputy's car out of sight, he sped up to get around the front trailer.

Nikki's phone rang.

"I hate to say it, but you might be right about Sammy falling victim to a crime," Andy said. "He's not in either truck, but those are his vehicles."

"I know you trust him, but I'm afraid his business might be laundering money."

"You're wrong." Andy's voice was firm over the speaker. "He's one of the most honest people I know. He's in trouble and I'm not going to abandon him. I'll follow the trailers to see where they're headed. You're the private investigator. Please help me."

"Start by toning down your reckless driving. You'll endanger all of us. Report Sammy's disappearance to the state police. Or you could have told that deputy about it." Nikki sighed.

"I did tell him. That was my friend Domingo. Told him I was speeding to see who had stolen Sammy's trucks and mules. I promised him I'd drive better, and he let me off with a warning."

Nikki asked what the deputy had said about Sammy.

"He reminded me that law enforcement is busy evacuating people. They're shorthanded as it is. He told me Sammy Amaya is an adult who probably arranged to move his livestock to prevent losing them in the fire." Andy spat a curse.

Nikki frowned.

"He recommended filing a missing person report if Sammy doesn't show up in a week or so. But you know how long they take to follow up on missing people, especially adult males." Andy suggested that they stood a better chance of getting law enforcement's attention if they knew more before filing the report. He pleaded again for Nikki's help.

Her brother was right about missing adults. Law enforcement does not act until it is certain a person is unaccounted for. Or foul play is suspected.

"What about the stolen vehicles? Didn't the deputy react to that?"

"Said he'd report it to the dispatcher."

"Okay, Andy, if you won't be reckless, I'll help you track the trailers. I have a GPS tracking chip with me." She reached for her purse and pulled out a real-time tracking chip from her last job. "If I give it to you, you can attach it to one of the trucks, but don't be irresponsible. Bringing attention to yourself is the last thing you should do."

He apologized, saying she was right. His temper got the best of him.

"Okay, watch where the trucks are going. After that, we'll regroup and figure out how to plant the chip. Given the right opportunity, attaching it to one of the trucks or even a trailer should be easy."

"Thanks, Sis."

The men could plant the GPS locator while she and Cindy drove to the rented house and barn. Olivia needed to be settled in the temporary quarters.

Nikki's phone rang.

Charlotte informed her there was nothing on any Sammy or Samuel Amaya living in New Mexico. Most of the Sammy Amayas she found were women. The men did not fit age, profile, or photo.

"Did you check Interpol?"

"Absolutely," Charlotte said. "Nothing there. Nada, nada." She added that she had run his picture through the FBI photo recognition database. Again, nothing. She had checked for a driver's license. Nothing there either.

Nikki thanked Charlotte. She ended the call wondering what to do next. A man who did not exist was now missing.

# SEVENTEEN

## NIKKI

The wildfire smoke had dissipated by the time Nikki saw Andy turn right onto State Highway 68, which connects Santa Fe to Taos. He followed the flow of traffic behind the trailers. He had taken her advice and kept several vehicles between his truck and the trailers.

Nikki called Eduardo and told him about the tracker, left in her purse from the Miami job. She kept Charlotte's call to herself. Cindy might not like that she was investigating Sammy. Cindy had heard Nikki's side of the conversation, but not any names.

"You're carrying a chip?" Eduardo asked, surprised. "That's convenient. But attaching it to a vehicle could be dangerous."

"Planting it might get us the information we need to convince the authorities to take Sammy's disappearance seriously."

She brought Eduardo up to date. Andy would follow the trucks. Nearing Taos, the drivers would have to choose one of three routes. At US Route 64, they could either go east toward Angel Fire or west to the Four Corners. Or they could remain on the state highway, which would take them north toward Colorado. Once Andy knew where the trailers were headed, they could figure out how to attach the chip to one of the stolen trucks.

"I'll load the GPS tracking app onto your phone. That way two of us can follow it," she said before ending the call.

Nervous, Nikki wanted to change the subject and she asked Cindy about her sleepwalking.

Cindy told her that it started in her childhood. "Like most people, I don't recall any of the episodes. My parents found out when I was three. Mom tucked me in bed and the next morning they were frantic when they couldn't find me in the house. Eventually, they discovered me asleep in the backyard, in my pajamas. A few weeks later my dad saw me walking down the stairs with a glassy-eyed stare. He talked to me, but I didn't respond.

"He remembered his mother had spoken of sleepwalking in her teenage years. That's when they took me to a sleep specialist. Rather than put me through expensive tests, the doctor recommended that my parents set up video equipment in my bedroom to monitor whether I got up or not."

"You haven't outgrown it?" Nikki asked.

"I wish. My grandmother got over it in her late teens, but then she suffered from restless leg syndrome. Still takes meds for it." Cindy added that with Olivia's birth, they'd set up sensors around their bed in case she sleepwalked. "It was scary that I took Olivia out of the crib when she was three months old. Andy found me holding her in the rocker on the deck. Now we have bells and whistles all around our bed. If they don't wake me up, at least they'll alert Andy."

"What about when Andy's away?" Nikki asked.

"I have a friend in Taos, Alicia. She stays with me to make sure everyone is safe."

Nikki glanced out the window and recognized the Church of St. Francis in Ranchos de Taos. "Which way do you think the trucks will go?"

Cindy told her the trucks would soon be approaching the intersection. Eight blocks later, they saw the trailers turn east toward Angel Fire.

Nikki's phone rang. Andy told her they should pull over on the road to the Taos hospital and watch the trucks from there while they planned how to plant the chip.

# EIGHTEEN

## NIKKI

The three crew cabs parked in an empty lot near the hospital. Cindy dropped Nikki off and drove half a block to a café to grab lunch. Nikki stayed with the men and watched the trailers heading east into the Sangre de Cristo mountains.

"If I'm going to help you, you need to level with me about Sammy," Nikki said. Her voice sounded as agitated as she felt.

"If you think I'm lying about Sammy," he said, "I'm not."

"Is it illegal drugs? Human trafficking? Money laundering?"

"You must subscribe to Cartel News." Andy's tone was sarcastic.

Nikki felt her face grow hot. "What's his real name?" She used her fedora to fan herself.

"Samuel Amaya Rendón, but his mother's surname is dropped in the US, as you know."

"Spell Rendón," she demanded. "I can't find any information on a Sammy Amaya. Not even in the FBI data base."

She texted Sammy's full name to Charlotte.

"Wait a minute," Andy said, grabbing his sister by the elbow. "You're investigating him?"

"You bet I am." She pulled her arm out of his grip.

"Cut it out. Sammy's like the brother I never had. He's no criminal."

So that was it? Nikki thought. Andy wanted a brother instead of an older sister. It stung.

"What are you thinking?" Eduardo moved closer to Nikki.

"Charlotte has checked Sammy out. No one exists by that name. Not anyone who fits Sammy's profile." Turning to face Andy, she added, "Do you realize he's completely off the grid? That's almost impossible to pull off."

"You know that anyone can come across the border these days," Andy said, ignoring his sister's comments. "Good people and bad ones. Like whoever stole Sammy's trucks."

"That could be," Nikki said, "or your friend is not as trustworthy as you think."

Andy told Nikki and Eduardo that they could leave. Continue their vacation or fly back to Florida. "I intend to help my friend. He needs me. Whatever's happening is not his fault. He's a good person."

Eduardo pulled Nikki aside and asked her what she wanted to do.

"I'd like to walk away. But I'd feel guilty as hell if something happened to Andy or his family. There's a chance Sammy's in the witness protection program. But I think he's a criminal."

"Then let's make a plan."

Eduardo waved Andy over and put a hand on his shoulder. "We need more information to file a missing person report. There's a way out of every box; we just need to work on the puzzle."

Andy looked down. "If you give me the tracking chip, I can plant it on one of the trailers. I'll call the state police tomorrow and give them the location of the trailers. There's no reason for you or Nikki to be involved."

"If you plant the chip, I'll help," Eduardo said. "Nikki and Cindy should continue to the ranch you rented. We'll get there after we attach the chip."

"Okay." Nikki exhaled. "That works. Olivia needs to be settled. As do the animals."

Eduardo suggested that he and Andy take the old Silverado. It was beat up and less noticeable than the white pickup, which might be recognized since Andy had driven it past the thieves earlier. "Besides, Sammy's truck is carrying all the lab animals. Nikki can drive that one to the ranch."

Andy nodded and moved Cindy's bags from the old Silverado to the back seat of Sammy's truck.

Nikki handed the locator chip to Eduardo and shared the locator app with both men. Andy gave her the keys to Sammy's pickup.

She looked toward the mountain highway and saw that both stolen trucks had pulled over at the very start of the ascent into the Sangre de Cristos. She yelled at her brother and pointed. The men jumped into the old Silverado and took off.

# NINETEEN

## EDUARDO

As they approached the trailers, Eduardo pointed out an SUV parked behind the second trailer. The flashing lights on all three stopped vehicles screamed for attention in the otherwise pastoral scene on the narrow two-lane highway.

He suggested slowing down to avoid passing them and catching anyone's attention.

"I told my friend, the deputy, about Sammy's disappearance," Andy said. "He'd report it to the state police, he told me. Maybe that's what this is about."

"I doubt it," Eduardo said. "That's not law enforcement. It's a road assistance service."

As they got closer, they cruised past the stopped trucks and mule trailers. A man stood by the front left wheel on the leading vehicle. The wheel was propped up by a hydraulic jack and the tire had been removed. The man was about to place the spare on. A short, burly man seemed to be supervising.

"I'd hoped the deputy had reported those trucks as stolen." Andy sounded disappointed.

Around the next curve, Andy drove by a firehouse, a school, and a smattering of houses. He pulled into a restaurant parking lot. "Let's grab a cup of coffee and see what happens."

Andy gulped his coffee, showing his anxiety.

Sipping his more slowly, Eduardo removed his hat and kept watch out the window.

"Here come the trucks. Let's go." Andy threw money on the table to cover the coffee and tip. Outside, they jumped into the old Silverado.

"Any chance Sammy made arrangements to send his mules to a safe place until the fire's over?" Eduardo asked, adjusting his fedora.

"Sammy wouldn't do that," Andy protested. "If he planned to send his animals somewhere for safety, he would have told me."

Eduardo thought about Sammy's house and the signs of a break-in. Andy's assessment was likely correct.

"Then boldly go where no GPS device has gone before." Eduardo tried to lighten the moment by recalling Andy's childhood fascination with Star Trek.

Andy laughed. "I like that. You must be a Trekkie too." He pulled out of the parking lot in the wake of the trailers.

The meandering switchback mountain highway offered beautiful vistas. It also kept the trucks inching slowly up the road ahead of them. Eduardo took photos of the landscape and the trailers, hoping to catch the license plate on the back trailer. When he checked, the tag was not clear. He tried to send a photo to Nikki, but there was no signal.

It was approaching midday, and he was hungry. He popped a piece of the gum that Nikki had given him. It might stem his hunger pangs. He offered a piece to Andy, who declined.

Two female elk appeared out of nowhere, crossing the road in front of them. Andy hit the brakes, skidded into the narrow shoulder, and turned the steering wheel sharply to the left to keep the cab from falling over the embankment.

The rest of the herd crossed the road, gracefully skipping down the mountainside with such elegance that it belied their speed. The elk stopped near a barbed-wire fence and turned to gawk at the pickup. A big buck, the last one to cross, stopped on the downward slope beyond the shoulder of the highway and glowered back. Then he hurdled the fence, followed by his harem.

"That got my adrenaline flowing," Eduardo said.

# TWENTY

## NIKKI

Nikki caught up with Cindy at the café and ordered a sandwich for the road. She drove Sammy's pickup, tailing Cindy to the rental property, shuddering to think about those creepy spiders in the back.

Once they arrived at the temporary lodging, she forgot about the spiders and focused on helping Cindy unload the animal cages and a few of the equipment boxes. Neptune ran around the yard, releasing pent-up energy and marking his new territory.

They fed and watered the lab animals first. That done, they got to work moving the boxes of household items. After all this, they should sleep well tonight.

Cindy left Olivia sleeping in the safety seat with the doors open as they worked so they could hear her when she woke up.

When babbling sounds came from the pickup, Nikki took Olivia out of the seat and kissed her on the forehead. Then she pointed toward the barn and with a very expressive voice, told her it was a rickety barn.

"Like the three little pigs," she said, holding up three fingers, "we don't want the big bad wolf to blow the barn down." She made sounds by blowing short bursts of air and making a face to symbolize the big bad wolf.

Olivia giggled and seemed to be imitating Nikki's words. They played for a few minutes until Cindy put Olivia back in the safety seat and gave her a stuffed bear, saying mommy and auntie had work to do.

Nikki could not believe how content and well-behaved Olivia was. She sat in the seat and cooed, gurgled, and chattered, entertaining herself, except when she dropped the bear. Cindy picked it up and gave it to her again. In short order, Olivia made a game of throwing the bear down and crying for her mother to retrieve it.

Nikki's phone buzzed with a message from Charlotte saying that her search for Samuel Amaya Rendón and variations had not yielded anything. Cindy must have decided to let Olivia cry instead of rushing to pick up the bear every few seconds.

Olivia kept crying. Nikki's rattled nerves could not take it. Dramatizing again the tale about the three little pigs and the big bad wolf, she blew short bursts of air gently into her niece's face and had her laughing in no time.

Cindy took Olivia, saying it was time for her nap.

Despite enjoying playtime with Olivia, Nikki could not shake Sammy, or whoever he really was, from her mind. She worried that her impetuous brother might pull something that would endanger him and Eduardo.

Her husband was smart, discerning, and insightful. Hopefully he could keep Andy in line, and they would return by nightfall.

Nikki grabbed her purse from Sammy's truck. Wishing she had her baby Glock with her, she remembered seeing a gun in the glove compartment when they'd gone mule riding. She opened the glove box and saw the revolver. A Smith & Wesson. She checked the cylinder. It was loaded.

# TWENTY-ONE

## EDUARDO

Between the tall pine trees at the top of a mountain, Eduardo caught glimpses of a little town nestled in a valley below.

"That's Angel Fire, a small ski resort," Andy said. "Nice little town."

The switchback road brought them closer to the trucks. As the narrow highway leveled out in the valley, Andy allowed more space between them and the trailers in front of them. They passed the turnoff to Angel Fire, and Andy followed the road signs toward Eagle Nest.

The trucks entered a gas station, each pulling into a lane. Eduardo suggested that Andy stop on the side street and stay there while he planted the GPS tracker. He noticed that his phone had signal again and sent a quick text to Nikki.

Careful to avoid attention, Eduardo jammed his fedora low over his eyes. A short, burly man with skull tattoos on his arm was fueling one truck. He looked like the one that had supervised the tire changing.

Two men came out of the small convenience store. Eduardo recognized the one carrying drinks as the driver he had seen. The other guy held an open box that smelled of hot dogs and was stacked high with bags of potato chips. He passed the hot dogs around to his companions.

Eduardo analyzed the scene and moved in to attach the chip to the undercarriage of the trailer, directly below the cargo door. Not the spot he wanted, but with the men milling around the trucks, this was the best he could do. Stepping back, he committed the license plate to memory. He had no good way to photograph this trailer's tag without being seen. Movement to his left caught his attention.

Eduardo was met with the stern gaze of the tattooed, burly man with heavy frown lines etched between his eyes.

"Gorgeous mules," Eduardo said. "Are they for sale?"

"They're sold," the man said in a heavy accent. He spat at the ground through nicotine-stained teeth and walked away.

From the corner, Eduardo saw the hot dog man climb onto the trailer. He opened and removed a combination lock, then lifted the cover on the front compartment. He passed a hot dog and soda to a hand that eagerly grabbed them.

"It's done," Eduardo said, jumping into the crew cab. He opened the app to make sure it was tracking the trailer. "One of the guys saw me up close. Sounded like he had a Caribbean accent. Puerto Rican, perhaps. No, no, it's Cuban. They have someone locked in the compartment near the escape doors."

"That's Sammy," Andy said. His voice echoed with excitement. "Let's follow them. When they stop along the road to sleep, we can make sure it's him."

Eduardo shook his head and sighed. "It's too dangerous. They'll take turns watching throughout the night. Besides, we need to help our wives at the rented place."

"Man, you're as bad as my sister. Why doesn't anyone believe me that Sammy's in trouble?" Andy slapped the steering wheel. "Something's wrong. I want to follow the trailers and make sure they've got Sammy."

"We don't even know if it's him. They could be hiding anybody. All I know is that there's a person inside that compartment." Eduardo dialed Nikki. On speaker, he told her that the GPS chip was attached.

They had arrived at the rental property, she informed him and

Andy. "The house and barn are a bit run down, but Cindy says it'll all work. She's happy that it's fully furnished, including a crib for Olivia. The place is old but serviceable. The one new item is a surveillance system, complete with cameras."

He and Andy had decided, Eduardo told her, to follow the trucks for a while to see if they could spot Sammy at some point.

She objected. "That could be too risky. By tomorrow, we can call the state police, report Sammy missing, and give them the location of the trailers. You guys need to get over here and help us."

Andy interrupted her and said they would just be trying to catch a glimpse of Sammy.

With a frustrated sigh, Nikki cautioned them not to take any unnecessary risks.

"We may not always get phone signal," Eduardo said, "so don't be concerned if we don't let you know what's happening." After confirming that the app on her phone was tracking the trailer, he told her he loved her and ended the call.

# TWENTY-TWO

## EDUARDO

A road sign told Eduardo they were entering Raton. He glanced at his phone. Three bars. It was late afternoon, and the trailers were still moving. Feeling pangs of hunger, he convinced his brother-in-law to stop as soon as they found a fast-food restaurant.

The trailers were parked at a diner. Andy drove past and pulled into the drive-through at the first hamburger joint they spotted. He ordered for each of them, and they wolfed their food in the parking lot so they could monitor passing traffic.

Eduardo watched the app as he ate. "They're moving again."

Andy responded with his mouth full, devouring the last of his burger. "They should go right past us."

After a couple of minutes, they realized the trailers had taken a different route. The app showed them crossing through town. Eduardo directed Andy to the new course. In the narrow neighborhood streets, they had to fall further back to avoid triggering suspicion. They followed the trucks to the outskirts of town. Signs showed they were heading toward Sugarite Canyon State Park.

Eduardo looked it up and relayed the information to Andy. "The park lies at the border of the Rocky Mountains and the Great Plains on the Colorado–New Mexico state line."

"They obviously know the terrain and have come here before," Andy said. He slowed to fifteen miles an hour and turned his headlights off, driving that way for over an hour.

On a dirt road, they lost sight of the trailers. Eduardo watched the tracker app and could see the trailers poking along until they stopped moving. Andy slowed to almost a crawl. About fifteen minutes later, Eduardo pointed to the trucks and trailers parked in the woods near a lake. Andy stopped behind a low hill near tall shrubs waving in the wind. The breeze whistled through the shrubbery. On foot, the two of them proceeded silently through the trees to get a closer look.

One trailer of mules had been partially unloaded. Two of them were tied to trailer bars, while a third one, a sorrel, was being unloaded. The burly man, hanging on the bars from the outside of the trailer, threw a rope over the mule's head, only to have him make a loud, high-pitched braying sound. The unhappy animal bared his teeth, lowered his ears against his neck, turned his back, and kicked the man through the lower bars, knocking him to the ground. The sorrel broke loose and ran in a circle, braying the whole time while the rope dangled from his neck.

Like a chorus, the other mules began high-pitched whinnying. One animal tied to the trailer kicked to get loose. When that failed, he took his head down and jerked it up, straining the rope tied to the trailer and shaking the whole vehicle. That behavior prompted the other tied mule to respond in the same manner.

The burly man got up, shook his clothes off, climbed onto the trailer, and squatted near the metal container. He must have removed the combination lock Eduardo had seen at the gasoline station. He lifted the lid. A head slowly emerged, and a hand gripped the edge of the metal box to help unfurl the attached cramped body.

Andy gasped.

It was Sammy. He stepped onto the trailer bed. The burly one unholstered a gun and pointed it at Sammy's head.

"Oh my god, they're going to kill him," Andy whispered.

"Be quiet," Eduardo said softly, holding his brother-in-law's arm. "They won't kill him. They need him to control the mules."

Watching from the clump of bushes, they saw Sammy step stiffly to the ground, obeying orders from the burly one.

They could hear Sammy's voice, but the wind made it impossible for them to understand his words. He moved rigidly toward the sorrel. The mule whinnied but soon stopped kicking and braying. Before Sammy could completely subdue him and bring him in, the sorrel took off into the woods.

Sammy walked to the second trailer and opened the gate. Very deliberately, he extended the ramp to the ground and got into the trailer to select an animal.

"A horse?" Eduardo asked, surprised. "I thought he only had mules."

"That's a mare, an old mare with a bell. She's the leader of the pack. Just watch Sammy use her to work the remuda."

For the better part of an hour, the two men watched as Sammy got all the mules to follow the mare to the lake for water. Even the sorrel, who had come back to the herd.

Brandishing his gun, the burly fellow barked orders while the animals slaked their thirst. Sammy led the mare back to the trailer and the mules followed.

"I'm going to grab my gun," Andy said, rising from his hiding position.

"Oh, no you won't. Unless you want to get us killed." Eduardo inched away from the bushes. "It's time to call in the law." He walked further away to avoid being overheard by the group holding Sammy. He punched numbers and glanced at his phone. "Damn, no signal."

Eduardo insisted that they leave, but Andy was just as determined to stay. They watched two men go into the woods and return with old, dry wood. While they were gone, the burly one, still holding the pistol, gave Sammy instructions. The man walked to one of the cabs behind Sammy. He opened the door and retrieved a Styrofoam box, which he handed to his hostage.

Sammy ripped it apart and removed a hamburger. He ate voraciously.

One man started a campfire. The orange-red flames rose high above the wood and a few embers sparkled as they landed on the bare ground. The men, save for one, took seats on the ground around it. The standing man returned to the same cab that had contained Sammy's food and came back with a couple of bottles of liquor and a soft drink that he handed to Sammy. Once their hostage had finished drinking, the burly one ordered Sammy at gunpoint to climb into the container again. He closed and locked the lid.

Andy seemed incensed at seeing his friend locked up again.

Fearing a verbal outbreak from Andy that would alert the group, Eduardo suggested going to the police station in Raton to report what was happening. "They can come out right now and take care of this."

Andy nodded. They crept toward the old Silverado, taking care to stay concealed behind the line of trees and bushes.

Halfway to the truck, a single shot sounded. Then a barrage filled the air.

Eduardo, panic stricken, plummeted to the ground. His fedora fell off.

He hit the ground hard, but that was better than being wounded or killed. Concerned for Andy, he raised his head slightly and saw him running toward the truck.

More bursts of gunfire came in rapid succession. Eduardo watched in horror as Andy toppled over.

# TWENTY-THREE

## NIKKI

Sleep eluded Nikki. She tried breathing exercises to relax, but her mind was filled with foreboding about her brother's decision to follow the trailers. She had texted Eduardo over and over. No response.

Instead of continuing to toss and turn, she went to the kitchen to heat herself a glass of milk. On a counter by the stove, she spotted a bottle of bourbon. She searched the fridge for a lime. Not finding one, she looked in a box Cindy had not yet unpacked and was elated to find a lemon and a pack of cinnamon sticks. While hunting for honey, she saw a half bottle of maple syrup in the pantry. All the ingredients for an improvised hot toddy.

She curled up on the sofa with her drink and a magazine advertising the art galleries and other tourist sites of Taos. Before long, she drifted off to sleep.

The sound of a car door slamming awakened her. The German shepherd barked from the entry hall. She jumped from the sofa and rushed to the front door. Turning on the porch light, she expected to see Eduardo and Andy.

Checking the yard, she saw a light inside the GMC pickup, the vehicle Cindy usually drove. Worse yet, the engine was running.

Was someone trying to steal the pickup? Had the mule thieves followed them?

In a state of panic, she reached for the doorknob to make certain the deadbolt was engaged. The door was completely unlocked.

She threw the deadbolt on. Nikki ran upstairs to grab the Smith & Wesson from her purse.

She grabbed the gun and dashed to Cindy's bedroom to wake her up.

A light blanket was partially draped over the bed with the rest on the floor. The bed was empty. She looked at the crib. Olivia was also gone.

Nikki dashed downstairs.

Cindy is sleepwalking, she thought, rushing outside. Sure enough, Cindy buckled Olivia into her safety seat. That awakened the sleeping child who started screaming.

Out of breath, Nikki walked up beside Cindy and asked what she was doing. Not getting a response, she gently turned her sister-in-law around and was surprised how easily she guided Cindy back to the porch. At the door, Cindy resisted and turned back toward the GMC. She slipped on the porch steps and stumbled.

The fall woke her. She sat up, looking confused. She blinked several times and stared at Nikki as if she did not know her.

"It's okay, Cindy, everything's fine. You're sleepwalking."

"Olivia. She's crying. Where is she?"

Nikki assured her that Olivia was safely in her seat in the crew cab.

"Did I do that? Oh, my god, tell me, did I bring her outside?"

When Nikki told her that she had, Cindy rushed to the truck. She burst into tears.

"I'm sorry, baby, I'm so sorry." She lifted Olivia out of the seat and hugged her.

Nikki climbed into the cab and turned the engine off.

Inside, they sat on the sofa where Nikki had been sleeping. Olivia climbed down and sat next to Neptune. He licked her face and Olivia giggled, covering her face with her hands.

"Have you heard from our men?" Cindy asked.

Nikki shook her head. "They must be out of range. The app shows the trailers a few miles northeast of Raton. If we don't hear from them tomorrow morning, I'll call the police." She glanced at her watch. "It's two a.m. We should go back to bed."

"I'm scared of falling with Olivia if I sleepwalk again. Or worse yet, that I take off in the pickup and end up crashing it. Please hide the keys to both trucks. Can we move the crib to your room? You can lock your door."

Nikki nodded and they went upstairs to transfer the crib. Cindy stayed until Olivia was asleep again. Nikki asked Cindy to turn the alarm system on, but Cindy objected. They were too loud and scared Olivia, she told Nikki. And wild animals made them go off.

Checking her phone and finding nothing from her husband, Nikki locked the door. She reached for a Harlan Coben paperback on the nightstand, knowing that sleep would elude her.

# TWENTY-FOUR

## EDUARDO

Three men raced past Eduardo. He held his breath and lay still in the scraggly clumps of grass, pretending to be dead. He lifted his head slightly to take a quick look at what was happening. Two of the thieves approached Andy, one pointing the automatic weapon at him, and the other one kicking him in the ribs. Andy failed to react in any way.

"Está muerto," one man uttered in the same accented Spanish that Eduardo had heard from the short, burly man. "He's dead."

Eduardo's heartbeat raced and his neck muscles tensed when he heard the man say Andy was dead. Terrified he was next, he prayed silently. The men were near the pickup. He turned his head to watch. Maybe an opportunity to escape would present itself.

Two thieves jumped on the Silverado's cargo bed and began opening the large boxes. They emptied them over the side of the pickup while the third one, a tall, lanky man rummaged through the contents. He periodically picked an item up and then threw it down again.

"Vámonos," the lanky one said. "Let's go."

Eduardo closed his eyes. He heard footsteps crunch the dry, irregular clumps of grass as they approached. One of the men kicked him.

The pain in his rib cage made him double up on the ground. A second kick to his torso was so hard, he thought his assailant might have broken his ribs.

"Éste si está vivo. Revísalo para ver si lleva pistola." Eduardo heard one of them say. "This one is alive. Frisk him to see if he has a gun."

They found no weapon, but they took his wallet and phone and ordered him to the camp they had set up. The burly man, who had stayed at the trailers, asked about the other one. The lanky one said that he was killed in the gunfire.

"Throw this one into the other box," the burly man said with a nod toward the front of the trailer. "He can clean the mule mierda out of the trailers."

Droplets of blood had stained Eduardo's shirt. He did not want to get mule shit on his wounds, but he would worry about that tomorrow. Unbuttoning his shirt, he saw several nasty gashes that were bleeding. They might have also broken a rib, but he was thankful his other bones were intact. It could have been far worse. He was alive!

"If you want me to clean out the mule shit, you'll need to pour your rum over my wounds to prevent an infection."

The burly guy pointed the bright light of his flashlight directly into Eduardo's eyes and studied his hostage. He emitted a guttural, frightful laugh. "Go on, throw the rest of the rum on him. I want to watch him squirm."

Eduardo was sure where this man came from. He had heard that accent in Cuba when he and Nikki had been there. The other men also spoke Cuban Spanish.

One of them knocked Eduardo to the ground. A second man poured the rum over his broken skin.

"Coño, parece que le dolió," the burly guy said, laughing. The laughter softened his cruel frown. "Holy shit, looks like it hurts."

It hurt all right, but Eduardo exaggerated his reaction to make sure he would get another dousing when he asked for it. He was willing to entertain the man's morbid sense of humor with his pain to keep the cuts from getting infected. He wanted to live. He wanted to get back to Nikki.

The lanky man ordered Eduardo onto the trailer. The man

removed the saddles and other mule gear from the metal container in front and piled them next to one of the escape doors. Eduardo put his shirt back on while he waited, and as he put his arm through the sleeve, throbbing pain deep in his ribcage caused him to double over. At that point, the lanky one ordered him to lie down inside.

"Ramón, si no se mete, dale un golpe con el mango de la pistola," the burly one ordered.

"Sí, Bembe," Ramón answered.

To avoid getting hit with the butt of the gun, Eduardo stepped into the narrow space. He eased his body into a lying position, the throbbing pain worse than ever.

The lid was lowered. He heard the lock snap closed. He inhaled deeply and searched for the breathing holes Sammy had drilled in the metal. It was impossible to see the tiny holes in the dark, yet he knew they were there. He ran a finger over the metal. Sure enough, he could feel the perforations. The air smelled acrid and stale, like the saddles and blankets that had been stored in the container. Ignoring the odor, he mentally reviewed what he had learned so far.

These men were obviously Cuban. Ramón was the lanky one and the burly man was the leader. Ramón called him Bembe. The other two were less involved in handing out punishment and their appearance was more refined. Could they naturally be quiet, or did they serve a special function in this operation?

Thinking of Nikki, he tried to stretch his legs. If only he could contact her. He needed to warn her not to hunt for him, but he had no phone. These men had killed Andy. Eduardo was worried about the fate that awaited both him and Sammy. More than anything, he wanted Nikki to remain safe.

Trying to get more comfortable, Eduardo turned to his side, the right side, the least injured one. His hand hit a small piece of metal. A nail. He placed it in his pocket. It might come in useful tomorrow.

The sound of engines starting up startled him. His body ached. The trailer moved over uneven terrain, making the pain worse. His entire body throbbed. The mules protested by braying loudly, somewhere between whinnies and grunts. Eduardo thought of talking to them, but his voice might spook them rather than calm them.

Why were they moving at night? Especially after the men had been drinking rum. It was obvious they wanted to get wherever they were headed.

The mules grew accustomed to the rhythmic swaying of the trailer and quieted down. For what seemed like an eternity, Eduardo considered how to escape. If there was a way to make a break for it, he would.

The road was smoother now. They must be on a highway. He focused on happier times to calm his mind.

His thoughts drifted to when he met Nikki. At a party in Colombia. But that was the second time. The first time he saw her was on the Gaudí rooftop terrace in Barcelona when they were kids. She lived in the US, and he was from Colombia. What were the odds they would ever meet again? He didn't believe in coincidences. Yet years later in Colombia, he had fallen for her the instant he saw her. Love at first sight, he always told her, love that started on that terrace in Barcelona.

To ease the pain in his ribs, he imagined her body next to his. He pretended his own heartbeat was hers. It made the cramped space more bearable.

Thinking about Colombia brought Keiko, his Japanese housekeeper, to mind. He would ask Nikki if they could invite her to live with them in Miami. Keiko was getting older. She had cared for him after his own mother died. He promised to take care of her, and he was sure Nikki would approve. They would need to find a place of their own instead of the luxurious Miami Beach condo they were housesitting. Eduardo's top priority, though, after getting out of this mess, would be to spend a full day in bed with his wife.

The thoughts of Nikki warmed his heart and quieted his mind. He fell asleep.

# TWENTY-FIVE

## NIKKI

Nikki checked her phone several times during the night. Nothing from Eduardo. When Olivia woke up, Nikki changed and dressed her, took her to the kitchen, and placed her in a highchair.

She was spooning scrambled eggs into her niece's eager mouth when her phone rang. She leaped for it. Eduardo? But the caller ID displayed Miners' Medical Center. With trepidation, she answered.

It was Andy. He sounded distraught. She asked him to repeat what he'd said.

Cindy started down the stairs. "Mm, coffee."

Nikki signaled her sister-in-law to be quiet and pressed the phone tightly to her ear.

"Where?" Nikki closed her eyes and reached for the table to steady herself. "You stay right there. I'll get to Raton."

Cindy had served herself a cup of coffee and was rummaging through the box of food.

Nikki bounded upstairs and slammed the door to her room. Yesterday, she had felt guilty about arguing with Andy over her suspicions that Sammy was up to no good. Now she was furious that her brother had brought all this on them by being loyal to his friend.

Cindy knocked gently on the door. "What's wrong? What did Eduardo tell you?"

Nikki opened the door about two inches. "That was Andy. Eduardo is gone."

"Gone?" Cindy asked. Her face turned ashen white. "What do you mean?"

Gasping, Nikki relayed that the men had been attacked while spying on the trailer thieves. Andy spent part of the night unconscious from a fall during the ambush. When he came to, he was alone.

Cindy, speechless, stared at Nikki with a terrified expression.

Nikki swallowed hard, fully opening the door. "Andy couldn't remember what he'd been doing. His head was covered in blood, and he couldn't find his wallet. A forest ranger on his way to work found him at five this morning."

"Is he okay? Where is he now?"

"A hospital in Raton. The ranger called for an ambulance to take him there. They were en route when he remembered that Eduardo had been with him. That they'd been following the mule thieves. Andy has a concussion and a gash in his right thigh, possibly caused by a bullet. And his ribs are bruised."

Olivia started crying downstairs.

"You stay here and take care of your daughter. I'll go to Raton to talk with the police and help them search for Eduardo. I'll never forgive myself if anything happens to him."

"I'm so sorry," Cindy said, reaching out to touch Nikki's arm. "Andy needs to remember what happened so he can help."

Nikki gave her a hard stare. "Andy's done enough. I don't need more trouble."

"Maybe Eduardo took the truck to get help," Cindy offered meekly.

Nikki's stomach gnawed viciously. She moved to the dresser to grab her purse and fedora. "The thieves did not take the truck. Andy was inside it, trying to piece together what had happened, when the ranger found him."

She flung the purse strap over her shoulder. "I'm leaving. I'll take

Sammy's truck." Yanking a jacket from the back of a chair, she stormed down the stairs.

# TWENTY-SIX

## EDUARDO

Eduardo had thought he would not sleep and yet he had. The first light that had filtered through the perforations made it possible for him to scratch a message for Nikki using the nail he found the night before. She would probably never see it, but it was the best he could do. A shadow cut the light streaming through the breathing holes.

A bang on the metal box startled Eduardo. He dropped the nail. The lid opened and bright, harsh rays of sunlight fell on his face. He could hardly move. He was stiff from lying in the container, and his ribs ached. The sky had a few high feathery clouds but other than that, it was clear.

"Levántate, comemierda," Ramón, the lanky one, said. "Get up, shit eater. If you need a bathroom, I'll take you to the woods."

Eduardo rose slowly from his uncomfortable bunk.

After they returned, Ramón gave him a piece of bread and an eight-ounce bottle of water and ordered him to climb back into the metal box. He drank half the water before recapping it. The other men were eating, but Eduardo had not seen Sammy. He was probably still in the other metal bunk.

"I don't have all day to wait on your majesty," Ramón said sarcastically.

Eduardo climbed into the container. He wanted to get that nail and etch another message to Nikki while he ate the bread.

Before long, Ramón raised the lid again and ordered Eduardo to get out.

The second trailer was parked beside the one he was in. Sammy was walking the mules down the ramp of that trailer.

"Help that comepinga over there. Saddle the animals so we can ride them out of here."

Ramón pushed his pistol into Eduardo's back.

"Okay, okay, I'll saddle them. How many?"

"All six, unless you want to stay behind." Ramón thrust the pistol into Eduardo's temple.

Once Eduardo climbed down, Ramón showed off by spinning the gun in his hand before holstering it again.

The mules from the head trailer were already out. Sammy was tying the reins of the third one to the metal bar like the other two. The saddles were on the ground with a blanket on top of each one. Eduardo, ignoring the pain in his ribs, picked up a blanket and placed it over the first mule in line—Jackpot, the one Nikki had ridden. He spoke softly and heaved the saddle onto the mule's back. Eduardo doubled over in pain from the motion, and he breathed deeply to keep from shrieking.

Sammy was already saddling the molly mule, Sassy. He ignored Eduardo, probably safest under the circumstances.

"Vámonos, vámonos," Bembe said. His permanent frown etched between his eyebrows was more prominent this morning.

They seemed anxious to get going. Eduardo saddled Gus, the third mule tied to the bar. Sammy got the other three mules and the old mare he used to control them from the other trailer. He tied the last mule he had brought down the ramp to the bar of the trailer where it would be saddled. The mule side-kicked him.

"Coño, don't you kick me, cabrón," Sammy cried out. As he always did to show who was in command, he slapped the mule with the loose ends of the reins. He seemed to do it a little harder than usual.

Eduardo recalled Sammy using the word *coño* once before, when Nikki was taking pictures of them on their mule ride near Montezuma. A common expression with Mexicans from the Yucatan peninsula or the Gulf Coast, but Sammy claimed he was from northern Mexico. So why use Cuban slang? Eduardo held his breath to keep his pain at bay as he pulled the cinch tight on Gus. He wondered if Sammy could be Cuban. Was all this a trap for him and Nikki after their undercover work in Cuba?

Bembe told the others to gather their belongings from the cabs, the personal items taken from the hostages, the keys to the trucks, and the registration and insurance forms in the glove compartments and throw it all into a duffel bag. After that they were to wipe the trucks and trailers clean of fingerprints. He walked away to make a phone call.

The other men hurriedly carried out his orders, providing Sammy an opportunity to make eye contact with Eduardo. He stepped in closer and whispered that they must find a way to escape. "Or hopefully Andy will bring help," Sammy said.

Eduardo shook his head. "Andy's dead."

Sammy's eyes flashed with pain, and he slapped the rein he held against his leg.

Bembe returned and ordered his men and the hostages to get on the mules. "Except for you, Celso," he said, pointing at one of the quiet men.

Eduardo was glad to learn another name.

Bembe handed his phone to Celso and conferred with him in hushed tones. He took his phone back and they each mounted a mule. Then Bembe, glancing at the mare, told Ramón to shoot her.

"No!" Sammy yelled. "If you kill the mare, I cannot control the mules. Let her trot along beside us. She's old. If she drops dead, so be it. But as long as she's alive, I'll use her to guide the others."

Bembe nodded and a stay of execution went into effect.

## TWENTY-SEVEN

## NIKKI

Before setting out, Nikki studied the simple route on the online map. Internet connectivity would impact her travels through the mountains. It would take her over two hours to get to Raton. She checked the tracker and saw that the chip was in the middle of nowhere to the east of Colorado Springs. She hoped it was still attached to the trailer. She dialed Eduardo from the secure phone she always carried for work purposes. The call went straight to voicemail. For security reasons, she left no message.

She glanced at the rearview mirror and saw Cindy running toward the pickup, carrying Olivia and a large bag. Neptune was right behind her.

"I'm going with you," Cindy said, out of breath. "Andy may need someone with him in the hospital." She circled to the passenger side, put Olivia on the seat and dropped the bag on the floor. "I need to get her seat from the GMC. It'll only take a minute."

While Cindy set up the safety seat, Nikki tapped the steering wheel impatiently. She hit the gas as soon as Cindy climbed in. Olivia fell asleep within fifteen minutes. Nikki remained quiet, hoping her silence made it clear she did not want to talk.

The paved road cut through Cimarron Canyon. The narrow gorge was formed by a forested mountain slope to her right and rust-colored granite walls rising hundreds of feet above them on the left. Nikki had kept her emotions under control until confronted by this natural beauty. She was worried beyond reason over Eduardo and felt guilty for being short with Cindy.

The narrow gorge reminded her of places she and Eduardo had hiked in the mountains near Medellin. Choking back tears, Nikki parked on the tight shoulder and told Cindy she needed a minute. She climbed out of the pickup. Her voice broke as she prayed for Eduardo. Wiping her tears, she got back in the cab and pulled onto the road, pressing harder on the gas pedal.

"I need to pick up the pace."

"We can talk any officer into giving you a warning," Cindy said.

"Or Neptune will take care of him," Nikki added.

Both women laughed.

Approaching Raton, Nikki asked Cindy to activate the directions to the medical center on the truck's GPS.

"Neptune has to stay in the truck," Nikki said, rolling down her window a couple of inches.

Cindy agreed.

The hospital's multicolored façade looked like several small buildings grouped together. Nikki stepped out of the truck and the odor of smoke assaulted her senses once more. It must be riding in on the wind. They had not seen smoke the entire trip.

The woman at the reception counter updated them on Andy's condition and emphasized how lucky he was. It was a serious concussion, and he was recovering well. She also directed them to Andy's room.

They heard his voice before they entered. He was propped up in bed talking with a nurse. Andy stopped as soon as he spotted his family. He waved them over, and the nurse took her leave.

"I'm sorry about Eduardo," he said. "We'll find him. My guess is the thieves have him. Just like Sammy. He's alive, so Eduardo is too."

"You don't know that." Nikki took a deep breath. "We'll talk about my husband later. And stop calling them thieves. They're criminals."

Nikki stepped away slightly while her brother embraced his wife and little girl. They spoke in hushed tones for a minute or so. Then Nikki asked if she and Andy could speak privately.

Cindy took Olivia outside. Nikki pressed him to tell her everything he could remember about the attack.

He gave her the highlights, most of which she already knew. A bullet had grazed his thigh. The doctor surmised that made him fall and hit his head on a rock.

"The Silverado was there, but you said your keys were missing. What else did they take?"

He paused before telling her that besides his wallet, his handgun from the glovebox was gone, the boxes of lab equipment and household goods had been opened, and the contents had been dumped on the ground around the pickup.

"They have your phone, too."

"No. The ranger found it. It must have fallen out of my hand when I fell. The criminals must have missed it among the equipment they dumped. The ranger said he'd pick up my stuff. I can get it when I return for the truck."

"Is anything else missing that you know of?"

"The registration and insurance card."

"Good god." Nikki rolled her eyes and tore into him in a loud whisper. "Your foolishness puts your entire family in danger. They know where you live, what your name is, your wife's name. Plus, Eduardo is missing…"

The words stuck in her throat, and she couldn't finish her sentence.

Andy groaned. "A paper copy of the rental agreement for the Taos ranch was with the papers they took. I'm sorry about Eduardo. He'll be okay, Sis. Trust me."

The stress gave her an instant headache. "We need to call the police. Right now. You obviously know that deputy in Peñasco. Ask him to go to your house. To see if anyone has been in there. And he needs to contact the state police in Taos who can guard you and your family until all three of you can evacuate the ranch."

"Aren't you exaggerating a little?" he asked sheepishly.

Nikki let out a long sigh of distress. "Do you have your phone?"

He tapped the pocket of his hospital gown.

"To be safe, you should get a burner. And one for Cindy."

Andy nodded.

"Good. Call that deputy now. And then find out when the hospital will release you."

He pulled his phone out.

"Hey, Domingo, I hate to bother you, knowing how busy you are with the evacuations and all, but I need a favor, hermano."

Nikki listened until Andy had asked the deputy to check out his house in Peñasco and to request protection for his family in Taos. Once her brother ended the call and began negotiating his release with the head nurse, she went outside. She added the two hours to convert to Eastern Standard Time. She would catch Floyd at lunch, a good time to speak with him. She waved at Cindy, signaling that she and Olivia could return inside.

The tracker app showed that the trailer had not moved since the last time she checked. Maybe the chip fell off or they had discovered it and removed it. They could be camping out. Or they could have abandoned the vehicles. There was one way to find out.

She needed a helicopter.

Nikki's voice broke upon hearing Charlotte speak. She took her fedora off and waited for Charlotte to get Floyd out of a meeting.

Nikki composed herself before speaking with her boss. She explained the situation, including that Charlotte had been unable to find anything on Sammy Amaya, with all the variations of names she had provided.

"I've gone over Charlotte's research, and it doesn't make sense. Have you considered he might be in the witness protection program?"

"That could account for his being off the grid," Nikki agreed. "But he could be easily found here by drug criminals from Mexico. Why wouldn't the WPP send him to Norway or the Philippines? Why does he own a mule farm in New Mexico? More likely he's a criminal."

"Hiding in plain sight might be on purpose," Floyd said. He asked what she was doing to locate Eduardo. Had she called his phone? Had she spoken to the ranger who had found her brother?

She had used her secure phone to call Eduardo, but it had gone into voicemail, she told Floyd. Law enforcement had their hands full trying to evacuate people from the wildfires. Without proof, they were unlikely to investigate two missing adults or guard those Nikki considered to be in danger, like Andy and his family. Eduardo was the most important person in Nikki's life, and she would move heaven and earth to save him. But would the police help?

"I've decided to rent a helicopter. I'll check out the Great Plains, where the signal is coming from, and maybe get some evidence. Then law enforcement should investigate what the hell is going on. Those criminals have stolen mules and equipment. They've kidnapped my husband. And Sammy. What do they want?" Nikki paced as she spoke. "My brother reported it to a deputy, but they haven't done anything that I know of. Plus, dealing with law enforcement in two different states, New Mexico and Colorado, complicates the issue."

Floyd offered to call the CIA and FBI and see if Sammy was on their radar. If so, it might be possible to get an agent or two assigned to the case. If not, he could fly out to help her. In the meantime, Security Source would pay for the helicopter, and she could check out the location herself. "Call me anytime, day or night."

She thanked Floyd and asked that he do the same. She put her hat back on. After a quick online search, she was pleasantly surprised to find a company in Raton that rented helicopters. It catered to vacationers who wanted to check out the foothills and the Front Range of the Rocky Mountains. Her heart lifted. She could reach the trailers. But terror of what she might find triggered heart palpitations.

At the reception desk, Andy told her that the doctor on duty had discharged him on the condition that Cindy drive. He needed to change into his own clothes before leaving the hospital. They spent a couple of minutes in the hallway discussing their next steps. She handed Cindy the keys to Sammy's pickup and urged them to return to the rental property and get ready to evacuate.

"If we leave, I have nowhere to take my lab animals," Andy said.

"Get serious." Nikki's voice rose in anger. "You still don't understand the danger we're all in. Give the critters enough food and water to last a few days."

Reluctantly, he agreed.

She feared the truck thieves were part of a mafia that could call in other members to harm him, Cindy, and Olivia. As for the old Silverado, lab equipment, and household goods, he could retrieve them once the situation was settled. "Be ready to leave the ranch, unless your friend the deputy arranges for round-the-clock surveillance that will assure everyone's safety."

"If we take Sammy's pickup, how will you get around?" Andy asked.

"I'm renting a vehicle. They're picking me up," Nikki said. She purposely neglected to add that the vehicle would be a helicopter.

# TWENTY-EIGHT

## EDUARDO

With Celso in charge, the group took off on their mules. He started off heading west, but before long, he reversed direction. Eduardo figured it was to leave tracks leading away from where Celso intended to take them.

Two of the four Cubans, Ramón and the quiet one, carried bags over their saddle horns with the personal belongings and other items from the trucks. Eduardo interpreted the bag carriers as the low men on the totem pole.

After three hours, the unnamed quiet man asked, laughing, how much longer he would need to endure the back of an ass. "This is not the kind of ass I like to ride."

Except for Sammy and Eduardo, the others laughed with him.

Celso studied his phone and said it would be at least a couple of hours.

The quiet man fidgeted with the bag on the saddle horn. It fell off and caught in the mule's hooves. The mule bolted. The rider lost his balance, the saddle shifted with the rider and slid down the animal's side. That spooked the mule even more. He bucked and the rider fell off, but the man's foot was tangled in the stirrup. The mule ran harder, and the fallen rider was dragged through the dirt.

Sammy took off on Sassy to catch the runaway. He guided Sassy next to Galaxy, the male mule, and reached for the reins. He missed. Lining up with the runaway again, he reached out and grabbed the reins this time, slowing the mule down and bringing him to a full stop. By then, Galaxy's rider was on the ground, his foot having disengaged from the stirrup. Sammy dismounted and walked both mules to the spot where the man had fallen.

Eduardo trotted toward the injured man, concentrating on reaching Sammy and the injured Cuban before the other men arrived.

"You're a doctor," Sammy said. "Play up your role to keep yourself alive. They need us both now."

The man's face was mangled and bloody. Eduardo checked the carotid pulse and found it beating. He examined the man's limbs and discovered broken bones in the right arm and leg, where his body was dragged over the rough terrain. A dirty mess, the worst part was a bone protruding through a tear in the jeans.

"Is he alive?" Bembe asked as he rode up.

"Barely. To save him, I need your shirts to use as bandages. And the rum you're carrying."

Eduardo removed his own shirt, ripped the sleeves off completely, and hung the two pieces of fabric around his neck. Taking the rest of his shirt, he pushed hard against the leg where the blood was gushing out and told Celso to get down and help him. He showed him how to push against the wound to control the bleeding. Instructing Celso to provide more pressure, Eduardo also ordered Ramón to help him bring a couple of large rocks that were nearby. Once they had hauled them and put them near the feet of the injured man, Eduardo placed the injured leg on top to help stop the bleeding. He aligned the joints and took over applying pressure to the wound. He asked Sammy for his shirt and exchanged it for his own shirt minus the sleeves. When the blood flow would not stop, he asked Celso to apply pressure again.

Eduardo took the ripped sleeves and tied them together to form a longer strip that would serve as a tourniquet. He tied it around the leg, slightly above the wound. He asked what time it was and requested a pen. He wrote the time on the inside of his left arm. The tourniquet had to be removed within two hours.

Sammy threw the blood-stained shirt into the brush.

The injured man opened his eyes and tried to speak. His words were mostly unintelligible, but Eduardo heard him mutter something about sandia and alamos. Was the man hallucinating? He was not complaining despite his injuries. His quietness was an extreme situation Eduardo usually encountered when a patient was in shock. With the tourniquet tied, he raised the patient's other leg and placed it on the rocks. If he was in shock, the elevation should help. Eduardo's own bruises and gashes were minor compared to this man's.

Eduardo told Ramón to hand him the bottle of rum and to take his shirt off and give it to him. When he poured rum over the open lacerations on the leg, the patient screamed so loudly that Eduardo decided this guy was no longer a quiet person. Now he was a screamer.

"Come here," Eduardo said to Ramón. "I need you to hold him down while I sterilize his lesions."

"Are you a doctor?" Bembe asked. Frowning, he passed his shirt to Eduardo.

Eduardo nodded and continued cleaning the blood from the man's face and head.

"What medications and supplies will you need to treat him?"

Eduardo asked for antibiotics to prevent the compound fracture from getting infected before the patient could be properly treated in a hospital where the bone could be stabilized. "I recommend an external fixator due to the open fracture. That cannot be done in our unhygienic conditions here in the field."

"I'm talking about supplies you need to treat him in the field, as you call it."

Eduardo protested. The risks were too great if he was not taken to a hospital.

"You're going to treat him here in the field," Bembe said in his husky accent. He pulled his phone out, opened WhatsApp, hit the speech-to-text icon, and held the phone up to Eduardo.

He spoke into the phone. "I'll need staples and a staple gun, antiseptic cleaner—preferably chlorhexidine, local anesthesia, a tetanus shot, surgery tissue forceps, nonocclusive dressings, towels, syringes, needles, and morphine. Splints for his leg and arm and a few hospital gowns. He needs a tetanus vaccine and penicillin. I need sterile gloves. The staple gun must also come with a removal device. Get a bedpan and a handheld man's urinal. Alcohol, gauze, pads, and oh, add three tubes of Bacitracin, the antibacterial ointment."

Bembe finished the message, ordering someone called Fausto to get the stuff. He moved further off and made a phone call.

Taking Ramón's shirt, Eduardo buttoned it up to use it as a sling. He carefully placed the patient's arm into the folded material, gently lifted his head, pulled the sleeves around his neck, and tied them to keep the makeshift sling in place. He asked Celso to help him keep the injured man as immobile as possible while he tended to the patient.

Bembe returned and asked Eduardo if his friend could be moved.

"A stretcher would be best. I'm not sure out here how we could make one ourselves."

"Can we take him out on a mule?" Bembe asked.

"It will be far riskier, but we can put him on the mule with Ramón. He can lean against Ramón's body for support, and we can tie him in place. Otherwise, he may not make it," Eduardo said.

The doctor continued cleaning the wounds, adjusting the tourniquet, and wiping the blood still oozing from several lacerations.

In the distance, the sound of a helicopter could be heard.

"Mira, que milagro. Look, what a miracle. Seems like we won't need the mules after all." Bembe laughed and searched the sky for the helicopter.

# TWENTY-NINE

## NIKKI

Nikki gave Martin Oliveros specific coordinates to the spot she wanted to fly over. The pilot of the lightweight Robinson R66 helicopter she had rented nodded. He went over how to safely get in and out of the craft as well as the in-flight rules. Then he put on his sunglasses and asked if she was ready.

The pilot tightened his seatbelt and checked hers. He handed her a headset. After she adjusted it, he gave her a pair of binoculars, saying they might be useful for picking up details in the mountains.

In the air, her headset came alive when Martin, accustomed to being an aerial tour guide, pointed out Pike's Peak in the distance.

"We have a beautiful clear day for flying. We're fortunate the smoke from the Hermit Peak fire has been blowing south," he said. Shifting in his seat, he continued speaking. "What you see to our left is the Front Range, the first mountains you encounter when traveling westward in the Great Plains. They rise ten thousand feet. On our return to Raton, maybe you'd like to fly over the Garden of the Gods for a closer look at Pikes Peak?"

"I'll decide after I see what I need to check." Nikki took her phone out and checked the location of the chip. It had not moved.

For the next half hour, she zoned out Martin's tourist chatter. She generally fixed her gaze toward the horizon, using the binoculars, expecting to see the trailers at any moment on the rolling, semi-arid, grassy plains. When she did spot them, her heartbeat sounded louder than the main rotor blades whirling through the air above the chopper's roof.

"Let's land," she said, pointing at the ground near the trailers.

"I can't do that without permission from the landowner. It's considered trespassing."

"Listen, my husband and a friend were in those trucks. Now they're missing. The trailers were carrying mules, and it appears they're gone. I need to land and check it out."

"Look, ma'am, the FAA does not allow random landings. If it's reported, I'd be in trouble."

"Please call me Nikki. I'm a private investigator from Florida." She took her wallet out and opened it to show him her license.

"This isn't Florida," he said.

Nikki pleaded with him.

"Why haven't you reported it to the police and let them check it out?"

The helicopter banked. Martin was heading back to Raton.

"I have reported it! So far, they've done nothing. It could mean life or death for my husband."

"I'm sorry, but . . ."

"What if it were your wife? Or your children?"

Martin turned and stared at her. He worked the collective lever, and soon the helicopter's blades were angling for a soft landing.

Nikki unbuckled and jumped to the ground, crouching below the turning rotors. She took a tissue from her purse and opened the door to the closest truck. It was empty. The second cab was also clear. The ramps where the mules had been unloaded made it easy for her to climb on the trailer beds. She went straight to the built-in container at the front of the unit. The cover was open. A combination lock was thrown to one side.

Getting on her knees, she caught a whiff of foul odors. She covered her nose and leaned in closer to examine the inside, and turning away, she yelled at Martin to bring her a flashlight if he had one. He descended the chopper with a twelve-volt battery type in hand and gave it to her through the bars of the trailer. He watched as she inspected every square inch of the container.

Martin glanced around nervously as she prepared to climb onto the second trailer. She opened the cover and almost fell backward from the stench. Covering her nostrils, she flashed the light inside and saw gum wrappers and an empty packet. Picking up the cardboard packet, she saw it was the kind of gum she had given Eduardo. But could it really be the same packet? Was Eduardo leaving a message for her? Andy had told her that the criminals were keeping Sammy inside one of these containers. Her heart told her it was a signal from Eduardo, yet her brain told her it was only a coincidence.

Moving away briefly to breathe, she turned back to inspect the interior using the flashlight. She started at the same end where she found the wrappers and discovered writing scratched into the metal wall of the container. Her chest quivered and her hands trembled.

"Fidel is here."

It was Eduardo. That she knew.

Below the message, he had etched a heart with a crude world tree in it. She touched the necklace with the world tree pendant around her neck. Eduardo had purchased it for her in the Yucatan a year and a half ago. It was the second world tree necklace he had given her. She gave the first one to Bibi, the ten-year-old they rescued from a kidnapping in San Miguel de Allende. She knew it was Eduardo's way of leaving a message that he loved her. Her eyes misted. She blinked and reminded herself that Eduardo's life depended on her investigation, not on her tears.

What had Eduardo used to create the etching? She looked closely at the corners of the container where she found his writing, but there was no clue at all. She flashed the light at the other end and spotted a rusty nail.

She carefully inspected that end of the container. Apparently Eduardo had left a message there too. Again, in Eduardo's handwriting, it clearly said *remember andrea*. The name was in lower case. He must have lain in both directions to get his scripts in at each end of the metal box.

What message was he trying to leave her about Andrea? Then the scribbling of the name Fidel. She concluded he was leaving clues about Cuba. But what? She would brainstorm with Floyd and Charlotte and together they would figure it out.

She recorded the evidence by taking photos of the writing and etching, the nail, and the trailer beds where the mules had been. Studying the pictures later, she might find clues she'd missed the first time.

Once more, she searched the cabs, this time going through the gloveboxes and under the seats. The criminals had taken everything, and they had probably wiped the trucks down. No visible fingerprints. Again, she snapped more photos. The cab interiors, the full trucks and trailers, and the ground where hoofprints and men's shoeprints were still visible.

She handed the flashlight back to Martin and followed the prints, which showed that the men had mounted the mules. The prints went west for another forty yards or so, then turned and headed east. They were traveling in a pack. She stopped to take more pictures at the point where the prints trailed off eastward.

Martin was noticeably edgy when she returned to the helicopter. She tried to put him at ease by telling him that with any luck, the wind would erase any evidence of a helicopter having landed near the trailers she had checked out.

"I hope you've found good clues," he said. "Back to Raton?"

"Not until I learn more. Let's fly east to see if we can spot the mules and riders."

"Seriously, the authorities should be searching for him, not you." Martin seemed annoyed.

She suggested they take turns behind a trailer for a bathroom break, since they would be flying for a while longer.

They climbed aboard the chopper and Martin complied with Nikki's request, though he remained silent. She searched the landscape with the binoculars.

A couple of times, she spotted animals, but closer observation revealed cows grazing on grassy patches in the open prairie.

At one point, Martin broke his silence by pointing to a long, narrow clearing. "It's a makeshift landing strip for small aircraft. Probably used by drug traffickers since there's nothing else around it."

They flew over the strip, but she saw nothing unusual and asked Martin to continue flying. For the next forty-five minutes, Martin flew a crisscrossing pattern to cover more territory. Nikki was about to give up when she saw what looked like a horse or mule. She adjusted the binoculars and asked the pilot to veer in that direction. She scanned the landscape and saw two more mules. Both were saddled, but without riders. Her stomach churned with fear.

Martin flew in a large circle, scrutinizing the prairie for more mules. Soon they spotted three more, obviously abandoned with saddles. In smaller crisscross movements, he maneuvered the chopper until he located a good place to land. A horse and another mule were nearby. They backed away when the helicopter landed.

Nikki and Martin descended to take a closer look. Her phone rang. It was Andy.

Martin moved away, perhaps to give her privacy on her call or perhaps searching for clues.

"Hey, Sis, no troopers or deputies can come out to protect the rental property. Seems they're all busy with the fires. He suggested getting a couple of guards."

"Forget about guards. We don't know how long we'd need them because I want you to pack up the essentials you need in case we evacuate. I'll head your way later today."

When she ended the call, she ventured out to the grass to take photos of the mule and the horse, looking down periodically to check for snakes. She managed to get closer to the mule and the horse without scaring them off. Then she saw that the mule was none other than Jackpot. He trotted toward her. She spoke softly as he approached and when she rubbed his nose, he leaned his bulky body into her.

"Ahh, you remember me," Nikki said. "I know you don't like having this saddle on all the time." She uncinched it, dropped it to the ground, removed the blanket, and rubbed Jackpot's back. She looked up when she heard the horse approach and saw that it was a haggard-looking mare.

Martin, sixty or seventy yards away, yelled and waved for her to join him. Feeling torn about leaving Jackpot on the prairie, she realized that he and the other animals were not in imminent danger, but her brother and his family could be.

She jogged over to Martin. On the grass next to where he stood was a pile of bridles. After snapping pictures, she told Martin she was ready to leave.

"Not yet," he said. "You've missed the main reason I called you over."

Nikki looked at him inquisitively.

"A helicopter landed here. Not long ago."

She glanced at the ground. Impressions the skids had left behind were embedded in the soil, and rotor wash had pushed pebbles and other debris into a large circle. "It looks like it, all right."

Taking more photos, she walked to the outer edge of the rotor wash. A piece of fabric was caught in a bush, and she stepped toward it. She screamed. It was Eduardo's shirt, the one he was wearing the day he disappeared.

Martin ran to her side and watched as she picked up a short stick and disentangled the material from the shrub.

Her voice trembled. She informed him that it was her husband's. "It's soaked with blood." She took a deep breath. "They've wounded him. Or worse."

They both walked the area looking for more evidence. Martin found a mule on the ground, shot in the head. The saddle and bridle were still on. Blood had stained the bridle and the dry dirt.

"This was very recent," Martin said, calling Nikki over. "The vultures haven't even found it."

Nikki's knees buckled and she lost her balance. Getting a grip on her emotions, she kept herself from falling.

"Maybe the blood on that shirt is from this mule," Martin said in a sympathetic tone.

She nodded and walked away.

After a fruitless half hour of effort to find more evidence, she called out to Martin that she'd seen enough. She put the shirt in a plastic bag that Martin retrieved from the chopper. Both sleeves were missing.

"Let's get to my brother's place as soon as possible." She gave Martin the address of the rental ranch, knowing that she needed to get her family out of there.

# THIRTY

## SAMMY

Sammy was sad to abandon his mules and the old mare on the prairie. But what choice did he have? Bembe had shot poor Galaxy—he could order the other mounts killed too. In the rush to get the injured man in the helicopter, they left the surviving mules saddled. Sammy had at least removed the bridles so the animals could graze.

Weary and shirtless, he leaned against the hard wall at the rear of the chopper. The sun warmed that side in the otherwise cold interior. Sammy figured that Bembe had arranged the helicopter to pick them up. Back at his mule farm, he had heard the burly man planning to ride the mules into the mountains, but then they went to the prairie instead.

Why? Sammy surmised that he changed the plan when he found out they had been followed. Bembe knew he had to abandon the trucks and trailers, and he used the animals to disguise their route. The man had obviously not factored in one of his comrades getting seriously injured.

The craft had been configured to fit in more equipment or merchandise or both. The only seat was in the cockpit where the pilot sat. A large box, covered in a white sheet, was near the back edge of the sliding door used for loading equipment or heavy items.

The chopper arrived with a stretcher for the injured man. Eduardo climbed on board. One of the men pointed him to two wool blankets, cotton sheets, a bag of headsets, and a first aid kit. Eduardo examined the headsets and tapped the one he passed to Sammy, communicating that they were not equipped with mics. They were just hearing protectors. Eduardo put one on and covered the patient's ears with another. He passed the bag to the Cubans and each one took a set. Before long, the chopper lifted into the air.

The stretcher holding the patient extended down the middle of the floor, like a battle line drawn to separate the space into two warring factions, the thieves on one side and their hostages on the other. Bembe had backed into the corner created by the box and the sliding door. After a few minutes in the air, he appeared to be snoring. His headset had slipped down to his neck. His other two companions, Celso and Ramón, had also fallen asleep.

Sammy watched Eduardo, also shirtless, care for the injured man as if there was no conflict at all with their captors. He had elevated the patient's legs by placing the foot of the stretcher on a small cardboard box and had covered him with a blanket. The doctor carefully monitored the man's temperature with an infrared thermometer from the first aid kit. The patient had been completely still for the last half hour in the helicopter. He assumed Eduardo may have given him painkillers or another drug that calmed him.

The patient looked like he was asleep, but his mouth moved as if in pain from time to time. It could be muffled cries, or inaudible screams.

The rotor blades made a distant whirring despite the earmuffs. It reminded Sammy of the day he had been extracted from Mexico nine years earlier. The difference was that this time the helicopter belonged to the bad guys. The sound brought back painful memories. His stomach cramped, and his heart ached at the thought of his lost loved ones. He thought of Andy too. Another death on his watch. And still more people could meet their death because of his decisions. His biggest concern right now was for Eduardo. And Andy's family. He knew what fate awaited him unless he managed to escape. If he wanted to survive, escape was his only way out.

Sammy was exhausted. He curled up on the floor, his arm serving as a pillow for his head, and he fell asleep. His nightmare started, as it always did, playing a gig at Sancho's Bar. Sammy beat the drums rhythmically, building intensity with sharp staccato, bringing a fevered energy to the entire band. The music deserved a better venue than this run-down hell hole. But he could not risk advertising in better places for fear of discovery. That limited the outlets where his band could perform. To Ana, his wife, he justified playing at Sancho's by insisting that his music might keep the violence down in that neighborhood. The next images in his nightmare shocked him awake. Sammy's entire body was shaking.

Opening his eyes, he looked at the men in the helicopter. Except for the pilot up front and Eduardo, who watched over his patient, they were all asleep. The doctor glanced at Sammy and eased to his side, keeping an eye on their captors.

Without mics, it was impossible to talk. Eduardo asked if he was okay, mouthing the words and wiping his forehead to show that Sammy looked feverish.

"It's nothing," Sammy mouthed back, with a dismissive gesture.

# THIRTY-ONE

## EDUARDO

The chopper landed and two more guys joined their captors, bringing Eduardo a couple of boxes of medical supplies. Bembe ordered Eduardo to put the supplies to good use. "I got new shirts for everyone, including you."

The Cubans left Eduardo and Sammy in the chopper with the injured man.

"Cheyenne Mountain," Sammy whispered. "Tell you more later. If we can escape, we'll have good stuff to tell law enforcement."

"Tell me now," Eduardo snarled. "Where are we? What the hell's going on?" He needed to remove the tourniquet before the patient ended up with nerve damage. He prepared to staple the laceration.

"First, I want to know how Andy was killed," Sammy said.

"We followed the trailers to the lake where you watered the mules. Andy was desperate to prove to the police that you'd been assaulted and abducted."

"He was like the brother I never had." Sammy looked at his hands, dejected. "He shouldn't have followed us."

"He considered you his brother too. That's why he did it."

Sammy asked again how Andy had been killed.

Eduardo explained it all to him, trying to be factual without showing any emotion. "Now tell me about this mountain."

"Are you sure he can't hear us?" Sammy asked motioning with his head toward the patient.

"Not with the ear defenders on."

Sammy looked out the chopper's window. "Whatever these guys are up to, it's not going to work."

"What's that mean?"

"The Space Force bunker at Cheyenne Mountain is one of the most secure installations in the country, carved into the granite of the mountain." Sammy's expression was serious. "These guys will never get inside the base. Foreign governments have found it easier to get spies into Los Alamos and Sandia."

Eduardo remembered hearing those words from his patient after the fall from the mule. Why would he have mentioned two of the country's national labs? Maybe it was making sense now. He gloved up and prepared a syringe of local anesthetic. He cut the man's pantlegs off and injected the patient's leg around the laceration. The man hardly reacted. Waiting for the anesthesia to act, he gave his patient antibiotics and a tetanus shot and emptied a dose of morphine into his mouth.

Eduardo asked Sammy to open the sheet-covered box that had traveled with them in the helicopter. "Try not to leave evidence that you've handled it."

Sammy wanted to know why.

"Just do it. I'd like to know what's inside." Eduardo worked the stapler over the patient's battered leg. He adjusted the forceps to hold the tissue in place.

Sammy removed the sheet. He lifted a flap and peeked inside the box. "There are bundles covered in bubble wrap."

"Get one out."

Glancing outside, he carefully removed the bubble wrap from one item. It was a piece of equipment that looked generic. There was no manufacturer's name or logo. He held it up for Eduardo. Dials, warning lights, ports, and indicators covered the front. As Sammy turned the device, Eduardo saw more ports on its sides. "This box must be holding six of these babies."

"It's a giant stingray phone tracker," Eduardo said, remembering the devices Floyd's office had trained him to identify before he and Nikki flew to Cuba on her last assignment.

He put the stapler down and fished a phone out of the patient's pocket. He swiped it and placed it in front of the patient's face. The phone unlocked the second time. He took pictures of the box and the apparatus. He eased his way to the sliding helicopter door and used the box to shield his body from view while he photographed the yellow pickup.

Sammy's face went red. "You're crazy. They'll find out what you've done. If we weren't already in danger, we are now."

Eduardo told Sammy to rewrap the stingray and put everything back the way it was while he tapped out a quick email. Acting as quickly as he could, he erased the email from the sent file, accessed the deleted mailbox, and deleted it again. Then he expunged the photos and tucked the phone back in his patient's pocket. Anyone searching a little deeper would still find traces, but at least no one would immediately discover the email and photos he'd sent. Nikki's secure phone would not help their captors if they retrieved the email. Still, they would know someone had seen the equipment and shared the information. Eduardo's adrenaline was pumping. He was sweating. He picked up the staplegun and got back to work on his patient's leg.

"Tell me more about this place," Eduardo said.

"The military collects intel here by using a network of satellites, radars, and sensors that cover the world. Since September 11, its mission also includes watching for terrorist attacks."

"You said we're at Cheyenne Mountain?" Eduardo kept working on the leg laceration.

"Very close to it. NORAD headquarters."

Having repaired the deep wound, Eduardo put the stapler down and picked up the hospital gown. He gently cut the remnants of clothes off his patient and put the gown on him. He used the splints to immobilize the femur and knee to prevent further damage.

"You know that guy you're saving would kill you if he's ordered to," Sammy said.

"Right," Eduardo said. "That's the way the spy business works, doesn't it? And if he dies on me, I'll be shot like a runaway mule. Sometimes life isn't fair."

Happy that his ribs no longer hurt, Eduardo was certain none had been broken. He spread Bacitracin ointment on his own ribcage wounds and reached for a couple of the new shirts. He handed one to Sammy. "Tell me more about Cheyenne Mountain."

"The facilities are inside the mountain, what they call the complex, all on steel springs meant to withstand a nuclear blast. Its entrance is all concrete and metal. Impenetrable."

"I'd love to see it," Eduardo said.

"So would the Russians, the Chinese, and the Cubans."

"Besides all that history, what other functions does it serve today?"

"Intel gathering," Sammy said softly. "It's collected here and then sent to whatever agency needs it."

"If intel is gathered in such a secure location, how can a few spies possibly break in?"

"Maybe they don't plan to breach it. They could be on recon," Sammy said.

Eduardo used alcohol to clean some abrasions on the injured man's head and arms and the skin around the staples.

"That might be how they'll use those large stingrays. What do you think?" Before he gave Sammy an opportunity to answer, Eduardo continued "Do you suppose those stingrays have quantum capabilities?"

Sammy looked surprised. After taking time to digest it, he smiled. "They could intercept incoming digital signals and take over the reception and resubmission of the messages."

"That's what I was thinking," Eduardo said. "Like a cell phone tower used to capture intel but operating with quantum technology rather than digital. I'll bet those stingrays are quantum."

"That would mean the Chinese are involved, not the Russians."

Eduardo asked why the Chinese.

"They have the capability. I read an article last month about the

Chinese testing quantum computers to intercept and decrypt satellite signals. The process could be so efficient that a lot of damage could be done before the US or Canada knows someone's stealing military secrets."

"You're brilliant," Eduardo said.

"But I'm a mule breeder, not a physicist, so I'm only guessing."

"Quantum computing sounds complicated. Let's go back to a simpler concept. Why did these people abduct you and take the mules?"

Sammy shifted his weight before answering. "I had packed the mules on the trailers to leave with you guys the next day. The thieves came along and said the mules would help them get to where they needed to be without being noticed by the authorities."

"How did they even know where to find mules?"

"It's easy. People in the Peñasco–Taos corridor know I sell them."

"And why did they take you?"

"To take care of the animals. At least that's what I heard one of the fellows tell Bembe, that muscular guy."

"I gather you think these guys are Cuban spies?" Eduardo asked.

Sammy shook his head. "They're Cubans, all right. But they're working for the Russians or Chinese. Probably the Chinese."

"There's one question I want an answer to, mi amigo," Eduardo said.

"Sure."

"Why do you know so much about this location? And about quantum computing?"

"I read a lot and I live alone. After I set up my mule farm, I had lots of free time on my hands. I took an interest in the history of Los Alamos National Labs and the Manhattan Project, where the atomic bomb was created. The innovative technology now is quantum computing, and it interests me."

"That's bullshit," Eduardo said.

"Wait a second," Sammy said. "Why the hell did you say that?"

"For an uneducated peasant, who crossed the border illegally, to grasp this scientific stuff is not terribly believable."

"But it's the truth."

Eduardo looked back at his patient and removed the arm bandage. It bled. He cleaned it up and used the staple gun to close the laceration. He put the stapler down, picked up the arm splints and worked on aligning the ulna and elbow to immobilize them. He finished and turned to Sammy again.

"For Andy's sake, for his family's wellbeing, tell me the truth."

"So, who do you think I am?" Sammy asked.

Eduardo looked straight into his eyes. "I suspect you're Cuban, despite your Mexican accent. These guys are Cuban. You must be working with them and pretending, for whatever reason, that you're not part of their group. Tell me what's going on."

"And you must be a CIA operative. Right?" Sammy asked scornfully.

Eduardo was about to tell Sammy where he could go, but he thought otherwise, and poured alcohol on a cotton pad to clean around the stapling on the patient's arm. Then he wiped the patient's face.

He wanted to ask Sammy another question, but he saw Bembe, the pilot, and the others heading for the helicopter.

# THIRTY-TWO

## NIKKI

Martin landed at the Colorado Springs airport to refuel the helicopter. Nikki called her brother from a porte cochere to take shelter from the hot sun. She avoided telling Andy about Eduardo's blood-stained shirt.

Instead, she told him she had rented a chopper and would soon be flying to the ranch. He sounded surprised and asked her when she had acquired her pilot's license.

"Hmm, maybe I should," she said, thinking about the times she'd flown in helicopters for work. This was different, though. Her family was in danger. It was not just a job.

He sounded disappointed that she was not a hotshot pilot.

"And make certain the security cameras are on and both your phone and Cindy's have the app connected to them. In working order. We'll need them for our safety tonight."

Andy told his sister he was sorry for all the trouble he'd caused. "I wish the criminals had taken me instead of Eduardo. Let me know if I can help."

She ended the call before she broke down. She stayed under the porte cochere a couple minutes longer. She reminded herself to replace the negative thoughts about Eduardo's situation with positive ones.

She gazed at the small airport grounds and admired the helicopter from where she stood. She would talk to Eduardo about becoming a pilot. After she rescued him, of course. Maybe they could both take flying lessons. Martin was removing the fuel nozzle and grounding cable, and she walked toward him.

Halfway there, her secure phone buzzed. It was an email from an unknown source. She activated additional security before opening it.

> Sammy & I are near Cheyenne Mtn, prisoners of 4 Cubans. They have a box full of equipment, like attached photo. I think it's Chinese made. I'm alive b/c they need a doctor. One guy was injured on a mule – he's in bad shape. I recommended hospital but leader won't consider it. Don't know our next destination. Get Floyd to involve FBI or CIA. Photo of yellow pickup has license plate – try to ID it. I love you. (You stay out of the investigation, that's an order.)

She read it again. Her heart fluttered.

Eduardo was alive! Yes! It was all that mattered. She pressed the office number to share this news with Floyd and Charlotte, and only them. They needed to act on this information. She signaled to Martin that she needed a few more minutes and returned to the shade of the porte cochere.

"I'm glad to hear from you," Charlotte chirped in her usual upbeat manner. "We've been so nervous about you and Eduardo."

When Floyd joined the call, Nikki felt giddy as she updated them on Eduardo's message.

Floyd cautioned her to be careful. Not to answer an unknown number. It could be a trap. "Send us the photo of the tag and equipment."

Charlotte gave her an email address where she could send the photos Eduardo had sent her. "In fact, send any photos you want to that email. I'll triple-check security on it."

"I'll also send pictures I took from the site where the trailers were. Eduardo was held inside a metal box. It had holes so he could breathe. He scratched two messages on the inside that I know were from him. And I found the shirt he wore the day he disappeared, all bloodied, on a bush." Nikki continued talking as she sent the photos of the equipment, the yellow pickup, and the ones she had taken of the abandoned trucks and trailers. The last ones she submitted, including those of the dead mule, were probably at the location where the men had been extracted by helicopter.

"When you get a chance, I'd like you to analyze the photos and send me your thoughts," Floyd said.

At that point, Charlotte must have shown him the piece of equipment Eduardo had photographed.

"Good grief," he said. "That looks like a stingray, with more capability than usual. No wonder Eduardo is recommending getting the FBI and CIA involved."

Charlotte mentioned she would enlarge the license plate on the yellow pickup and see what she could get on it.

Floyd promised a safehouse for them. The helicopter would fly them from the ranch house to that secure hideaway the following day. He'd arrange for DNA tests on the bloodied shirt although they knew Eduardo was okay at this point. Before ending their call, Floyd asked her to contact him again once she had arrived at her brother's place.

# THIRTY-THREE

## NIKKI

"Let's hope the smoke won't affect our visibility on the other side of the mountains." Nikki checked a wildfire website on her phone.

"Taos Ski Valley is clear, but that can change," Martin said. "I'm licensed for zero-visibility flying, but I'd be obliged to file a flight plan. I'd rather rely on visual flight rules again."

He explained that flight plans were mandatory for helicopters when the pilot planned to use instruments to navigate through conditions such as fog, clouds, rain, or smoke from wildfires.

Nikki suspected that he was avoiding filing a flight plan given the nature of the work he was doing for her, and she was pleased.

Flying over the Sangre de Cristo mountains in a relatively small helicopter made the trip a bit longer. Or maybe it was Nikki's anxiety to get where she needed to be that made it feel long. Wisps of smoke resembling cirrus clouds could be seen above them, but a glance at the southern sky made her thankful the fire was far enough away that it did not impact their visibility. Dark, menacing clouds of smoke rose above the mountains to the south. She shuddered. Through the haze hanging over the southern sky, she thought she recognized the outline of Hermit Peak. She recalled the traveling monk. In this century, he could have flown to visit many more places.

Neither she nor Martin had spoken on this leg of the trip. Nikki thought about what she had discussed with Floyd. She also examined her photos and sent several more to Charlotte, using her encrypted email. They would stay in her outbox until she had connectivity. Her concern for Eduardo's life remained very high. He was a physician and his captors needed him. But what if the patient died? Would they sacrifice Eduardo the way they had killed that poor mule?

She described in detail what she had found at the site of the trailers, Eduardo's messages scratched into the metal container, the hoofprints that had traveled west before turning east as if to confuse anyone investigating. But that seemed irrational. They had traveled east before the helicopter picked them up and took them west toward Cheyenne Mountain. Could the criminals—or the spies, as she should think of them now—have been headed somewhere else? Maybe when one was injured, they called for help and changed course. None of it made sense. She held the plastic bag with the bloodied shirt in her lap.

After writing up her analysis, she instructed Charlotte to discuss it with Floyd. That way they would all be prepared to strategize once she called them from her brother's place.

Martin interrupted her work to point out Mount Wheeler, the tallest peak in New Mexico. "It's three miles southeast of Taos Ski Valley. Your brother's place is off the highway to the north from there. We'll arrive shortly."

"Circle the ranch before we land. I want to get a feel for the terrain," she said, looking down at the beautiful landscape and thinking that the trip could have been enjoyable under other circumstances.

Ten minutes later they were circling the rental property. Nikki appreciated the panoramic view the helicopter's vertical reference windows allowed. She was glad to see that the dirt road leading to the ranch house was longer and curvier than she had remembered. The house, up on a rise, had good visibility for vehicles making their way toward it.

Martin pointed to the people who had come out of the house on the lot where they were to land.

"My brother and his wife."

"My fear of landing on private property is that I endanger people. As I've told you, I shouldn't land without the express permission of the landowner, and I don't want to be fined or lose my license."

"Not to worry," she said, knowing he had not filed a flight plan. "My brother has sense enough to keep his family safe as we touch down."

Nikki jumped out of the chopper, and ran, hunched over, to throw her arms around Olivia, who planted a big, gooey kiss on the side of her aunt's face.

Martin remained in the helicopter, jotting notes in an electronic log. By the time he descended from the craft, the rotors had stopped. He used chocks to immobilize each wheel. Next, he took rope and stakes to secure the chopper to the ground. Then he took off his sunglasses, snapped them into a case, and dropped them in his flight bag.

Nikki introduced him, adding that Martin would stay with them overnight. It was late afternoon, and he could not return to Raton at this hour without filing a flight plan. Besides, he might fly them to a safehouse tomorrow morning if Floyd had found one for them.

"In fact, I'll call Floyd now to figure out how to keep us all out of harm's way. Are you ready to leave at a moment's notice?"

"I'll show you both," Andy said.

Nikki frowned but followed him to the entry hall. She and the pilot stepped past seven suitcases lined up near the front door. The pilot frowned at the luggage.

"We've packed our essentials," Cindy said.

Martin made a soft tsking sound, as if in disapproval.

Nikki nodded slightly, a nonverbal assurance. She turned to Andy. "Essentials mean a change of clothing, maybe two for Olivia, toiletry items, such as toothbrushes and toothpaste, and medications. That's all. While I call my boss, why don't you and Cindy repack. Put everything you'll need into one duffle bag."

"Otherwise, the helicopter might not lift off at this altitude," Martin added.

"What about Neptune? He belongs to Sammy, but he's a member of the family. Is there room for him?" Cindy asked, patting the German shepherd's head. She looked ready to burst into tears.

"Of course, he'll go with us," Martin said. "He's family. Speaking of family, can I call my wife from here? And my office too?"

Cindy showed him to a room down the hall for privacy. Nikki took the stairs to the second floor to call her office.

# THIRTY-FOUR

## NIKKI

Nikki tried to relax as she waited for Charlotte to pick up. When she answered, Floyd joined in immediately. He asked for the latest developments and thanked her for the emailed analyses.

Nikki fought getting choked up. "My emotions have been all over the place. I was so happy when I got the email and photos from Eduardo. Now I fear for his life again. It won't be easy to find him."

Floyd sounded empathetic, telling Nikki not to lose hope. "Eduardo is smart. He'll do whatever it takes to stay safe. I've arranged to test the DNA on the shirt at a first-rate lab in Denver. One thing is good. He told you he's okay, so we're sure it's not his blood."

He told her an operative would meet her once they landed at the safe location in Colorado. She was to turn the shirt over to him.

"You found us a safehouse?"

"Of course. A couple of CIA contacts helped us out. You and your family need to get out of that rental safely. It's a short helicopter trip from where you are right now."

She swallowed hard. "I don't know how to thank you for taking care of my family. I'm not even on assignment."

"You're like a daughter to me, Nikki. You know that," he said, "I suggest you fly up to the safehouse first thing tomorrow morning. There's a helipad in the forest about half a mile away. A Jeep is in the hangar. The chopper can be stored there."

"Can you give me the operative's name?" Nikki asked.

"Charlotte will send you an encrypted message with his name, the safehouse address, a passcode for the hangar, and where to find the key for the Jeep. Just in case the operative isn't there when you arrive."

"What about helicopter fuel?" Nikki asked.

"There should be plenty in the hangar. And I've ordered you a baby Glock. You'll find it attached to the underside of the toilet tank, like we've done before," Floyd said. "The safehouse has been fully stocked with food and anything else you might need."

"Does the Agency know who Sammy Amaya is?"

"They're checking. I should know in a day or two. It's so big now that one department doesn't always know what the other one is doing."

"What does your gut tell you about him?" Nikki asked.

"The other men are likely mercenaries. On Sammy, it could go either way. He could be a double agent, he could be on our side, or he could be either Mexican or Cuban." Floyd reminded her to be cautious regardless.

Nikki finished her call and joined everyone in the living room. She informed them that Martin would fly them out to the safehouse the next morning. In the meantime, she suggested they eat and go to bed early. They could take turns as sentry to make certain no one surprised them. She asked her brother if there were any guns on the property.

"Not that I know of."

She had Sammy's revolver in her purse. But she did not want to announce it to anyone. "Okay. We must be ready to clear this place quickly. If we're going to be attacked before daybreak, we'll sneak up the mountain and find a place to hide."

"Excuse me for interrupting," Martin said. "I can fly the helicopter at night. That would be safer than trying to hide in the forest."

"I thought zero-visibility meant you had to file a flight plan," Nikki said.

"Except in an emergency. I'll wear night goggles and we'll be fine."

"Okay, we'll do the chopper if we need to exit quickly," Nikki said.

"Hopefully nothing will happen and at the first light, we'll fly out. Understood?"

They nodded.

They spent time planning an emergency getaway. Nikki and Andy would carry last-minute items that would be left by the exit door, and they would lock up the house. That would leave Cindy to take care of Olivia and provide Martin the time he needed to start up the helicopter.

Nikki instructed Andy and Martin to find hammers, baseball bats, brooms, or anything else that could be used should they be surprised. She suggested placing them by the exterior doors and on the floor beneath the living room windows.

"They won't be very good against automatic weapons," Cindy said.

"Hopefully, we won't have to use them," Martin said.

Nikki set the security cameras up to cover the grounds and connected the app on her brother's phone, on Cindy's, and her own.

"What about me?" Martin asked.

"You're the pilot, you need to sleep."

He stared at Nikki. "With all this talk, you seriously think I'll sleep?"

"If we need you, I'll wake you up," Nikki assured him.

Martin did not look convinced.

Cindy volunteered to take first watch, starting at seven-thirty. They would all keep track of their surroundings from the cameras and through the windows. The phone apps would alert them, but there was a twenty-second delay. In life-and-death situations, even a minuscule delay could be critical.

Nikki offered to stay up with Cindy. Then Andy would take the second four-hour watch. Olivia would sleep in the bedroom with her parents until it was Andy's turn to be the watchman, and then he would wheel her crib to Nikki's room.

"Once my four hours are over, I'll wake you up, Sis. You can keep watch while I feed and water my lab animals before we leave. Plus, the barn's back door offers a good view of the road where it breaks away from the highway."

"You should put them into a hibernation state, and they won't need to eat or drink," Nikki said.

Andy laughed.

"At daybreak, I'll awaken everyone," Nikki said. "No breakfast. I'll pack a bag of those apples I saw in the kitchen. We can munch on those if we get hungry."

Andy took Nikki aside and apologized for the mess he had made of the situation.

"We'll work together and get Eduardo and Sammy back," she said, touching his arm in a conciliatory gesture. *Fake it till you make it*, she thought, still not sure if her feelings toward Andy were softening.

# THIRTY-FIVE

## EDUARDO

Eduardo put away the stapler and other supplies he no longer needed. The Cubans and the other men, the ones that had brought the medical supplies, were returning to the chopper. One of them jumped in and pushed the sheet-covered box of instruments closer to the door.

"Catch it, Fausto." With a grunt, he pushed the box to the man on the ground.

The weight of the box threw Fausto off balance. "Caramba, this shit is heavy." He continued cussing with a lopsided smile.

His coworker laughed and got out of the helicopter. Together they carried the box away from the aircraft and outside the range of the rotor blades.

Eduardo had heard Bembe on the phone with this man, but now he had a face to associate with the name.

Bembe climbed in and looked at the man on the stretcher. "How's he doing?" he asked gruffly.

Eduardo summarized his work: stapling the major lacerations, injecting him with a tetanus vaccine and penicillin, giving him a painkiller by mouth, and cleaning up all the minor wounds. "He's running a slight fever, which is expected. I've given him an antibiotic to prevent infection. The compound break puts him at high risk."

Bembe grumbled and sat on the floor next to the door, no large box to lean against this time.

The pilot waited for the passengers to settle down before sliding the door shut and starting the engine. The main rotor hummed, reminding everyone to prepare for takeoff. Some buckled in and put their headsets on, others merely adjusted earmuffs. The helicopter lifted at an angle.

Eduardo guessed their destination would be a hideaway near Cheyenne Mountain. But soon he saw that they were flying away from the mountains. First north of Colorado Springs and then east toward the prairie. He had been dead wrong.

The patient awakened. He thrashed about in the stretcher. Eduardo could tell he was in pain and gave him another dose of morphine.

Eduardo wiped his hand with disinfectant and checked the man's temperature. His fever was holding steady, which was a good sign.

Everyone but the pilot and Eduardo had slept on the first trip. Flying over the prairie, Eduardo drifted off. The slight banking of the helicopter awakened him. He felt the chopper slow for landing. Rubbing his eyes, he looked out and saw a large barn and a two-story house. Nothing else. The sun was low in the sky. It must be around six in the evening.

A quick glance at his patient confirmed the man remained asleep as they descended. It was good news that the place was so isolated. He doubted that they had a doctor on staff. Eduardo would be worth more alive than dead for a few more days. That would give him time to figure out an escape.

Two of the thieves helped hand the stretcher off to the pilot and Sammy, who were first to descend. Eduardo concerned himself with the medical supplies and handed them to Celso before he descended. Bembe led the way into a huge but dark kitchen. The late afternoon sun streaming through shutters on a large window above the sink provided the only light.

On closer inspection, Eduardo noticed a stove, built-in microwave, and two refrigerators set on the far wall. The other three walls, except for doorways, had built-in stained-wood cabinets. A granite-topped island also had matching wood cabinets. A few feet away from the island was a long dining table with eight chairs.

Bembe opened a door and ordered Sammy and the pilot to take the stretcher downstairs. He pushed Eduardo ahead of him.

The cabinets Eduardo passed all had locks on them. What could be inside? Surely not porcelain dishes.

Downstairs, he was shocked to see a well-equipped clinic, including four hospital beds already made up with sheets, two exam tables, and lighting good enough to perform surgery. What had they done or expected to do that they needed emergency instruments and resources like defibrillators, anesthesia, electrocardiogram, ultrasound, and x-ray equipment in addition to basic laboratory devices and supplies? Besides, who would know how to operate all this equipment?

"Here is your hospital. Now take care of him," Bembe commanded in a booming voice.

"Let's get him into a bed," Eduardo told the two men carrying the stretcher. He turned back to face Bembe. "We'd like something to eat. And a soft meal for him."

"I could cook for us all," Sammy said.

Bembe stared back, ignored Sammy's offer, and went up the stairs.

"Why did you volunteer to cook," Eduardo asked in a whisper once they were alone.

"I'd like a chance to get into those locked cabinets."

Eduardo searched the drawers and cabinets for IVs and discovered that the clinic was not quite as well stocked as he originally thought. Still, it was better than the field.

"This must be their intel headquarters," Eduardo said, keeping his voice low. He looked around the clinic. "My guess is the stingrays retransmit the captured info to whatever they have on the first floor. Maybe into whatever's in the cabinets."

Sammy whispered that he would sweep the room for hidden recording devices.

"They are decrypting the intel somewhere along the line," Eduardo said softly, as if whispering to himself. "Either within the stingrays before they rebroadcast, or through the equipment they have upstairs. If they realize we know, they'll kill us both, whether they need a doctor or not."

"They'll kill us when we're no longer useful," Sammy said.

Eduardo hated to think about it, but he had no idea why they were keeping Sammy alive now that the mules were no longer being used. That gnawing feeling that maybe Sammy was part of the ugly scheme returned. But surely, that could not be true.

# THIRTY-SIX

## SAMMY

The patient was sleeping, so Sammy put his dinner in the refrigerator. He stacked the chipped white plates that he and Eduardo had eaten from at the top of the stairs, as Celso had instructed him. He surveyed the clinic from that vantage point. Nothing suspicious. But they must have hidden cameras somewhere. Tired, he dreaded sleep for fear of the nightmare.

A shower in the back of the clinic beckoned, but he offered to take care of the patient while Eduardo used it. After taking a shower, the doctor laid a fresh hospital gown at the foot of the bed to use after cleaning the patient again.

Sammy leaned in and whispered to Eduardo. "On the way here, we flew over Schriever Space Force Base. It fits with the retrieval of intel."

Eduardo shifted closer to Sammy to hear better.

"Schriever's Missile Defense Center controls communication satellites for the Department of Defense that provide early warning and navigation information."

Eduardo raised his eyebrows. "I didn't know Colorado had so many important military and defense sites."

The patient opened his eyes, lifted his head slightly, and asked in slurred, Cuban-accented Spanish where he was.

"The clinic," Eduardo said.

"Aww," the man said slowly, "we made it to the control center."

Eduardo nodded and asked the man his name.

"I'm Macario." He winced. "You saved my life."

"We still have to work at getting you healed."

Sammy warmed the food in the microwave and handed the plate to Eduardo. After a few bites, Macario pushed the plate away. Eduardo cleaned the patient.

Sammy asked in hushed tones about the other men as he helped Macario's good arm through the sleeve of the clean hospital gown. He especially wanted to know about Bembe.

Macario snickered softly. "Bembe," he whispered. "In Cuba it means the prophet. Be careful with him."

Eduardo eased the injured arm into the gown.

"Three times a week, we leave in the mornings. You have time to plan your escape."

"Escape?" Eduardo looked surprised.

"If you want to live." Macario moaned and stretched the fingers on the hand of the broken arm.

Sammy and Eduardo exchanged glances.

"Is the clinic bugged?" Sammy asked, taking advantage of the patient's willingness to share.

"Nah, but keep your voices down. Up there"—he pointed to the top floor using his good hand—"we have cameras, but never did put any in the clinic. All the best equipment is for the job. They bolt the door at the top of the stairs."

Sammy would like to believe the basement did not contain listening devices. But could he trust Macario?

"What's upstairs?" Eduardo asked.

"Control center." His eyes were half-closed. "We catch intel on the airwaves and pass it on."

Before long, the patient had fallen asleep again.

"Why'd he say so much? Encouraging us to escape, sharing what they do?" Sammy asked, still whispering.

"It's the morphine. It can work like a truth serum on some people."

"Do you think that's all true?"

Eduardo shrugged. "We'll find out."

# THIRTY-SEVEN

## NIKKI

Nikki climbed out of bed, still dressed. Her eyes felt gritty. She squinted at the security camera app and turned to Andy, who stood at the foot of her bed. "I'm awake. You can go feed your lab animals."

"Olivia and Cindy are asleep in the main bedroom," he said. "Let's leave Olivia there."

"And the pilot?"

"Asleep."

Andy left for the barn.

She checked the cameras again, one by one. No movement recorded on any of them. She wanted the soft light of dawn to appear over the mountains so she could get her family to safety. But that was two hours away.

Her phone buzzed, showing the alert for the camera app. She stopped abruptly on the stairs, heart palpitating. Her shaking hands brought up the camera app. A big dark figure appeared. Panic hit her for a split second, until she saw, to her relief, that it was a bear. A female—followed by a cub. They ambled out of range and disappeared into the forest. This time, Nikki smiled at seeing a mother bear and her cub.

In the kitchen, Nikki packed a bag of apples. She left it by the door, where she already had her purse, fedora, and a small case. According to Floyd, the safehouse had extra clothing. Andy and Cindy's luggage was in the helicopter already. Only last-minute items were piled by the exit.

The wait was getting to her. She texted Andy that she was going to awaken Cindy and the pilot. He responded with a thumbs-up emoji.

She knocked on Cindy's door and waited until she heard her sister-in-law's response. Then she continued down the hall to Martin's door.

They joined Nikki downstairs in minutes.

No sooner had they gathered in the kitchen than Andy called. Nikki put him on speaker. "Headlights leaving the highway, coming this way. We need to clear out."

It was still dark. Nikki asked Martin if he could be ready to take off shortly. In a nervous reaction, she touched the world tree pendant on her necklace.

He nodded. "Let's go." Martin dashed outside to start the helicopter.

Cindy ran upstairs to grab her sleeping daughter.

Andy hurried through the kitchen door and locked it. He took the few bags and other items by the front door to the aircraft. Neptune followed him.

Inside, Nikki monitored the cameras while she waited for Cindy. Headlights appeared in one of the feeds. She stiffened when a second set came into view. She finally heard the chopper engine starting.

Cindy rushed down the stairs carrying a crying Olivia and she ran through the door Nikki held open for them. Nikki locked the door behind her and sprinted to the helicopter. She took Olivia while Cindy climbed in.

The last one to board, Nikki collapsed into the seat and strapped herself in. Martin told them to put their headsets on. She placed a headset on Olivia while Cindy held her daughter's arms tight to prevent her from removing it. With her niece taken care of, Nikki put on her own headset. Olivia kept crying. Martin turned her mic off.

"Up we go," Martin said.

The red glow from the cockpit lit up the entire cabin. From the back, where Nikki sat, the glow outlined Martin's right shoulder and reflected off the pilot's night vision goggles, making him look like a ghostly robot. She closed her eyes and braced herself as she felt the craft lift into the air.

She dared to look out. Light streamed through the windows of the two-story house. They were gaining altitude when two vehicles raced into the front yard, the very spot the helicopter had been only minutes before. The headlights illuminated four men with semiautomatic weapons running around like ants. One aimed upward. Nikki flinched, waiting for the impact. When nothing happened, she opened her eyes and got one final view of the ranch house. The attackers were no longer visible.

# THIRTY-EIGHT
## EDUARDO

A soul-wrenching cry awakened Eduardo. After he screamed, Sammy called out a woman's name. "Ana, forgive me. It's all my fault, Chiquita."

In a prolonged wail, he repeated it twice more.

Eduardo went to his side, gently urging Sammy to wake up. "It's a bad dream. You're okay. You're safe."

As safe as anyone could be as captives of mercenary spies.

Sammy sat up.

In the dim light from the lamp that Eduardo had left on, he saw the man's catatonic expression. This was not the Sammy he had known for the past several days. He was reliving a trauma. Recent events had probably triggered bad memories.

Despite the screams, Macario slept on. Probably due to the morphine.

"Talk to me," Eduardo said softly, resting a hand on Sammy's shoulder.

Sammy walked to the bathroom. He left the door open as he washed and dried his face and hands and returned to his bed. Before sitting down, he stepped into his pants and threw his shirt on.

"You're reliving a severe trauma," Eduardo said. "If you talk to me, maybe I can help."

Sammy shook his head.

"Is it about your life before you came to this country?"

Sammy stared blankly.

"Anything to do with the drums you play?"

Sammy lowered his head and mumbled. "How do you know about the drums?"

"When you didn't show up, Andy and I went to your house."

When Sammy would not talk about the nightmare or the trauma that caused it, Eduardo tried another tactic. "Look, it's clear you're no uneducated peasant. I doubt you're even Mexican. I think you're Cuban. Our only chance to get out of this alive is to trust each other and work together."

"I should have killed myself, but I was a coward."

"Is your nightmare about suicide?"

Sammy shook his head. "Guilt. Now Andy's dead, and that's my fault too."

Macario groaned. He called for Eduardo. "I need a bedpan."

Eduardo hated the interruption but tended to his patient.

Half an hour later, the door at the top of the stairs creaked. Macario gestured for Eduardo to step away from the bed.

Celso balanced a tray with their breakfast, permeating the clinic with the aroma of bacon. He asked if Macario had screamed in his sleep.

Eduardo glanced at Macario. He appeared to be sleeping. Sammy had climbed back into bed, also pretending to be asleep.

"That was me." Eduardo shrugged. "I had a nightmare."

"Is the patient better?"

"Somewhat, but he's still running a fever."

"Leave the plates at the top of the stairs when you're done." With that, Celso left. Eduardo heard the bolt slam home.

Macario opened his eyes and smiled. "I'm hungry."

Sammy got up too. "Breakfast smells good."

Eduardo cranked Macario's bed into an upright position and

arranged the pillows. "Remember to keep your splinted arm and leg still."

"Están fritos si no se escapan," Macario said, taking a mouthful of scrambled eggs. "You guys are toast unless you escape."

"I gather you're willing to help us?" Sammy asked.

Macario nodded.

"Why?"

"You because I admire what you did. The doctor because he saved my life."

Macario admired something that Sammy had done? Eduardo wondered what it was. Maybe some show of courage when they were taking him from his ranch. But escape was the more pressing issue.

"And just how do you propose we break out of this fortified basement?" Eduardo asked.

"Ahh, there's a secret passageway. I will reveal it to you, on one condition."

# THIRTY-NINE

## NIKKI

Nikki prayed during the flight to the safehouse in Montezuma County. Irritable from worry and lack of sleep, she reminded herself: positive thoughts. She turned her attention to the place where they were headed. Montezuma was apparently a popular name in this part of the world.

She and Andy's family were on their way to safety and Eduardo was still in harm's way. She could think about other topics, like the spies that had taken Eduardo, yet that upset her. Floyd seemed to think Sammy was Cuban. She worried more whether Sammy was a spy too, or if his life, like Eduardo's, was in danger. She shuddered.

Martin pointed out Mesa Verde National Park. He suggested that Andy grab the binoculars and look at the cliff dwellings that were coming up. After he enjoyed the view, Andy passed the binoculars to Nikki. She gasped at the houses built into alcoves on the cliff's face. Martin explained that they were the best-preserved cliff dwellings in the country.

"The overhanging rocks protect them from the elements," Martin said.

Turning to share the binoculars with Cindy, she saw that her sister-in-law and Olivia had fallen asleep. Neptune, too. Andy and Martin had talked the whole flight. Granted, Martin knew a lot about the terrain and the history of the state, but Nikki needed sleep. She could have turned the mic off and slept, but she felt responsible for their escape from the rental property. She was ready to land, find the safehouse, indulge in a shower, and take a nap. Would her family be safe there? She shuddered thinking about Andy when he told her the criminals had taken the documents from his pickup, including the rental agreement on the ranch house. That was how they knew where to look. She hoped they would not trace them to the safehouse. She considered the weak points, such as phones. Hers was secure, Cindy stopped using hers last night, and Andy used his in the early hours of the morning. She worried.

A man stood at the edge of the makeshift heliport. Must be Clive Underwood, the CIA operative Floyd had arranged to meet them. He wore an army cap, cutoff blue jeans, a sweatshirt, sandals, and aviator-style sunglasses. Once the rotor blades slowed down, he took Olivia, who was crying again, from Nikki. The child looked at him in surprise, took his cap, put it on her head, and giggled.

Neptune jumped out and sniffed the ground.

Clive, probably a cover name, introduced himself as the manager of the cabin. "You filled that helicopter to capacity. Glad you made it safely."

He walked them to the small hangar. Another man, rather young, stood close to a green truck. Clive introduced them and asked Nikki to give that man the shirt that was to be sent for DNA testing. She ran back to the chopper to get it. At the hangar again, Clive gave Nikki a key ring, with a key for the Jeep and two for the house.

The young man climbed into the truck and took off.

"The cabin's along that road. You can't miss it. Other cabins are scattered around on other roads. I'll help Martin service the helicopter and put it in the hangar. We'll join you shortly."

Martin objected, saying he had to head back to Raton as soon as he refueled.

"I've been instructed to pay you in cash," Clive said.

Martin told him the fee and stashed the payment in his flight bag. He scribbled a receipt, tore it out, and gave it to Clive.

"It's been quite an adventure. Glad I could help," Martin told Nikki. "Call if you need anything else."

"Next time I hire you, I'll be on vacation, and you can file flight plans," Nikki said.

They laughed at their private joke.

# FORTY

## SAMMY

If there were listening devices in the basement clinic, Sammy and Eduardo would not be able to escape. Yet common sense told Sammy that the kidnappers upstairs would not have asked Macario to set the abductees up. They could kill the two men anytime, anywhere. The Cubans only needed him for the mules, so why was he still alive? As for Eduardo, they needed his skills. At least until Macario recovered.

"You said you had one condition to help us escape." Sammy decided it was worth the risk to inquire. "What is it?"

"Freedom. I want my freedom."

Sammy snorted and asked if they had to carry him out.

"Freedom from what?" Eduardo asked.

"From everything and from that comemierda. That shit eater."

"Who's that?"

"Bembe. Es un comemierda."

Eduardo touched the man's forehead even though he had only recently taken his temperature. "Are you hallucinating?"

Before Macario could respond, Sammy asked him if it was the morphine talking.

"I'm very conscious of what I'm telling you. If you two promise to come back for me, I'll tell you how to get out of here."

"Tell us your plan," Eduardo said in a much softer approach than Sammy had taken.

"First, we wait until the men leave for work. That should be soon," Macario said, stretching his neck and glancing at Eduardo. "You'll need to save that woman of yours. Bembe sent four men to hunt her down. To get her and her brother's family too."

Eduardo's hands trembled. He rubbed them against his pants to hide it, like any good spy would, but Sammy had noticed. Sammy was not yet certain if Eduardo was a CIA operative or not. Or could it be that Nikki worked for the Agency? Andy had told him Nikki was a private investigator, but was that a cover for her true employment?

"How..." Eduardo sputtered. He looked genuinely terrified. "How do they know about her?"

"From your telephone. And from documents in the pickup's glove compartment. The pickup you were traveling in with that other man, the one who was killed in the park. They got an address from a rental agreement. They were going to check that out."

"Tell me about the work they do." Sammy was testing the man's honesty.

Macario sighed. "They'll set up those new communication units that I saw you photograph when the three of us were alone in the helicopter."

"You fooled me," Eduardo said. "I thought you slept through that."

Macario chuckled. "I'm well trained."

"How do we get out of here?" Sammy asked.

"First, there's a tunnel Bembe had us build in case of emergency. It takes you out to a small shed. The entrance and the exit are well hidden. If they suspect I helped you, it's my death sentence."

"I can tape your mouth down and tie your legs to the bed," Eduardo said, "if you think that will convince them you were not our accomplice."

Macario held his good hand up and told the doctor that would not be necessary.

"Tell us where that tunnel is," Sammy said more forcefully, yet still speaking softly.

"Promise you'll come back for me," the patient said.

They vowed to do their best.

"That's not enough. You must swear you will come back for me, and I'll tell you how and when you should break out."

"You'll tell us how we're supposed to rescue you?" Eduardo frowned.

"That's the easy part," Macario responded in his Cuban accent. "Call in the FBI and the CIA."

Sammy held up his hand and solemnly swore he would come back for Macario. Eduardo followed his example.

"If you do what I say, you'll make it out alive. The end of the tunnel opens next to a shed that's protected by an overhanging cliff where the prairie drops, creating a glen."

"It can't be too far from here, can it?" Eduardo asked.

"Quarter of a mile."

Eduardo whistled. "That's a long tunnel."

Sammy thought the Cubans must have been inspired by the one at Cheyenne Mountain.

"It's an escape route should your government find out what goes on here," Macario explained. "The cliff camouflages the shed."

"What's in the shed?" Eduardo asked.

"Survival food and equipment, but it's locked. You'd need a torch to get inside. Don't waste your time."

"Where can we walk for help?" Sammy asked.

"We are east and a little south of Schriever. You'll see the mountains to the west. Best route on foot is to head north to State Highway 94. From there, catch a ride along the highway or keep walking west to the nearest gas station, where you can find a phone."

The men were silent for a couple of seconds before Sammy asked how long Macario's comrades would be away.

"Depends. When they take the helicopter, it's usually five hours. In the Suburban, it's six or seven."

"Where's the tunnel entrance?" Eduardo asked.

Macario pointed with his good arm in the direction of the bathroom. "The linen closet in the back corner has removable shelves. After that there's an interior that slides to the right and opens to the landing at the top of the tunnel stairs."

They heard the door opening from the kitchen. It was Celso.

Sammy stepped into the bathroom. Eduardo opened a bottle of pills, handed one to Macario, and passed him a glass of water. Just a doctor taking care of his patient.

Celso came into the clinic with a platter holding three plates. It was mid-morning and too early for lunch. He put the tray on the side table, grunted a hello to Macario and asked how he was feeling.

"Better," he responded.

Sammy stepped back into the clinic.

Celso reminded them they knew what to do with the empty dishes. He walked to the bathroom before returning upstairs.

"Friendly fellow," Eduardo said. "And he checked the bathroom."

"He has to be careful around the two of you," Macario said. "They must be going somewhere. Otherwise, he would not have brought lunch so early."

Worried, Sammy repeated Eduardo's concern that Celso had looked inside the bathroom.

"He's making sure we have not discovered the tunnel," Eduardo said. "We should prepare supplies, like water, to take with us. Food would be difficult since Celso cooks meals not easily packaged." He rummaged through drawers and retrieved two flasks which he filled with water.

"Take breathing apparatuses for the tunnel," Macario said. "In the cabinet by the fridge."

"Do you suppose they've heard us?" Sammy asked.

"I don't think so," Macario said, "but I agree he was checking the tunnel. You'll have to wait and see if they leave. Let's eat while the food is hot."

# FORTY-ONE

## NIKKI

Nikki took a hard look at the cabin. It needed repairs—a paint job, a few planks on the deck, and the front door, which looked like it could fall off its hinges. She worried the interior would be as bad or worse.

She opened the rickety door into a mud room with a built-in bench along the wall. A solid metal door prevented her from going further. She unlocked it.

In amazement, she saw a cozy living room, a small dining area, and a fully equipped kitchen. An open floor plan, all tastefully decorated. A high ceiling graced the interior. She imagined bringing Eduardo here. They could enjoy a glass of champagne every evening after hiking to their hearts' content, to places like Mesa Verde National Park. Eduardo would be fascinated by the cliff dwellings and the history of the Ancestral Puebloans.

Andy followed her into the cabin, carrying their scant luggage and the bag of apples no one had eaten. Cindy came in, carrying Olivia.

"What a marvelous place!" Cindy gazed around the room. "If only we were here under happier circumstances."

"Do you think this will do?" Clive asked with a sly grin.

"It's beautiful. Such a contrast to the outside." Nikki set her purse on a nearby chair and removed her hat. "But we're not vacationing. My husband is missing."

"As soon as you get settled, I want to ask you and your brother a few questions about his disappearance. And Amaya's too."

Andy suggested they sit down and get started.

"Let's use the back room for that," Clive said putting his sunglasses in his shirt pocket. "I'll start with the two of you. That way, Cindy can take care of Ms. Olivia."

Nikki, picking up her purse, said she needed to visit the bathroom. She wanted to retrieve the baby Glock that Floyd had arranged to be hidden there. It was unlikely that Olivia would find it, but Nikki needed to make certain. She figured it had been Clive who had hidden it there, but he'd apparently followed Floyd's instructions instead of handing it to her himself.

She reached under the toilet tank and found the handgun. A note attached to it said the ammunition was in a drawer of the same bathroom. Placing both items in her purse, she left it on a high shelf in the closet. It would be safe since there was no way Olivia could climb up there. Now she had two guns. She could give the Smith & Wesson to Clive when she had a chance.

On her way back, she grabbed three apples. A small cactus in a planter sat on the countertop next to the bag of apples. It reminded her of Keiko's ikebana arrangements. She wondered how Keiko was doing. Colombia was not an easy place for a single woman of Japanese descent to live. *When this is all over*, she thought, *Eduardo and I should invite her to Miami to live with us.*

"The refrigerator is fully stocked," Clive said, "and the pantry has tons of food, a few bottles of wine, vodka, and whiskey. Plenty of beer in the fridge. If you need anything, let me know and I'll make sure you get it." He led the way to the back room. "The artwork is by Colorado artists. Native Americans, most of them."

Nikki glanced at the prints and original paintings on the walls. They were very appropriate for the house.

# FORTY-TWO

## CLIVE

They sat at a round table in the room at the end of the hall. Clive told them he would interview Andy first for background on Amaya.

Andy described how he met Sammy, the way he became a family friend, and his help with the hibernation studies.

"Does the man have any relatives?"

Andy shook his head. "Not that I know of. He's spoken about his parents, but they're both dead."

"No children?"

"None that I've heard about."

"Besides you, does he have any friends?"

"He knows a few people but actual friends, I'd say Cindy and I are the only ones."

"He spends a lot of time with you, then?" Clive asked.

Andy nodded.

"Does he travel?"

"To Spain a few times a year to call on customers that buy his mules. He'll take two to five days every month to meet with prospective clients in this country. Or to deliver an animal."

Clive asked about the length of the trips to Spain.

"Usually three weeks, give or take a couple of days."

"Who takes care of the mules when he travels?"

Andy grinned. "You're looking at him."

"During the season when he helps you with the bear studies, has he gone off on a trip?"

"Oh, for sure. Once, when I needed his help the most, he left for Spain. He cut that trip short and was only gone for a week so he could get back and help me."

Next Clive asked about Sammy's background.

"All I know is that he's from northern Mexico and that a family tragedy occurred. That's when he came to the US."

"Tell me about the family stuff."

"He's never provided any details. All he said was that the family trauma made him move here."

"Do you trust him?" Clive asked.

"With my life."

Clive inquired about the day Andy and Eduardo had followed the trucks and trailers into the mountains. He asked him to be very specific about what he remembered the night they were assaulted.

Andy glanced anxiously at his sister.

Nikki reached for an apple and took a bite.

"Go on," Clive said.

"We followed the trucks out of Taos. Nikki saw they'd pulled over before starting the climb into the Sangre de Cristo mountains. We thought troopers had stopped them, but we didn't know for sure. As we got closer, we saw they'd stopped for a flat tire and a man from a road assistance service was changing it for them."

"It's my understanding the trucks kept going, all the way to Colorado," Clive asked. "And Sammy was with them."

"How do you know that Sammy didn't plan all of this to mislead you," Nikki interrupted. "Sammy is not the trustworthy guy you claim he is."

Explaining that he knew how sensitive this situation was for them, Clive asked Nikki to understand that they needed to discuss it to bring Eduardo and Sammy back alive.

She apologized.

Andy went over the events of that afternoon and evening. After Eduardo attached the GPS tracker on the trailer, they followed the trucks until they parked near a lake in Sugarite Canyon State Park.

"We stopped where my crew cab could not be seen and hid in the brush to watch the criminals. They let Sammy out of a built-in metal container on one of the trailers. He took the mules to water at the lake."

"Did you notify the state police?" Clive asked.

"Our plan was to call the police station in Raton, but there was no signal. We left our hiding place to return to my vehicle. Something alerted the criminals to our presence. They came running after us, shooting automatic weapons. They could have killed us, but they didn't."

"Why did they take Eduardo and not you?" Clive asked.

Andy looked down before answering. "My guess is they thought they had killed me. Don't know for sure since I passed out when I fell and hit my head on a rock." Andy pointed to the gash on the side of his head.

"Go on," Clive said.

"I came to early the next day. Totally confused. I didn't know what I was doing out there or that Eduardo had been with me and was missing. It took me a while to remember. When I looked for the trucks and trailers, they were gone. A park ranger found me and radioed for an ambulance."

# FORTY-THREE

## NIKKI

Now Nikki took her turn to tell Clive what she knew of Amaya, though she had only known him for a few days. She hoped something she said would help find Eduardo. Gathering her thoughts, she stopped eating the apple. She could understand Andy's lack of caution. He had always been impulsive. But why had Eduardo gone along with her brother's decision to follow the criminals?

"Contrary to my brother," she told Clive, "I don't trust Sammy."

"Why is that?"

"My office searched several databases, including Interpol's, to locate him. Nothing turned up."

"How confident are you that your office did a thorough job?"

"Totally," she responded. "Charlotte, our office manager, is also our researcher. She's outstanding."

Andy cleared his throat as if he wanted to speak, but Clive asked him to remain quiet. "Speak only if you're asked. You can add your opinion when I'm finished with the interview."

"Do you think he's a criminal?"

Nikki hesitated and then shook her head. "I don't know what to think. But he's lived in this country for nine years and owns a business here. Yet there's no evidence that he even exists. Charlotte could not locate a driver's license for him, but he presented one to a sheriff's deputy the day that he took us mule riding in the Pecos Wilderness. On the plus side, I can say he's affable and witty."

"Did you happen to see the driver's license?"

"No, but it must not have been in the name of Sammy Amaya. In fact, the deputy handed the license back to him and called him 'Mr. San.' But Sammy interrupted him, so I didn't hear the rest. It might have been Mr. Sanchez, Mr. Santos, Mr. Sandoval. Who knows?"

Clive suggested that maybe she'd misheard Mr. San for Mr. Sam.

Nikki shook her head. "I'm certain he said Mr. San."

"Do you know the name of his business?"

"I don't, but Andy should know," she said.

Andy laughed. "It's incorporated and it's public record."

"It's probably a limited liability corporation. That way you don't have to reveal as much personal information." Nikki took another bite of apple.

"Can you provide the name?" Clive asked.

"I think it's Windswept, LLC."

"You think?" Clive asked. "Or do you know?"

Andy cleared his throat and turned to face his sister. "You might as well know that I'm the registered agent and the only member."

Nikki choked on the apple. After coughing several seconds, she asked Andy if the LLC was engaged in criminal activity.

"You keep thinking Sammy is involved in shady business deals, but I can assure you that he's not. Neither am I."

Clive intervened and asked Andy to simply answer the question.

"Look, I'm tired of you and my sister thinking the worst of him. I repeat, Sammy is not involved in criminal activity."

"As the agent and only member, that makes the LLC your entity," Clive said. "If Sammy is the manager of the business, and he's involved in unlawful activities, you would not be liable. Unless you're also participating in them."

"There's nothing illegal going on," Andy insisted.

"Then why was Sammy kidnapped?" Nikki demanded.

# FORTY-FOUR

## EDUARDO

"I hear the helicopter," Eduardo said. He climbed the stairs and listened by the door. He heard a low rustling, and then a door slammed. After that, the house was silent. Still, he waited until it was clear the chopper was airborne. Returning to Macario's bedside, he asked if he thought they could get out and get somewhere safe before Bembe and his men discovered their captives had left. He and Sammy would come back for him after that.

"You must. They will hunt you down once they know you've escaped."

"Your infection could get worse if you don't take antibiotics. If I leave them where you can get them yourself, they could suspect you helped us. The best place is on the overbed table. I'll leave them there with a pitcher of water. You can wheel it closer if you need a pill and move it away when you don't. Make sure to take the antibiotics."

"Coming back for me may take more than twenty-four hours. Call the CIA and FBI so they can organize a raid on this place. Tell them I know all the sensitive intel we've captured and passed to the Ministry of State Security. I can provide details of the operation, names of those involved here, and the ones receiving the intel."

"The MSS, did you say?" Eduardo asked. "Not the Cuban DGI?"

Macario snorted. "Cuba doesn't have the military might to do much with the intel except sell it. It's going to China. I thought you knew that."

"Call me ignorant. I'm only a doctor and what I know is that you need a hospital to get the care you need. I've done the best I can. If we get you out, I'll personally take you to a hospital for surgery."

"If you get me out of here, I'll be happy. I want to defect and work out a deal to get protection, like the WPP. I have information that the CIA will find useful."

Eduardo nodded. He did not want to dampen Macario's enthusiasm, but getting the agencies to act quickly might be an issue. Floyd could get the information to the right people, maybe he had already acted on the stingray pictures he'd sent Nikki. But it takes time to organize a full-blown investigation.

Macario's condition worried Eduardo. Controlling the infection was only part of the issue. Getting the bones properly set became more urgent as each day passed. Bembe either did not care about Macario's condition or did not understand its seriousness.

And Nikki was ever in his thoughts. Her dedication to her work, even in the face of death, had always amazed him. But his abduction was not just a job. That would make her more emotionally involved than ever. Her safety was his major concern. Especially after Macario had told him about the four men sent to capture her. Eduardo knew her life was in danger.

Eduardo had been sending telepathic messages to Nikki throughout the day, hoping they would reach her. He had never given extrasensory perception much credence. Yet, as a neurologist, he knew the brain was the most powerful organ in the human body. In his current predicament he remembered times the two of them seemed to understand each other without speaking. ESP? Maybe. In the past two days, he had felt close to her despite their physical distance and inability to communicate. During brain surgery, technicians monitored the patient's brain waves. He did not doubt that his thoughts could travel. The only question was whether Nikki would receive his messages.

Sammy nudged him. "No noise upstairs since the helicopter left.

We should make a break for it. Is he going to make it?" Sammy asked, nodding slightly toward Macario.

"I'm working on it. We can't leave until Macario is set up." Eduardo arranged the meds, the pitcher of water, and paper cups on a stainless-steel tray on the overbed table. He added a bedpan at the center of the bed so Macario could reach it easily.

"Why don't you take a look at the entrance to our escape route?" Eduardo asked Sammy.

# FORTY-FIVE

## SAMMY

Sammy listened at the top of the stairs for a couple of minutes to confirm no one had been left behind to guard the captives in the basement. Then he headed to the clinic bathroom.

He opened the corner closet and removed the towels, soap, and tissue. The shelves came out easily enough. The remaining wood paneling had narrow slits the full length of the closet, along the bottom and the top. He pushed one side of the back wall to the right. It moved like a sliding door on tracks, opening to a small landing. The stairs disappeared into a pitch-black tunnel.

Did he trust Macario enough to enter this dark underground passage? What about bugs, spiders, snakes? A dank, stale odor hit his nostrils. He had never thought of himself as claustrophobic. He had no problem going through caves for Andy's bear research. And though it was unpleasant, being forced into that metal box of his trailer caused no panic attack. But the caves and the metal container had been far less scary. They were about to enter a long tunnel from which escape might prove to be impossible. What if the tunnel collapsed? Flashlights and water would be essential. What about oxygen? Could this be a setup? He used his sleeve to wipe the sweat off his forehead.

Sammy called for Eduardo, who joined him, carrying a flashlight, a couple of water flasks, and two portable breathing apparatuses, each with an attached tube and a breathing cushion that covered the nose and mouth.

"How did you know that was my main concern?" he asked, pointing at the breathing equipment.

"We wouldn't get very far in a primitive tunnel without these." Eduardo set them on the counter surrounding the wash basin. "Macario told me the tunnel has ventilation shafts, but it's best to be cautious."

Eduardo donned the small backpack and slipped a flask of water into the side pocket. Sammy did the same. He flipped the breathing cushion into place.

Sammy pulled on the headgear and adjusted the mouthpiece. Then he moved aside and let Eduardo lead the way, shining his flashlight into the tunnel.

# FORTY-SIX
## CLIVE

Nikki's interview with Clive was over, but Clive asked her to stay behind. As soon as Andy closed the door behind him, the agent wanted to know if she thought her brother could be involved in some sort of scheme with Amaya.

"I hope not, but I can't be sure. I'm suspicious of Sammy but Andy thinks he hung the moon. Finding out that Andy's the front for the mule farm gives me pause, I hate to say."

Clive suggested calling Floyd in Miami. Charlotte was included in the conference.

Nikki asked her to investigate Windswept, a registered New Mexico limited liability corporation.

"I'm searching now," Charlotte said. "Ahh, here it is. The articles of organization for the LLC are filed as well as the document called 'Statement of Acceptance of Appointment by Designated Agent.' Oh! That agent is Andres Manuel Garcia. Your brother?"

"Yes. Please check the number of members."

"I'm scrolling down. Here it is. Again, it's your brother."

"Can you find the stated business purpose?"

Charlotte took a couple of minutes to search while everyone else remained silent. "The articles don't have a general business purpose statement. Ahh, here it is, an industry classification code. Let me look it up."

Nikki told Floyd that Andy had already revealed he was the agent and lone member of Amaya's LLC.

"In other words, it's really Andy's LLC, not Amaya's. Is that right?" Floyd asked.

"Correct."

"It's an LLC for operating a ranch," Charlotte said.

"I don't get it." Floyd coughed. "I thought your brother had a grant from the European Space Agency to study the hibernation of bears and other animals. How does ranching fit into this?"

"He's helping Amaya stay off the grid." Nikki sighed. "At least that's my guess."

Floyd asked Clive if he'd found anything out about Amaya.

"Not yet. I've got a couple of inquiries out there. The guy is off the grid, all right."

Floyd told them he had submitted the photos Eduardo had taken of the stingray phone tracker to Hank, Clive's boss. "That should get some action rolling."

"I hope so," Nikki said.

Clive noticed that Nikki kept twisting the wedding band on her finger as she spoke.

Floyd wanted to hear their plan to find the two men and their kidnappers.

"I'll interview Andy again, without Nikki," Clive said. "Find out more about his business relationship with Amaya. I'm hoping he'll spill his guts."

Floyd suggested taking a helicopter to where Nikki found the mules loose on the prairie. "Something else out there might help us find them. Until the FBI opens an investigation, Security Source will pay for the chopper."

"You can take it out of my pay," Nikki offered.

Floyd ignored her.

Before ending the call, Floyd said he was prepared to fly out and help on the ground if he was needed.

Clive and Nikki continued in the room to discuss follow-up, like hiring a helicopter. He wanted to call Daniel, a pilot that he trusted. "I'm sure your guy is fine, but I'd rather have mine work this."

"One last item," Nikki said. "I have a Smith & Wesson that belongs to Andy. I took it from the glove box of his crew cab."

"What are you planning to do with it?"

"Give it to you once we leave the safe house," she said.

Their meeting was over. She left and Clive asked Andy to return to the room for further questions.

# FORTY-SEVEN

## NIKKI

Nikki entered the open living room to see Cindy on the sofa, scrolling through her phone. Olivia played with Neptune on the floor.

Nikki asked Cindy what she was reading.

"I looked up Montezuma." She read from her phone. "Montezuma County, in the southwestern corner of Colorado, was created by the state legislature in 1889 and named for Moctezuma II, a revered Mexican chief of the Aztec Indians."

She glanced at Nikki and continued. "You're right about the spelling of the chief's name. It's Moctezuma with a 'c,' not Montezuma. The article states that at some point in history, the name was changed to Montezuma. At least in the US."

"What else did you find?" Nikki asked, absentmindedly.

Gunshots rang out.

Nikki ran to get her gun.

Cindy jumped and grabbed her daughter. Clive and Andy burst into the living room.

More gunfire.

Clive bolted to the refrigerator and pulled it away from the wall. "Go down these stairs to the saferoom," he ordered.

Cindy went first, Olivia in her arms, followed by the German shepherd.

Clive pushed Andy to go next.

Nikki rushed back, clutching the baby Glock in one hand and her purse in the other.

Clive was the last one in. Nikki watched as he pulled a hook on the back of the fridge and locked it in place, hiding the entrance. He closed and bolted the door between the top of the stairs and the refrigerator. A soundproof curtain rolled down when he punched a button.

"We'll be safe here until we know what the gunfire was about. I need to report this to my office and the state police." Clive picked up a land phone and spoke into it. "We're under attack."

# FORTY-EIGHT

## EDUARDO

Eduardo scanned the tunnel ahead of them in the dim glow of the flashlight. He sensed Sammy's fear. Sweat had soaked through the man's shirt and beaded on his forehead before they even began the descent into darkness. Sammy's reaction would seem illogical unless he suffered from post-traumatic stress disorder. The doctor did not want his friend, if he could think of Sammy that way, to panic as they fled to freedom.

Eduardo talked to keep Sammy free of whatever terror had broken through during his nightmare. He made sure to illuminate only a few feet at a time. That kept the shadows from appearing to jump at them as the tunnel curved. The light reflected off the crown of the underground passage.

Sammy jumped and screamed.

"What's going on?" Eduardo asked, pulling his mouthpiece off. He turned in time to see Sammy writhing on the ground. Had he been bitten by a snake? Eduardo asked again what was happening.

"Up there," Sammy gasped, removing his mouthpiece. "Worms."

"Listen to me," Eduardo said forcefully. "Our only threat is from the men who abducted us. If we don't get out of here, they'll catch us."

"Flash the light on them," Sammy pleaded. "Straight up. They're right there."

Not knowing what else to do, Eduardo aimed the light upward. Wriggling earthworms caught the light.

"These babies are not going to take you anywhere. Earthworms are our friends," Eduardo said.

"They're waiting to eat my flesh," Sammy moaned, curling into a fetal position. "I should not have come here. This place will be my coffin."

Eduardo sat on the damp ground next to his friend. In soothing tones, he reminded Sammy that they were on a mission to escape from the men who had abducted them, the men who had stolen his mules. They had to get through the tunnel. "Otherwise, we won't get your mules back. They'll go wild, out on the prairie."

"But the worms—"

"These worms make it possible for your mules to eat grass. They keep the cycle of life going on this planet."

"Hmm, are you sure?" Sammy asked, his voice trembling.

"I'm positive."

"How do they breathe down here?"

"Through their skin. They pick up oxygen and release carbon dioxide."

"Do they have brains?"

"Very primitive ones, yes. Let's go, Sammy. It's important."

"Do you suppose worms dream?" Sammy asked, sounding more like himself.

Relieved that Sammy was coming out of his PTSD episode, Eduardo took a quick inhale from his mouthpiece and suggested they keep walking while they talked.

A few minutes later, Eduardo beamed the flashlight on stairs leading up to a landing. Just like the entrance they had taken out of the clinic.

"We still need to be careful." Sammy sounded wary.

Eduardo was not certain if Sammy was concerned about their kidnappers or the worms, but he trudged ahead to the landing.

A metal bar ran horizontally across the entire width of the low metal door at the top of the stairs. Eduardo took a deep breath and pushed against the door. Nothing. He tried lifting the bar, and then pressing it down. Still nothing.

Shining the flashlight, he noticed a mechanism, a latch embedded in it. He ran his fingers across the bar. Almost immediately he located a narrow clasp. Turning it gently, the mechanism moved. The door creaked to life. He pushed his knees hard against it, sending a cloud of dust into the air. Grime fell on the landing. The debris crunched under his feet. He ducked and beckoned for Sammy to follow. They entered a space as restricted as the tunnel had been.

# FORTY-NINE

## NIKKI

Olivia crawled on the floor. She was unusually quiet. Nikki assumed that she was picking up the adults' fear. They could not hear any noise from outside the soundproof safe room. The phone Clive had used to call his office and the police was their only communication method with the outside world. She could not even guess how long it would take for the authorities to respond.

Clive opened the refrigerator and told the group to help themselves to the food and refreshments inside. "I'll make coffee. Anyone join me?"

The other three adults raised their hands. Olivia, watching, raised hers too. That got them smiling.

"Any news, the police will notify me," he assured them. He made coffee, grinding fresh beans.

Nikki watched him prepare individual cups. Black, sugar, hot milk, or both, according to each person's preference. She marveled at his patience and wondered how worried he might be, or if this was tame compared to other situations he had encountered. She guessed he was a full-time operative and that coming here to the safehouse was in the line of duty, even though he had claimed originally to be the manager of the property. He was clearly much more than a cabin caretaker.

She thought of Eduardo. There were times when she felt as if he were right there with her. In a spiritual sense. It gave her comfort, a feeling that he was alive and just needed to be rescued.

Except for Olivia, by now sitting in her mother's lap, they all sipped coffee.

Neptune growled and ran up the steps.

Cindy put Olivia on the floor. She and Clive followed the dog up the stairs.

"It's okay, boy. Settle," she told the dog. "Settle."

He laid down on the tiny landing. After a couple of minutes, she released him. She went downstairs and he tailed her.

Clive complimented her on the dog's training.

"His owner, Sammy, trained him."

"We could do a puzzle," Clive said. He opened a cabinet and pulled out some puzzles. He put a few dog biscuits on the floor for Neptune and he also opened a bag of jellybeans and another of gummy bears.

"How about the puzzle of our predicament?" Andy asked, sounding testy.

"Since you're responsible for *our predicament*, let's hear your suggestions," Nikki responded in an equally testy tone.

"Now, now, kids. Let's sit back and relax. There's nothing we can do but wait. The authorities will come soon enough."

"Or the gunmen will break in here and kill us all," Andy said.

"Cut it out," Clive told Andy.

Andy took a handful of jellybeans and sat on a step, popping the candy into his mouth.

Nikki took a seat at the table and Cindy did the same. Clive spread out an old newspaper on the table to build the puzzle on. The two women selected a serene European scene with a castle on a hill in the background and a quaint town in the foreground, complete with a church steeple, houses with balconies and hanging flowerpots, and people walking dogs on the main street. Clive emptied the box and mixed up the thousand pieces.

Sheepishly, Andy joined them. "Sorry. Just nervous."

Clive nodded.

# FIFTY

## EDUARDO

The high Colorado prairie spread out in all directions from where they stood, the front ridge of the Rocky Mountains barely visible in the west. The two men silently admired a yellow carpet of wildflowers that spread as far as they could see. A breathing, living organism that belied the dry desert.

The flowers all seemed the same to Eduardo until they had walked into the prairie, the tunnel well behind them, when he noticed that they might be from the same family yet there was a diversity with each variety displaying distinguishing traits—black-eyed Susans, dwarf golden asters, and desert mule ears. The rounded petals of one type sprouted out from a darker center while another had pointed petals, and yet a third type had smaller blossoms. A vast blanket of color in the bright sunlight, with different kinds preferring the rock outcroppings and others hugging the sandier parts of the plains.

Eduardo said a silent prayer for Nikki's safety. He took a few extra minutes to meditate as they walked.

Soon he would find a place where they could borrow a phone and he could call her. He hoped Sammy would not have another PTSD episode. He should be fine since they would not be sleeping. He hoped nothing else would trigger his traumatic memories.

"I'm leaving my breathing apparatus here," Sammy said.

"Why?"

"It's hurting my back." Before dropping the backpack on the ground, Sammy removed the water container from the side pocket.

The men considered which way to go. Sammy pointed in a northwestern direction, saying that would take them to highway 94 as Macario had told them. Shadows indicated they still had four or five hours of daylight ahead of them.

"We've got to find a phone," Eduardo said. "We won't be safe until we call the people we need to notify."

They walked about twenty minutes. The carpet of yellow flowers was not as thick as it appeared when they had first observed the prairie from the higher ground near the cliff. Yet the flowers buzzed with insect life.

Sammy took a swig of water. "We should pick up the pace if we expect to get somewhere that has a phone."

Looking in the direction they were traveling, Eduardo saw a dust cloud. "We've got to catch the truck."

He took off running, Sammy following him.

"Wrong way," Sammy yelled. "Truck's heading south."

"Phone," Eduardo yelled back, not slowing down.

As Eduardo got closer to the dirt road, he waved his arms to catch the driver's attention.

The truck barreled straight past Eduardo's flailing arms.

Dejected, Eduardo turned away. Then he heard the truck apply its brakes. He spun around and saw the pickup skid across the road, spitting loose gravel like a machine gun firing random bullets, before stopping and turning around.

A freckle-faced young man, maybe fifteen or sixteen, pulled up beside Eduardo. With a silly grin, he asked if he could help.

"I need to borrow your phone. I must make an urgent call."

The kid unplugged his earbuds from the phone and handed it to Eduardo.

Sammy chatted with the teenager while Eduardo moved away to call his wife.

Nikki did not answer. Eduardo dialed her again and this time, he left a long, detailed message about breaking out of a two-story farmhouse with a barn southeast of the Schriever Space Force Base. In his estimation, they were still southeast of Schriever. The clinic had an injured Cuban who had helped them escape. The injured person, named Macario, wanted to defect to the US and had, in his own words, plenty of information the CIA would find useful. Macario confirmed that the stingray devices, like the one he had sent photos of, were for capturing digital intel. He further explained the Cubans were spies for hire that worked for China's Ministry of State Security, the MSS.

He and Sammy, he explained, would walk toward highway 94 or Schriever, whichever they encountered first. The cell he was using belonged to a young man he had stopped on a dirt road. "I love you, Nikki." He ended the message.

Why hadn't she answered? Eduardo worried she might be hurt. Maybe even abducted. She *always* took her calls. He hoped Bembe's men had not found her or Andy's family. He dialed Charlotte and got the recording about office hours and telephone numbers to call when the office was closed. One was Floyd's number, which he punched into the keypad.

At the third ring, Floyd picked up. "I'm so glad you called. Are you safe?"

"For the time being. But I called Nikki twice and she didn't answer."

Floyd said he had spoken to her earlier that day. She was with a CIA operative, probably out of range. He would update her about Eduardo's escape.

Eduardo gave Floyd all the information he had on the ranch house, the helicopter, the Cubans who were working for the Chinese, the intel they were obviously gathering, and their own escape from the basement.

Floyd expressed concern for their safety. "Spies won't let you get away. I'll get my guys moving, but you'd be better off in a more secure place. How quickly can you get to a police station?"

Stepping back to the driver's side of the pickup, Eduardo asked the teenager if he could drive them to a police station.

The young man looked alarmed. "I don't have a driver's license. My dad will whip me if I get caught driving. He doesn't know I took the truck out today." He glanced at his cell in Eduardo's hand and continued, "maybe I should get my phone back and head home before I get in serious trouble."

"How about a ride to the nearest gasoline station?" Eduardo asked.

The teenager shook his head, reaching out to take the phone back.

Eduardo moved away.

Sammy offered to pay him. The young man still refused and insisted on getting his phone back.

"We're stuck here," Eduardo said, updating Floyd. "We cannot force this young man to give us a ride to the police or the nearest gas station."

Floyd would call the necessary authorities and get someone out to pick them up, but first he asked to speak to the young man to ask for directions to their current location.

The teenager kept the phone after speaking to Floyd but handed Eduardo two bottles of water. Eduardo got a whiff of alcohol on the teen's breath. He sped away before Eduardo had a chance to cajole him into taking them to safety.

After the call to Floyd, Eduardo and Sammy decided they should stay put. Law enforcement would come to pick them up.

# FIFTY-ONE

## NIKKI

Nikki jumped at the ringing of the landline. Clive dashed to answer it. The others in the room dropped puzzle pieces and moved to the edge of their seats, straining to hear his end of the conversation. After responding, he went silent. His back was turned to them.

"Three individuals?" Clive asked before going silent again.

Olivia pulled Neptune's tail and he barked. Olivia cried, afraid or surprised at the dog's reaction. Cindy picked her up.

"It's okay, sweetie," she whispered. When the crying continued, Cindy offered her a gummy bear. The child pushed it into her mouth with her little fingers, chewing and drooling.

"You're certain that's all it was?" Clive asked. "Do me a favor and leave a guy out there anyway."

Nikki whispered to her brother and sister-in-law at the table. "Sounds like good news."

Clive listened again for a few seconds and thanked the caller. He hung up the receiver and returned to the table where three anxious people were waiting for an explanation.

"It appears there was a bachelor party at the cabin behind us. The fellows had a bit too much to drink and decided to have a little target practice."

"At a bachelor party?" Nikki asked, surprised. "Surely you're joking."

"I'm dead serious," Clive said. "Apparently, they thought they were out here by themselves and could shoot their guns. My colleagues arrested three guys. This is a protected park area. No shooting allowed."

"You don't think they were spying on us?" Nikki asked.

"Not according to the officer who called me. They were drinking too heavily to do deliberate harm."

Andy wanted to know if it was safe to return upstairs.

"Yeah, I'll open the door," Clive said. "We can move the puzzle to the dining table and finish it there."

Nikki realized Clive had placed the puzzle on a newspaper so he could move it. Not having played games or cards or put together puzzles growing up, she did not know the subtleties that came with such activities.

Neptune was the first one up the stairs. Cindy, holding Olivia, followed Clive.

He opened the soundproof curtain, unlocked the door, and pushed the refrigerator out of the way. Clive stepped aside to let Cindy and Olivia pass.

Neptune growled.

Clive yanked Cindy back into the safe room. She screamed. A man stood at the entrance. He'd snatched Olivia out of Cindy's arms. With his free hand, he pointed a gun at Cindy.

# FIFTY-TWO

## EDUARDO

Waiting on the prairie with nothing to do put Eduardo on edge. If only law enforcement would show up soon. He sipped from a water bottle the young man had given him.

"That kid looked scared out of his wits when you mentioned the police station. I wonder if he's been in trouble with the law," Sammy said, also sipping water.

"He'd been drinking, and my guess is that he was high on some substance. That's why he was scared." Eduardo took his backpack off and dropped it on the ground.

Eduardo searched the horizon, hoping to spot a vehicle. When he saw nothing, he stretched his arms and lowered himself into a squat. Rising, he did the exercise again. Sammy joined him. They completed a set of five, rested for a minute, and performed another set of five.

A sound caught their attention. They looked up.

Before they could move out of the way, a drone hit Sammy in the head, knocking him to the ground. Eduardo saw blood oozing from his forehead.

The drone swooped up, gaining altitude. Eduardo grabbed his backpack and waited for it to come around a second time. He talked to Sammy to make certain he was conscious as he watched the drone make a big loop around them before dropping in altitude and coming straight in for another pass. He prepared the backpack and secured his stance, feet spread slightly wider than shoulders. He bent his knees like a baseball player at bat.

The drone zoomed toward him.

Eduardo hit it as hard as he could. The drone dipped close to the ground before gaining its balance and climbing again.

It circled above them and made another pass. Eduardo hit the bull's-eye and brought the drone down a few feet from where he stood. He picked up a rock and smashed the whirring parasite.

Glancing up, he checked to make certain there were no further threats. He bent down to examine Sammy. Blood streamed down his face and the side of his head. He looked dazed.

Eduardo grabbed the water flask in the side pocket of his backpack, but it was broken, and the water had leaked out. In the high, semi-arid prairie, they must conserve water for drinking. To clean Sammy's injury, he had no choice but to use the water the teenager had left for them.

"Do you know where we are?" Eduardo asked.

"I do. On the plains near Schriever Space Force Base. Now the Cubans also know where we are," Sammy said.

Eduardo quizzed him about the date and his birthdate and asked him to touch his nose with his index finger while keeping his eyes closed. After running him through several other exercises, he told his friend he was okay.

"It's a nasty injury but the hematoma is superficial, not enough to cause real damage. You'll have a bruise for sure."

"Didn't you hear me?" Sammy asked. "The Cubans will be here in no time."

"Yes, yes, I know. Maybe we'll get lucky, and Floyd's group will find us before the mercenaries do."

"We should move further north on this road and not be sitting ducks, as they say."

"If you're really up to it, then let's do it," Eduardo said, helping Sammy up.

Eduardo tried to tear a piece of his shirt off, but he had no luck. It was the one the Cubans had provided, and the material was too new to tear easily. He glanced at the ground, looking for a sharp-edged rock. He took his shirt completely off and placed it on a large rock. With the sharp edge of a smaller stone, he managed to rip a jagged piece off. He handed it to Sammy. "Hold this to your forehead to stop the bleeding."

Eduardo put his shirt on and the two started walking.

Scanning the horizon, Eduardo wondered if help would arrive in time.

# FIFTY-THREE

## CLIVE

The man aimed his gun at Cindy. In a heavy accent, he told her to hold her arms up and march out.

Clive moved slightly.

"Stay where you are, or I'll kill her."

Nikki, behind Andy on the stairs, pulled her gun. Using the baby Glock was impossible with Olivia in the man's arms plus the three adults between her and the assailant.

Neptune jumped at the attacker.

The man hit the floor, losing his grip on the gun, but still holding the screaming Olivia.

Clive dived for the gun. He aimed it at the man. "Release the child."

"Put the gun down or I'll snap her little neck."

Clive put it on the floor.

"Now go back inside your hiding place." The assailant pushed himself along the floor to grab the gun.

Neptune lunged at the man again, and sank his teeth into his arm, the one reaching for the gun.

Nikki ran up the remaining steps, her gun ready.

Relentless, the German shepherd held on and shook the man's arm as if trying to kill him. To fight the dog, the assailant let go of Olivia. Her mother sprang to pick her up.

Nikki aimed at the man's head and held the baby Glock steady.

Clive grabbed the intruder's gun off the floor and leveled it toward the man's torso.

"How did you know where we were?" Nikki demanded.

Clive pulled his phone out and called for backup. He asked Cindy to call the dog off. Blood from the assailant's wound was spreading on the floor.

"Tell me how you knew where to find us," Nikki grilled him again.

"Kill me, go ahead and kill me," the man said, holding his bleeding arm. "My comrades will be here before your help arrives."

"Your comrades," Nikki scoffed, "have been arrested."

"Not the ones coming here."

# FIFTY-FOUR

## SAMMY

Sammy and Eduardo walked for several minutes. Finally, Sammy broke the silence. "I need to talk about why I came to New Mexico. In case I die. Call it a confession if you want."

"Sure, I'll listen." Eduardo sounded matter of fact. "But we're not going to die. At least not today."

Sammy said his parents were Cuban, though he was born in the US.

Eduardo remained silent, waiting for Sammy to continue his story.

"My father was a Cuban operative who spent almost three decades in Miami. I was just a kid. I grew up in this country, went to school here. I graduated from the Massachusetts Institute of Technology on scholarships. I was an American. My father behaved as if he were a Cuban exile, but that was just a cover."

Eduardo apparently mulled over Sammy's words. "An MIT graduate sounds more likely than your story of an uneducated peasant."

Sammy could tell that Eduardo thought some of his other stories were lies too.

"In his private life, my dad was an idealogue. He believed in the Revolution, and he raised me to become a spy, like him. He was dying from cancer when he asked me to serve the Revolution."

Sammy glanced at Eduardo who seemed intent on watching the horizon, probably hoping to see a vehicle coming their way.

"Didn't the Cuban Revolution end when Fidel took control?" Eduardo asked.

"The Cuban government claims the Revolution is still going on. Until the Yankee imperialists are overthrown."

Eduardo seemed uninterested and did not respond.

Sammy continued undeterred. "My dad was relentless in his influence over me. He spoke to his handler and told him that with my studies and flawless English I was an attractive candidate for the Directorate of Intelligence, where I could do intel or commercial spying."

"The DI? And you joined up?" Eduardo asked.

"I did it to please my dying father. Not having lived in Cuba, I didn't know the difference between the two systems of government. Not until later when I returned to the island to be trained. At first, I too believed in the Revolution."

Eduardo asked what had changed his mind.

"The fact that Cuban society was so divided. Those on the inside lived like kings and queens. The rest of the population lived in poverty. Those who opposed the regime were either killed or incarcerated in deplorable conditions."

Sammy sighed.

"My mother was not an idealogue. She had seen the difference in lifestyle, and most of all, she appreciated the freedom young people had here to choose their studies and their careers instead of having the government decide for them."

The two walked in silence for a few minutes.

"Did your mother advise you to study computer science?" Eduardo asked.

"She urged me not to follow in my dad's footsteps. As a teenager, I played percussion in the school orchestra, and as a drummer, I formed a band. We played gigs wherever anyone would hire us. I had dreams of my band becoming the next Beatles or Queen fad. My mother, being Cuban, loved music and encouraged me to become a professional."

"Do you regret not following a musical career?"

Sammy nodded. "On occasion."

"So, I wasn't wrong. You are undercover for the DI," Eduardo said with some hesitation.

"I left that fifteen years ago. I met a woman from Mexico, and I thought it was the right time to start a new life, so to speak. Since I was a citizen, admitting what I had done meant that I would be prosecuted. I devised a plan to turn over the intel I had on Cuba, my handler, and others who were spying, in exchange for not being prosecuted and for getting into the witness protection program. It's a long story."

Sammy looked at the ground in front of them and studied their shadows to guess at the time.

Eduardo interrupted his thoughts when he asked him to continue his story.

"I spoke to the CIA, but they were not interested in taking me. The operative I contacted was very supportive. If it'd been up to him, we would have negotiated a deal, and I would have been put into the WPP. My timing was not good. I went to the CIA at a time when the US was normalizing relations with Cuba, so the higher ups felt there was no need for the intel I had.

"During that time, the number of Cuban spies in the US did not diminish, but the laxer attitude toward Cuba made it easier for spies to infiltrate national laboratories, like Sandia, Los Alamos, Lawrence Livermore, Fermi, you name it. Universities and research facilities too."

"Did you remain with the DI after the CIA refused you?"

"No, I followed my heart to Mexico, where I changed my name and married my sweetheart. We had twin boys. Incredible boys—Carlitos and Arturo." Sammy looked out over the horizon. A few drops of blood slid down the side of his face. "I also went to Mexico to avoid prosecution here."

"Where is your family now?"

Sammy stopped. He clenched his jaw. He looked at Eduardo. "They died." His throat tightened and became dry.

Eduardo apologized, saying he had no idea.

"It's okay. It's part of what I need to talk about."

"If there's any way I can help—"

"It goes back to the late 1990s. I was a programmer on the Blue Mountain computer project at Los Alamos."

"You worked at a national lab?" Eduardo sounded surprised. "How did you get top secret clearance?"

"I was an American citizen. I'm sure they looked at me more closely because I had Cuban ancestry, but organizations were recruiting minorities. I was Latino with a doctorate from MIT."

"Hmm, makes sense," Eduardo mumbled.

"Getting back to Blue Mountain, in case you haven't heard about it, the project was a supercomputer, probably the most advanced at the time. It could run simulations for the National Nuclear Security Administration."

"Nuclear simulations? I don't quite get it."

"Instead of doing live nuclear testing, the computer could simulate all kinds of nuclear conditions and provide analyses of weapon reliability. It could also predict their performance."

"A much safer way to test," Eduardo said.

Sammy nodded. "I passed information on that project and the subsequent one for almost twelve years. A lot of what I stole, especially in the beginning, was innocuous. I was a novice. My heart was not into espionage. If not for the spying connection, I would have been very happy at Los Alamos. I didn't want to be a spy and I wanted out."

A prairie dog must have sensed their approach and scurried into its hole. Sammy kicked the dirt piled up on the rodent's mound.

"Yet I could not just resign. You don't do that from the DI. At least, not if you want to stay alive."

"And you were never caught by the US?"

Sammy shook his head. "Being a good spy meant that you took information without leaving evidence of stealing anything. I was careful not to set off any suspicion, more to save my skin than to be a good spy."

# FIFTY-FIVE

## NIKKI

Still panicked by their surprise attacker in the safehouse, Nikki would not lower her gun. Not even after Clive handcuffed their suspect and tied a belt around the man's feet. Andy paced the room. Cindy, in the bedroom, sat on the floor with Olivia on one side and Neptune on the other.

Her voice carried softly into the living room. She told her daughter a story about a baby duck that got lost in the forest and quacked for its mother, but the wind distorted the duck's call and mama duck couldn't hear him. Cindy used sound effects, like quacking and the swishing of the wind. She repeated the sounds and the names of the duck, the mother, and the wind, until she had Olivia giggling and repeating after her.

Clive, ready to shoot, stood behind the suspect. Nikki sensed he was watching her too. Perhaps to make sure she wouldn't pull the trigger and kill the assailant.

For her part, Nikki worried other attackers would arrive before the police or the FBI. If the spies got there first, she intended on using the suspect for negotiations. She wondered if they would even care if she shot him.

The Cuban mercenaries had located them again. How had they

done it? She analyzed details and figured they had tracked them through one of the phones. But which one? Hers was encrypted. Cindy had used the app when they took turns being sentry at the rental property, and again today, though only sparingly. That left Clive's, which was unlikely, and Andy's. For sure, it was his, she decided. She hoped today's events would teach her brother a lesson.

Neptune ran to the living room, barking and growling. He jumped on the metal door Clive had locked.

"Get down, Neptune," Nikki ordered.

Clive yelled for Andy. "Get your family into the safe room. And that means your sister too."

Nikki remained steadfast in aiming for the criminal.

Andy rushed to the bedroom to help Cindy with Olivia. Bringing them with him, he pulled the refrigerator away from the wall and opened the door to the cellar, and told Cindy to hurry in. "Down, Neptune," he said to the German shepherd standing behind the refrigerator.

Gunfire went off outside. Someone shot the lock off the metal door.

Andy rushed into the top of the cellar.

Someone kicked the door in, and two men came through swinging semiautomatic rifles.

Andy had failed to close the cellar door. And the refrigerator remained away from the wall.

"Drop the gun and put your hands in the air," a muscular man of about forty said to Nikki with a hardened voice. He turned his rifle toward Clive. "And you, too."

"I'm putting it down now," Nikki said in a weak voice.

Clive laid his on the floor too.

The second assailant must have caught the motion of a door closing behind the refrigerator and moved toward it. "I see you. Come out of there." He shot a waist-height round at the top of the cellar. Nikki held her breath, praying not to hear a body fall.

"Get over here, Cruz," the other man said. His voice was as hard as when he'd ordered Nikki to drop the gun.

Cruz turned and glanced at his comrade bleeding on the floor. "I will get all you comemierdas for doing this."

"It was the dog," the injured man said feebly from the floor.

"A shitty dog did that to you?" Cruz asked. "Where is it?"

"They call him Neptune."

Neptune, still behind the refrigerator, pounced on the man called Cruz and knocked him to the floor.

The assailant with the hardened voice aimed and shot toward the dog.

Cruz let out a sharp, loud cry.

Neptune yelped and ran into the cellar.

More shots followed.

Cruz lay motionless on the floor. On the other side of the room, the hard-voiced man contorted in pain. He'd been hit by a bullet.

In the confusion, Nikki dived for her gun. She looked up and saw another man standing by the metal door. He was wearing a sheriff deputy's uniform.

"What took you so damned long?" Clive asked the newcomer, picking up the rifle the hard-voiced man had dropped.

"It's over now," the deputy said, holstering his gun. He moved to shackle the hard-voiced man. "The FBI should arrive shortly."

Nikki stood and walked toward the cellar. "Are you guys okay down there?"

"Scared out of our wits," Andy shouted.

"Neptune's been hit," Cindy cried.

# FIFTY-SIX

## EDUARDO

Eduardo thought that with Sammy's background, it was no wonder he suffered from PTSD. He wanted to keep him talking. Maybe it would be therapeutic. Or he could find out important information. He asked if the labs had kept him assigned to simulated nuclear tests.

"Basically, yes. After a few years, Blue Mountain was replaced by a new computer that had the capability to maintain the nuclear stockpile. I spent another six years downloading just enough information to keep my handlers happy. Sometimes I gave them disinformation."

"How did you deal with the double life?"

"It messes with your mind. I kept to myself. I didn't have friends. In my spare time, I hiked the mountain trails around Los Alamos or practiced my drumming. Not having a social life did take a toll. What really created mental havoc for me was that I loved this country. My father got to me in a moment of weakness and then the Cubans hooked me."

Eduardo took in Sammy's story as he gazed at the wildflowers. From the carpet of yellow after they'd left the tunnel, the colors had changed to the red and orange hues of the Paintbrush plant and the red bell-shaped Prairie Smoke. He continued walking and pumping

Sammy with questions. It had become therapy for Eduardo, keeping his mind off the danger they faced. He took a couple of deep breaths, enjoying the crisp, clean air.

"Wasn't the remote location the reason the labs were built there to begin with?" he asked.

Sammy nodded. "Robert Oppenheimer recommended Los Alamos for the Manhattan Project because of its remoteness."

"Interesting," Eduardo said, "Los Alamos must be the ideal place for a loner spy."

Sammy rubbed the lump on his forehead where the drone hit him. "Or for a person who can befriend people easily, be the life of the party, but not get close to anyone. If people like you, they won't suspect you."

Sammy was certainly easy to like, Eduardo thought.

"During my time at Los Alamos, we developed ways to minimize nuclear proliferation. That eased my conscience somewhat."

"Rightfully so," Eduardo said.

"In fact, from its highest point, the US has reduced its nuclear arsenal by ninety percent."

Eduardo raised his eyebrows. "I had no clue it had been reduced. And certainly not by so much."

"Unfortunately, other countries have increased their arsenals. In the end, we're probably no better off. But during my time in Los Alamos, other aspects of the place fascinated me."

"Such as?"

"Meeting famous physicists."

Eduardo wanted to change the subject back to Sammy's family life, but he had the impression that the pain over losing his family made Sammy avoid the topic. He steered the conversation to his personal life while he worked at the labs.

"After three years," Sammy said, "I started going into Santa Fe to remind myself what life with a few friends could be like. I needed something positive to occupy my mind. Music always made me feel better. A band in Santa Fe needed a drummer on the weekends when they had work, and I joined them whenever they needed me."

"Did that get you in trouble? Like losing your cover?"

"On the contrary. We did a wedding gig in Santa Fe. That was a weekend in 2009. The guys in the group introduced me to Ana. She said I was the best drummer she'd ever heard. I realized my mother was right. If I'd only listened to her, I could have had a career in music."

"Have you thought of starting your own band? It's never too late."

Sammy blotted his injury again. He wiped away perspiration, not blood, that had formed on his forehead. "Meeting Ana encouraged me to leave the DI. I wanted a normal life. To marry Ana and have a family."

"But you didn't defect."

Sammy shook his head. "I couldn't. I was a US citizen. I was a mole, and the CIA wasn't interested in me. I was in danger of being arrested for my betrayal. I told Ana everything because I could put her in danger too. She suggested we move to Mexico. I had cosmetic surgery there to change my appearance. Changed my name too and built a whole Mexican persona for myself, including Mexican accents, a northern one and the Mexico City sing-song."

Eduardo asked about Ana's friends in Santa Fe. Did they know she'd married him?

"We kept that to ourselves. Before the surgery, I flew to Guatemala and bought a death certificate, stating I'd been killed in a hiking accident. I had it sent to the HR department at Los Alamos. My work colleagues assumed that's what happened to me. The programmer from Los Alamos had simply died."

"But the Cuban government," Eduardo said, "wouldn't be so accepting. They would verify their man had died. And they'd follow whatever tracks you'd left."

# FIFTY-SEVEN

## NIKKI

Without flinching, Nikki ran downstairs. Cindy and Olivia were there and neither one of them should see the mess upstairs. If the police wanted to question Cindy, they could do it in the cellar.

Neptune's left hind leg had been hit. Cindy had already taken a couple of towels from the cellar bathroom and was cleaning his wounds. He kept trying to lick them, whimpering in pain.

Nikki told him what a good dog he was. He lifted his head and looked at her with sad eyes. "You'll be okay," she said. "And because of you, the rest of us are alive."

"That comes from Sammy's training. He's so good with animals. He should be featured on TV as the dog and mule whisperer," Cindy said.

"I hope you're feeling better about Sammy," Andy said.

Nikki ignored his comment and continued to talk to Neptune as Cindy bandaged the dog's leg.

"Let's see if he leaves it on," Cindy said as she cleaned blood off the floor with the dirty towels.

Clive came down. "The FBI just arrived and a couple of police investigators too. They're doing forensic work upstairs. They will get a statement from each of you, starting with you," he said, speaking to Nikki.

Cindy asked where they would be sleeping that night.

"That depends," Clive said. "This is a crime scene. You'll probably move to a hotel in town. If they get all the forensic evidence they need, you can probably stay here, but that's very doubtful."

"That's just my point," Cindy said. "I don't want to be here after the shooting today."

"You have blood on your pants and your shoes," Nikki said. "Did you get hit?"

"Superficial," Clive said, with a wave of his hand. "When the deputy arrived, he shot the Cuban's kneecap from behind. As the Cuban fell, he let go a barrage of bullets toward the cellar door. He dropped his rifle. The last bullet out must have been the one that grazed my leg."

Cindy told him to get his pant leg up while she went for the bottle of alcohol and clean washcloths and bandages. She had returned and was examining the wound when an officer came down and told Nikki he wanted to interrogate her.

She followed him upstairs to the same room where Clive had questioned her about Sammy.

After all the usual technicalities about name and what she was doing there, he asked her who had killed Cruz Batista.

"His own colleague."

"Which one?"

"The husky voiced one. I don't know his name. He has an injured leg."

The officer asked her to explain.

"The one with the injured arm was on the floor. The other two Cubans arrived later. They had automatic rifles. By then, Clive and I were unarmed. Cruz must have seen movement at the top of the cellar because he shouted for people to come out. He shot his rifle into the half-closed door."

Nikki took a deep breath before continuing. "The German shepherd was crouched behind the refrigerator. The dog leaped onto Cruz and knocked him down."

The officer asked if the dog was trained for combat situations.

"From what I saw today, I'd say he's extremely well trained. We're alive because of Neptune."

"Go on," the officer said.

"The shooter either thought there were people hiding behind the door or he was trying to kill the dog and accidentally hit his comrade. In any case, he blasted the door. You can check all the bullet holes. He killed Cruz. About that time, the deputy, whose name I don't know either, came in and shot him from the back and hit his knee. Otherwise, we might not be alive."

An ambulance arrived to take the two injured Cubans to a nearby hospital. And Cruz's body would be taken to the morgue.

Clive spoke with the police officers, three in total. One of them accompanied the ambulance. They told him the Cubans would be well guarded in the hospital.

One by one, the officer who questioned Nikki interrogated everyone. Once he finished, he told them they were free to pack up what they needed so they could check into a hotel.

They had arrived with so little luggage that they were soon ready to leave. Clive put on his sunglasses before walking them to the Jeep. On the way, he offered his house. "I live alone, and I travel so much with my job, that the house will welcome the company."

Andy protested, but Clive said they would be safer at his place than they would at a hotel. Besides, the CIA did not have another safe house in the area.

# FIFTY-EIGHT

## SAMMY

Sammy checked the horizon, searching for a dust trail or any other sign that an emergency crew was on its way. No movement except for a couple of buzzards that were so busy eating the entrails of a small animal that they ignored the men.

He glanced at Eduardo.

"Ana was smart," Sammy said. "She came from a family with connections in Mexico and got me an interview at the engineering firm where I ended up working. She encouraged me to keep playing drums, and I formed my own group. We played in venues where I thought I'd never be found. Never advertised the band. My appearance and identity had changed, and I was sure there was no chance the Cuban government would find me."

His voice broke. "One evening, I loaded my drums onto the pickup. The garage door was open. A car drove by slowly. The two passengers stared at me. It was Mexico City, one of the biggest cities in the world, and I figured they were looking at the drums. I dismissed it.

"At the gig that night, my gut told me something was wrong about that car. It could not be a coincidence. That gnawing feeling kept growing. Like I should have stayed at home and told Ana about the strangers. If they were checking us out, we'd have to move."

Once the gig was over, he told Eduardo, he packed the drum set onto his pickup. His stomach clenched at the thought of abandoning the life he had built with his family in Mexico City. Driving home, traffic was light, so he risked speeding back to his family.

In a somber mood, he shared with Eduardo the plan he made that night. A mental list of tasks—cashing out their accounts, acquiring new identities, leaving their lives and their loved ones behind. And most important, how would he minimize the emotional toll on his family?

They would move back to the US. The US presidential elections in 2016 had brought to power a man intent on reversing the coziness with Cuba that the previous administration had established. He would apply at the CIA again. He had been out of the spy business, but he could help them on Cuban matters if they gave him a chance. He would call his contact from 2009, a man who had wanted to help him, but whose superiors had nixed that possibility.

Sammy had been certain his timing was better this time.

There was only one hitch. It had been easier to disappear and reappear as a new person in 2009 when the world was not completely online. In a mere six years, going off the grid was more difficult due to face recognition technology and computerized records. That complicated maintaining a clandestine identity.

It would require much more than just avoiding credit cards and a bank account. The Cubans obviously had his new identity, probably photographs of his new appearance, and they could trace him through facial recognition cameras in airports and along the streets of many cities.

That was why he chose to live in a rural part of New Mexico.

"But what about traveling to Spain?" Eduardo asked. "You mentioned selling mules in Spain."

"Ahh, I shipped the mules to Europe," Sammy said. He gazed at the horizon and sighed.

He went back to telling Eduardo his plan to get new identities if the CIA did not want him. They might have to live in a Central American country for a while. "I was thankful my sons were only four years old. They'd adapt to the new life."

Sammy continued his story. His beloved drum set and their personal effects would be left behind.

On the computers they owned, he would download the data they needed, and destroy hard drives and all traces of personal information. Not that he stored sensitive data. He had been extraordinarily careful not to leave a bridge between his current life and his past.

Sammy felt like a ghost as he related the rest of his story. He'd never told anyone, not even Andy, about returning to his house in Mexico City that fateful night. He'd abandoned his pickup on the street. He left the engine running, his prized drums on the back. He bolted up the steps to the front door. It was crooked, off one hinge, and the deadbolt dangled in the slight breeze, reflecting the light from the hall.

The door creaked as he pushed through. The house was eerily quiet.

For an instant he thought he was sleeping. A nightmare. He hurried into the kitchen, still refusing to believe what he was seeing. A sense of wrong hit him hard and he yelled for Ana. No response. He rushed to their bedroom.

Blood. Blood everywhere. A mirror above the dresser was shattered, but the few remaining glass shards were smeared with red. A chair was turned over. He thought he'd faint, but he had to find his family. He looked around. The closet door was open a crack. Were they hiding?

He whispered Ana's name. Hardly able to speak, he told her he was here to protect them. Not to fear anything since they would leave the house tonight. Leave the country a few hours later.

His fingers touched the closet door with hesitation.

Ana leaned against the closet wall, her clothes soaked in blood. Carlitos was on one side of her, his bruised and battered head nestled in her lap. Arturo lay across her outstretched legs. Blood pooled around them on the hardwood floor.

He fell to his knees and banged his head on the wall. His family was dead. It was his fault for not being home. He might as well have done it himself. He had failed them by not being home. With a shaky hand, he reached out and touched Carlitos. A Desert Eagle handgun,

Ana's, fell to the floor. It had been lodged between the child and his mother. Ana must have tried to defend herself and their children.

"I wanted to kill myself," Sammy said in an anguished whisper, "with that handgun."

Eduardo nodded and touched Sammy's shoulder sympathetically.

"Why had I gone off to play that night? I should have paid attention to that car, the one with the passengers watching me."

Sammy paused and took a deep breath.

"I thought about revenge, but it was cowardice that kept me alive. I never went looking for the bastards. I would have had the entire Cuban intelligence apparatus after me." Sammy used the blood-stained cloth in his hand to wipe the tears rolling down his face. "I was such a coward."

Eduardo turned his head at the distant sound of a helicopter.

"They're coming for us! This nightmare is almost over."

# FIFTY-NINE

## NIKKI

After they all climbed into the Jeep, Nikki asked Clive if they should destroy their phones to prevent being followed again.

"Great idea. Should have thought of it myself. Mine's encrypted and should be okay, but I'll destroy it too. We should keep yours just to have something available in case of emergency. It's encrypted, right?"

"Of course," Nikki said. "We could wipe them clean if you have the appropriate tools to destroy all the data."

"It could leave traces that can be reconstructed," Clive said. "I'll demolish them."

He took his own, Cindy's, and Andy's phones, removed the chips, and cut them into tiny pieces with a set of heavy garden shears from a toolbox in the hatchback of the Jeep. He handed the bits to Nikki and told her to toss a few out at a time as they drove. He removed the batteries to get rid of them later. Then he took a hammer from the toolbox and destroyed the phones.

"That will hopefully do it," Nikki said. "I think that's how they found us. But I want a burner as soon as possible."

They drove in silence for a few minutes.

She offered to cook dinner at Clive's house. Cindy volunteered to be sous chef.

"I can't believe the two of you want to cook. Are you serious?" Clive asked. He sounded surprised.

"Cooking keeps my mind occupied," Nikki said. "While you drive, I'll check my phone."

Floyd had called her. She also had a message from an unknown caller. That one could wait. Her fingers trembled as she pressed the listen button on Floyd's message.

She shouted with joy when she heard that Eduardo had escaped. Neptune's ears shot up and he looked around.

But Floyd's message warned her that Eduardo and Sammy were not out of danger yet. He was sending a team to rescue them, but he would not be happy until he had them safely out of there.

She replayed Floyd's message on speaker so everyone could hear it.

The message from the unknown caller was Eduardo. She listened to it twice and wiped away tears of happiness. She longed to call him back and tell him she loved and missed him. But he had borrowed a phone.

Instead, she bowed her head and prayed silently for a minute.

Cindy asked if she was okay.

Nikki responded that she would be as soon as Eduardo was safe. She glanced at her watch and dialed Floyd.

He sounded upset when he learned about their day. "I'm sorry you had to deal with three spies today. They've thrown a lot of assets on this job. Shows how important it is to them."

"It's okay. Two of them are in jail and maybe they'll talk. The other one was killed," Nikki said.

He repeated what he said about Eduardo in the message. Law enforcement had organized to pick Eduardo and Sammy up. As soon as that happened, Eduardo would call her using a borrowed phone, since his own had been taken away.

Before ending the call, she told Floyd she would get a burner and destroy her secure phone. When she ended the call, she shared Floyd's conversation with the rest of the group.

"What a relief," Andy said.

"Whoa, it's not over yet. We know they're alive, and Floyd is sending people in to get them, but let's not declare victory yet."

Clive informed them that they were close to his place. He would take a detour to destroy Nikki's phone, to avoid leaving a trace of their location for the night. Clive finished off the phone and handed the bits to Nikki.

Clive drove past a small rural airport. "It's about two miles from where I live. One reason I bought that house."

They arrived at Clive's home. He drove up the driveway and parked inside the garage. Clive showed her to a bedroom. She reminded him about Sammy's gun.

"Didn't Floyd arrange for you to get a baby Glock? I hid one under the toilet tank in case I wasn't there to give it to you when you arrived."

"Yes, the Glock is mine. Sammy's is the Smith & Wesson." She took it from her purse and handed it to him. "It's loaded."

They walked back to the kitchen, and Nikki said she still wanted to cook.

"Use whatever you want. Despite being gone a lot, I do keep a well-stocked pantry. We can order pizza if you prefer."

Cooking kept her mind busy, she told him again. She opened the door to a small pantry full of every imaginable pasta, cereal, rice, boxes of chicken broth, flour, beans, canned fruit, canned tomatoes, herbs, and jars of spaghetti sauce. The fridge held fresh vegetables, whole and low-fat milk, and a variety of cheese. The freezer section contained ground beef and chicken. Nikki pulled out ground beef and set it on a plate to thaw in the microwave. On a side counter were fresh tomatoes, onions, and garlic.

"Sous chef reporting for duty," Cindy said.

"Take a break from cooking," Nikki said, "I can handle it."

"I like doing it. Call me old-fashioned," Cindy said. "I enjoy being a mother and housewife."

Andy, carrying Olivia, settled at the dining table in the combined living, dining, and kitchen area. Neptune hobbled in behind them and laid down on a plush rug by the sofa.

Clive handed burner phones to everyone. Cindy and Andy agreed to use theirs only in case of emergency. Nikki notified Floyd about the number to her new phone.

Almost without thinking, Nikki gathered ingredients for spaghetti and placed them on the counter. She handed the Parmesan to Cindy and asked her to grate.

"Looks like we're having Italian for dinner," Cindy said.

"That's right," Nikki said. "Who doesn't like Italian?"

Clive chimed in saying he loved spaghetti, glancing at the pasta on the counter. "It calls for a good wine. I'll uncork one."

Nikki hummed an Italian song. Happy that Eduardo was alive, she broke into the song "Felicitá."

"Your song about happiness is contagious," Andy said, joining in a couple of stanzas.

Olivia took a few steps to the sofa and sat down next to Neptune, not touching him, as if she knew about his injury and shouldn't bother him.

"We won't be getting a concert tour anytime," Nikki said, laughing. She put Andy to work on cleaning and dicing onion and garlic. She browned ground beef in a skillet, then removed it to sauté the onion, garlic, and herbs.

When Cindy placed a jar of spaghetti sauce next to the stove, Nikki asked her to wash and chop the tomatoes. "Sauce made with fresh ingredients is so much nicer."

Clive poured wine into stem glasses. They all stopped what they were doing to make a toast.

"To a safe rescue for Eduardo and Sammy," Andy said.

"Amen," Nikki said, lifting her glass.

# SIXTY
## NIKKI

Nikki kept the burner at her side during dinner, expecting it to ring at any moment. At first she enjoyed the conviviality. But time passed and Eduardo still did not call. Glancing at her watch every few minutes, she thought of dialing her boss. But he would call her if he had news, good or bad.

Unable to stand the tension, Nikki got up and peered outside, then returned to the table. She tried to focus on the conversation, which had turned to the wildfire in New Mexico. Cindy wondered how their lab animals were faring. Did they have enough food and water?

Andy must be worried about them too, she thought. Typical man, no talking about his worries. Instead, he held it all in until subjecting them to his tantrum in the safe room.

Andy had always been awkward, even rude at times, but she thought he was ethical. Finding out that Sammy's mule farm basically belonged to Andy made Nikki wonder if she knew her brother at all. She could not shake the idea that he could be involved in something illegal. Or was there a valid reason for him to help Sammy run a successful mule business? Sammy had not seemed like an ignorant peasant to her. But was she too judgmental? Andy coughed, and she turned her attention back to the conversation.

"How close is the fire to your home in Peñasco?" Clive asked.

"Too close for comfort," Andy responded. "The morning we evacuated, it was about nine miles away, but the smoke made it seem closer."

"The fire was so strong," Cindy said, "because the winds made it impossible for the firefighters to fly planes to drop repellant on it. Those same winds spread the fire faster. We could see the red reflection in the billowing smoke. Our whole town will burn down if they don't control it. So sad."

"And think of all the people who've lost their homes. Who've lost everything," Andy said. "Everything they've worked for."

Clive asked if it was true that the wildfire started as a controlled burn done by the US Forest Service.

Nikki nodded. "Then it got out of hand. Everything was tinder dry. It's no wonder the rangers couldn't control it."

"Yesterday I read that almost four hundred houses in Mora and San Miguel counties have burned." Andy shook his head ruefully. "Looks like we won't be going home yet."

"There are other factors that keep us from returning home," Cindy said.

Andy looked at her like she'd just punched him in the ribs.

Nikki checked her watch, paced back to the window, and fidgeted with her phone. When her excess anxiety became apparent to the others, Clive assured her that it would take time for law enforcement to locate Eduardo and Sammy.

"Forty minutes ago, you were singing about happiness," Andy reminded her. "Don't worry, you and Eduardo will be reunited shortly."

# SIXTY-ONE

## EDUARDO

The helicopter got closer. Eduardo's heart beat faster. Then it almost stopped. That looked like Bembe's helicopter.

Eduardo sensed that Sammy was thinking of running. "Don't you dare move. I need you to help me."

"If I run, they'll kill me," Sammy said. "Not a bad alternative."

"We're going to get them arrested. You hear me? The FBI and CIA will come. I know they will."

"It's not like they didn't have time to get to us. Bembe and his cohorts are better at this game."

The helicopter banked and landed forty yards or so from them. Eduardo and Sammy turned their backs to avoid the pebbles and other debris the wind kicked up. Eduardo wished he still had his fedora. That made him think of Andy. He hoped someone would find him in Sugarite Park before the vultures did. Eduardo felt a tinge of pain for his brother-in-law.

Bembe was the first one to jump out of the chopper, followed by Celso. Bembe held an assault rifle.

"Comemierdas, thought you'd get away with this. Heh? You'll be sorry. No one double-crosses El Bembe."

Celso put handcuffs on both men and ordered them to the helicopter.

Given the time it took them to fly back to the control center, Eduardo was surprised he and Sammy had walked as far as they had. He thought about Sammy's story. The man had so many ghosts, it was amazing he had not gone completely mad.

The helicopter landed. Eduardo wondered what awaited them. He was afraid it would not be good.

# SIXTY-TWO

## NIKKI

Nikki could stand it no longer. She left the table and dialed Floyd from the bedroom. He told her he was also concerned. The rescue crew was still searching for Eduardo and Sammy.

She suggested bringing Clive into the conversation and waved at him to join her. She closed the door behind him and put the phone on speaker.

"I want to organize a search party at daybreak tomorrow morning," she said. "Can you get a helicopter ready for six-thirty?"

Floyd asked her what she had in mind.

"I'm planning as we speak," she said. "First, we should fly over where that teenager saw them. If we don't find them, we'll fly a wider circle and locate the two-story farmhouse and barn that Eduardo described in his message to me. He said the Cubans called it their control center."

Floyd took a few seconds before asking Clive what he thought.

"It can't hurt. My only concern is whether the Cubans have found them and taken them back to their control center. A helicopter in the area would make them suspicious. They could harm Eduardo and Sammy," Clive said.

"We can use binoculars," Nikki said, "so we don't get too close to any property that resembles Eduardo's description."

"And then what?" Floyd asked.

Nikki sighed. "Clive can call the FBI. They can SWAT the place."

"That's as good a plan as any," Clive said. "Let's carry out this first phase, see what's there, and call the assault team in once we have more intel."

A phone rang in Floyd's background. He told them it was the rescue team. He would call right back.

Nikki paced.

She jumped to answer the phone when it rang again. She told Floyd that it was on speaker.

"The rescue team didn't find a trace. I told Eduardo not to move away from that road. It's flat out there. There's nowhere to hide. I hate to say this, but my guess is the Cubans picked them up. Otherwise, Eduardo would have borrowed a phone to call you. And he'd probably call me too."

Nikki asked if the rescue team had a helicopter.

"No," Floyd said. "They were in two heavy-duty vehicles, and they canvassed the area completely."

"We're back to where we started," she said, frustrated. She was furious they had not used all available land and air teams to locate the men. Didn't the FBI and the state police have helicopters?

Clive reminded her that Eduardo had left good information for them. He would call his pilot and get him down from Denver first thing the next morning.

Nikki chewed a fingernail. Her nail polish was chipped, like paint peeling off the side of an old house. She stripped the remaining flakes off. She wished she could pilot a helicopter herself and she'd mount her own assault on that compound.

# SIXTY-THREE

## EDUARDO

"Why not get rid of these comemierdas right now?" Celso asked Bembe, leading the two handcuffed captives down the steps into the basement.

Bembe was silent.

The tension in the room was palpable. Eduardo tried to read Bembe's thoughts, but the man showed no expression other than his perpetual frown.

Once they were standing by Macario's bed, Celso removed Eduardo's handcuffs. The patient's face was flushed. His wounded leg was much more swollen than earlier that day. Eduardo realized his captors would not kill him for a couple of days, not until he stabilized Macario again.

Eduardo told them he would wash his hands before examining the patient. Scrubbing his hands over the basin, he noticed the corner cabinet in the bathroom had been completely boarded over. The towels, gauze, paper towels, and miscellaneous toiletry articles were on a counter in the clinic, next to the bathroom. He helped himself to a second clean towel and wet it down.

Stepping back into the clinic, he placed the towel on Macario's forehead and examined him. His leg was very red and hot to the touch.

"He has cellulitis," Eduardo said. "You either take him to a hospital or I need more meds to treat him."

Bembe snorted.

Celso handed Eduardo a pen and pad. "Write down what you need."

Eduardo scribbled two antibiotics, dicloxacillin and doxycycline, and a painkiller. He wanted a variety of antibiotics in case his first choice did not work. He added the name of a cream to moisturize the skin.

"Get this stuff tonight," Eduardo said, handing the handwritten note to Celso. "He needs it right away."

"If he dies," Bembe said, looking straight into Eduardo's eyes, "I'll kill you."

# SIXTY-FOUR

## SAMMY

Sammy wondered why the Cubans were keeping him alive. The doctor's life was spared, at least for the moment, because Macario was so sick.

As for Sammy, he was certain the Cubans would kill him in the end. They had a plan. Maybe torture him, break him, and find out the truth. Was that why they spared him? He had confessed his past to Eduardo. At least the parts Eduardo needed to know. He felt better after talking to the doctor. There was only one other person who knew as much, or more, about his clandestine past. That was Andy, but the Cubans had killed him.

Macario reached for Eduardo's hand and pulled him close. "It's my fault. I skipped the antibiotics while you were gone. I brought the overbed table closer and then pushed it out of reach."

"Why?"

"To make sure they didn't think we were in collusion."

Sammy approached the bed. "Now you must survive. Otherwise, they'll kill the doctor."

"I'm aware," Macario whispered. His voice sounded tired. He wanted to know how far they had gone before they were captured again.

"We thought we were going to make it," Sammy said, "until a drone attacked. Then we knew they'd found us. It was just a matter of time." He left out the bit about Eduardo's phone call. He would not be surprised if the Cubans had installed listening devices in the clinic in their absence.

"It was bad luck," Macario said softly. "They returned sooner than I would have thought, and they came down to check on me. I pretended to be asleep. When they awakened me, I acted surprised that you had escaped. By then, my leg felt more inflamed and was looking infected. It was easy for them to believe I knew nothing about your escape."

"What can we do now?" Sammy asked, whispering.

"I'm not a magician," Macario said. "No more tricks up my sleeve."

Eduardo prepared distilled water, cotton, and gauze to wash Macario's leg. "You must convince Bembe to get you to a hospital. I can only do so much, but this compound break is tough to treat without all the proper equipment. I'm afraid you need surgery to reset the bones."

"Do the best you can," Macario said. "If they take me to a hospital, they won't need you anymore."

Sammy stepped away and left the patient and doctor talking. He took a closer look at the back areas of the clinic, like the corners, and the area under the stairwell. It was a closet of some sort with a huge padlock on the door. Why keep it locked? He heard the door open at the top of the stairs. He stepped away quickly. The aroma of chicken soup permeated the clinic. This time, the person delivering their dinner was not Celso, but Ramón. Celso followed him, holding a gun. He stared at the two abductees.

Sammy stood next to Macario's bed as Ramón put their dinner on the table. Two plates were filled with a Cuban arroz con pollo—savory chicken and rice—and a bowl that contained chicken soup. The soup was obviously for the patient. He looked at the tray with their food, trying to suppress his growling stomach. It had been a long day, and a disappointing one. Yet Sammy was hungry. He glanced at the food again. This meal could be his last.

# SIXTY-FIVE

## NIKKI

Nikki was fixing breakfast when Clive came into the kitchen. He told her the helicopter had arrived at the small airport. She asked him if they should take their food to go. Helping himself to a cup of coffee, he said they could take ten minutes to eat and then take the Jeep to the chopper.

He gulped the coffee and took the plate of scrambled eggs, bacon, and toast that Nikki handed him.

Andy stepped into the kitchen with Olivia in his arms. "Cindy's sleeping in," he announced. "Breakfast?" When Nikki nodded, he grabbed a piece of bacon and sat Olivia down to chew on the bacon while he served his own dish.

Nikki shoveled scrambled eggs into her mouth as fast as she could. She told Andy she was sorry not to chat, but the helicopter was waiting on them. She ran to the bathroom when she finished.

While she was gone, Clive cleaned his sunglasses and asked Andy to drive them to the small airport. That way Andy would have the Jeep. He handed him a slip of paper with a couple of names and phone numbers in case he had an emergency.

Nikki returned with her purse flung over her shoulder, ready to leave.

Andy carried Olivia to the Jeep and buckled her in behind the driver. Nikki ignored the baby's babbling. This morning, her priority was finding Eduardo. The longer those spies held the hostages, the more likely the outcome would be tragic.

At the airport, Clive introduced Daniel. The short, red-haired man had a ruddy complexion. Clive called him his favorite investigator pilot. Daniel's deep voice belied his physical frame.

Thanking Andy, Clive told him to take care of his family. They would fly back as soon as they could. "With good news, I hope."

Nikki wasted no time climbing in next to Daniel.

Once they were airborne, she found herself mentally urging the helicopter to fly faster. She bit her nails and watched the shadows and vegetation change over the Rockies.

Flying over the mountainous terrain, she considered how they could gather intel that Clive or Floyd could pass on to the FBI and CIA. That was the only way her husband would be rescued now. He escaped once. The criminals would not allow that to happen again. Then the most terrifying of thoughts hit her. What if they had already killed him?

Daniel announced over the headset system that they were over the area where the men had been waiting for the troopers to pick them up the afternoon before. She looked out the window over the orange and yellow colored prairie.

Clive suggested he slow the chopper down a bit. "We need to have a better look at the terrain." He also took a box and unwrapped two sets of binoculars. He handed one to Nikki in the front seat.

Both passengers were busy searching the ground for any signs indicating the men had been there yesterday. She looked for tracks left by a helicopter that might have landed, but the wind would probably have swept away all evidence.

"Can we make a bigger circle to search for that two-story house and barn?"

Daniel's deep voice said he had been briefed the night before when Clive had called him. "I won't take any unnecessary chances, but we'll gather the intel you need."

His assurance did little to calm Nikki. She chastised herself for wasting energy being nervous. Through the binoculars, she searched the horizon for the house and barn Eduardo had described in his voice message. They were flying eastward, and she adjusted the binoculars to keep the sun out of her eyes.

# SIXTY-SIX

## EDUARDO

Eduardo ached to remove the handcuffs that locked his hands to the metal bar at the head of the bed. He brought his knees up, and that relieved the intense discomfort for a while. His thoughts drifted to Nikki. He prayed she was safe and hoped that none of the Cubans had followed her trail. If only he had been able to speak with her when he had the teenager's phone. He would have told her the danger she was in.

About half an hour later, he heard the door at the top of the stairs swing open. The welcome aroma of breakfast hit his nostrils. They would live another day. Nikki and Floyd could mobilize the troops to save them. He longed to see his wife and hold her in his arms.

Celso banged the platter loudly as he placed it on the metal overbed table near Macario's bed, awakening the patient and Sammy as well. It was Ramón's turn to stand guard at the bottom of the stairs, holding a gun.

"Son of a bitch," Sammy said, struggling with his handcuffed hands. "Hey, Celso, can you take these fucking shackles off?"

Celso took a gun tucked into the middle of his back and hit him across the face with it.

"Whoa," Sammy said. "What side of the bed did you wake up on? All I want is to go to the bathroom."

Celso pointed the gun at Sammy's head and gestured for his colleague to release Sammy. After Ramón removed the handcuffs, Celso took the keys back and walked to Eduardo's bed, taunting him.

"If you try to escape again, we won't spare your life. Even if you are a doctor." He unlocked Eduardo's cuffs and pocketed the key.

Turning to Sammy, he repeated the threat.

Sammy retreated to the bathroom. Eduardo also visited it after his friend was finished. He brought wet washcloths and a towel to clean Macario. Despite the new meds he'd administered the night before, the man's fever was still high. Eduardo cranked the bed upright to make it easier for him to feed the patient. He took only a few bites. Then Eduardo took his own plate and ate.

When the patient and captives finished, Celso stacked the plates on the platter. "If you need any medications, let me know now." Celso glared at Eduardo.

"I can't think of anything," Eduardo said after considering for several seconds.

The Cubans headed for the stairs. Eduardo and Sammy were left unshackled, free to move around the clinic.

What Eduardo wanted was a telephone to call Nikki. The Cubans would never allow him to use a phone, nor could he endanger her life. As Macario had told him, other men in the group had gone after her. He kept replaying Floyd's words about Nikki not answering the phone because she was working with a CIA agent. Those words were his consolation.

# SIXTY-SEVEN

## SAMMY

Macario called for Sammy. "I'm going to die."

"You can't do that. If you die, they'll kill the doctor."

"Get closer, Carlos. I need to talk."

Sammy, shocked, leaned in.

"That afternoon in Mexico City when a car drove slowly past your house…"

Sammy pulled away. "You killed my family. You dirty bastard." He lunged, grabbing Macario's neck.

Eduardo leaped in to get Sammy off the patient. Sammy knocked Eduardo away.

Regaining his balance, Eduardo grabbed Sammy from the back. "Stop. Right now. Or we'll all be dead."

"He killed Ana, my boys. He's going to pay."

Eduardo clung to Sammy with all his strength.

"I didn't pull the trigger, but I might as well have done it," Macario said. His voice, barely a hoarse whisper, trembled. "Listen to me. Like you, I've been dead since that night."

Sammy pushed Eduardo away and looked at Macario, breathing hatred.

"I'm sorry. Words are not enough, I know. You can kill me if that makes you feel better. Just know that my guilt over their deaths has eaten me alive. I've been a ghost since they died."

"You're evil, you dirty son of a bitch," Sammy said.

Macario closed his eyes. "I was depressed. My wife left me. My kids don't want anything to do with me. Yet I could not quit the DI. They would go after my family. So, I never quit. That's been my punishment."

"Cut out the bullshit, you damned fucking comemierda." Sammy pulled the stainless-steel tray from the overbed table, spilling medications on the floor. He lifted the tray high and with a crazed glare, calculated where to hit Macario's head.

"Stop!" Eduardo shouted. "That won't bring Ana or the twins back."

Sammy glanced at Eduardo and raised the tray higher.

He brought it down with force, dropping it short of Macario's head. It fell on the bed. It bounced and hit the cement floor with a loud, metallic clang. Sammy kicked the scattered medicine bottles and backed away, sobbing.

# SIXTY-EIGHT

## CLIVE

The helicopter crisscrossed the plains for more than an hour. They saw a few isolated ranch houses and dirt airstrips, but nothing that matched Eduardo's description. Both passengers swept the landscape with binoculars, searching for the location where the Cubans held their prisoners.

Clive saw two bumps on the horizon, and asked Nikki what she thought. She adjusted the lenses to get a better view. Could it be the barn and farmhouse Eduardo had reported? When she clearly saw the two-story house and the second tall structure, she confirmed it fit the description.

Nikki asked the pilot to give Clive, in the back seat, a better view. Daniel banked the helicopter for both passengers to study the distant structures.

"By god, I think we've found it." Clive instructed Daniel to keep a good distance while giving them several perspectives to determine if it could be the place Eduardo described as the control center.

After they had several viewpoints, Clive and Nikki discussed the points that made them think this spot was indeed the one they were looking for.

"What happens if we're wrong?" Nikki asked. She turned down the volume on her headset.

"We'd lose time. Beyond that, we'd surprise some unsuspecting folks at their tranquil ranch property. I've seen enough that I'll call my office and get operatives moving on this mission."

"I need to call Floyd," Nikki said. "Are we going to land?"

Daniel's voice came over the sound system recommending that the phone call be made from the air. "It might be noisy, but it won't interfere with my communication or navigation systems."

Clive called his office and spoke to Steven, his second in command, who had already been briefed about the mission. He removed his seatbelt and looked over Daniel's shoulder to provide approximate coordinates for the location of the ranch house and barn.

"You'll need to land at the clearing near the intersection of Ellicott and State Highway 94. We'll use both helicopters. I'm going in with you," Clive emphasized.

"I'm going in too," Nikki said.

"You're joking." Clive shifted back in his seat and put his seatbelt on again.

She shook her head. "I'm dead serious."

"You know I can't have a civilian on a mission like this. I'll contact you as soon as I can."

"Then let me stay with Daniel. I'll be close in case you need my help."

Clive looked at her as if she had not understood him and he repeated his earlier remark, adding, "I've made other arrangements for you. Trust me on this. I'll need Daniel to take us in and drop us off."

# SIXTY-NINE

## NIKKI

Nikki inhaled and dialed Floyd. She had a lot of interference in the call, but she brought him up to date about finding the ranch house where presumably her husband was being held captive. She also said Clive had called his team in. Despite speaking over a burner phone, she gave no specifics for fear the radio waves carrying her voice frequencies would be picked up. It would endanger the men they were attempting to rescue.

Ending the call, she reminded herself to stay calm and let Clive do his job without her interference. But that was damned hard. She wanted to rush in, help in the rescue effort, and make certain the others made no mistakes.

Stan, the pilot of the second helicopter, landed about a quarter of a mile from State Highway 94 near Ellicott, as Clive and the FBI team had agreed. Arriving in the chopper were Steven, Clive's backup, and two FBI agents. Along with the second chopper, a patrol car met them. Two men stepped out and joined the FBI and CIA group, but the driver remained at his seat.

Clive had arranged for the driver to escort Nikki to the luxurious Broadmoor Hotel in Colorado Springs. Not allowed to join the mission, at least she could await the outcome in a nice hotel.

Clive probably thought she would protest being chauffeured into Colorado Springs. She must have surprised him when she headed toward the car.

She waved and asked him to call her when he had news.

She slid into the back seat. "I'm Nikki," she said to the driver, taking her hat off and setting it on the seat next to her.

"Agent Apollo," the man said. "I'll stay with you until we hear from Agent Underwood."

"Did you say Apollo?" she asked.

"Yes, ma'am. My grandparents emigrated from Greece. It's a common surname there."

She asked if he had nothing better to do than babysit her.

"No ma'am."

# SEVENTY

## CLIVE

Clive gathered his team. Seven men, including the two pilots, stood before him. He needed at least six, including himself, to take over the ranch house. Daniel and Stan would remain with their helicopters. The rest were the assault team. Enough to subdue a group of well-armed, well-trained men.

"I want a surprise element to this attack. We'll fly in as close as possible and land far enough away that they won't hear us. We'll hike in the rest of the way. Bring water and a couple of pouches of food. It will take at least an hour.

"We don't know what kind of surveillance equipment protects their control center. But we can assume they have some sophisticated stuff given the type of equipment they've been planting around Cheyenne Mountain. And perhaps Schriever too."

"Are we all going in at the same time?" one agent asked.

Clive removed his sunglasses and looked at his team. "We get to the property in ones or twos. Assemble behind the barn."

The first one in would be covered by the second and third operatives he explained. Those making their way toward the barn would be covered by those waiting to move toward the target. "If we get four of you behind the barn without being seen, we can storm the house. Steven and I will come around on the other side to provide cover."

He turned to Daniel and Stan. "You guys need to stay at the helicopters. At least one craft must be ready to rescue us if we require evacuation before taking the house. That will be Stan." He instructed Daniel to be the lookout and to keep his chopper further away from the Cuban command center once they went in unless he gave him clearance to approach.

The pilots handed out Kevlar jackets.

Clive asked if there were any questions. "Let's get on with it," he said when no one spoke.

The men split into two groups and climbed into the choppers.

Clive put his sunglasses back on and took the copilot seat next to Daniel, who took the lead. He had a reasonable idea where the choppers should come down.

Daniel landed in an area that was clean of shrubbery. Clive jumped out while the rotors were still whirling. He ducked and ran out into the open to signal the other pilot where to land.

The assault team regrouped a few meters away from the helicopters. Clive led the way toward the control center. He checked his compass several times. After catching sight of the ranch house, he told his men to break up into groups and spread out. He kept the front position until the barn was visible. He talked over the wireless system, emphasizing they would go in two at a time. He would fall in with Steven and they would take the farthest route to the back side of the house.

Using his binoculars, Clive saw the first two make it to the back of the barn. One stepped into a ditch and lowered himself into a defensive position. They had made it to the target without gunfire. The next two arrived as easily as the first two. Clive was worried. Had the compound been abandoned? Or were they lying in wait to see how many were coming before the men defended the control center?

Holding his AR-15 in position, Clive signaled his companion to cover him as he moved to hide behind a woodpile near the house. Two large windows that overlooked an open veranda on that side could easily give away his location if people were patrolling from inside or if silent surveillance was set up outside.

Ducking and moving steadily toward the wood pile, Clive noticed the front room was bathed in subdued lighting. He wondered why no one was visible. Why he had seen no early warning devices. Perhaps the Cubans were out in their own helicopter, placing intel gathering equipment near Shriever and Cheyenne Mountain, as Eduardo reported to Nikki in his message.

This mission was too easy. Something was wrong. Very wrong.

# SEVENTY-ONE
## CLIVE

Clive ran from the woodpile to the house, took two steps to the open veranda and ducked under a window. He peered inside to find a sparsely furnished room with a pool table in the middle. He eased his head below the windowsill and signaled for Steven to follow him. Steven sprinted to the veranda and crouched as he followed Clive to the front door. Steven tried the handle, but the door was locked.

Clive spoke into his wireless microphone, telling his men that he was going to blow the lock off the front door. They should stay put unless they heard more gunfire. Removing his sunglasses, he put them in his shirt pocket.

Holding his AR-15 with his left hand, he removed the pistol from his waist and shot the lock and handle completely off. He held his breath as he holstered his gun and opened the door. Hearing no noise, he signaled Steven to follow him inside.

Steven declared the large living and dining room clear. He checked a closet and a bathroom. "Clear."

A heavy door to another room was also locked. Clive notified his men again that they would hear one more gunshot they could ignore. The door almost fell off when he shot the lock mechanism. Steven followed Clive into the large room. It was equipped with kitchen appliances against one wall and floor-to-ceiling cabinets on the other three walls. The only window was over the sink and dishwasher.

The room had two more doors, one that led outside and another one with three reinforcing bars padlocked into metal brackets.

"They don't want visitors in there," Clive said. "They're hiding something important. Let's clear the upstairs first."

Each man took a bedroom. The closets and drawers contained men's clothing and underwear. After checking all four bedrooms and a hall bathroom, they returned downstairs to open the barred door.

"We need a crowbar to tackle this job," Steven said.

Clive shook his head. "I'm going to blow the door lock off. Then the door should open, and we'll crawl between the middle and lower bars. They're meant to keep people in, not out."

"Brilliant," Steven mumbled.

Once again, Clive notified his people outside that he had to use his gun. "This door might take two shots." He paced the kitchen as he talked, and he examined the door to the outside. It had a heavy-duty deadbolt. "I'm also going to blow the kitchen door to the outside. That'll be the third shot. Make sure none of you are standing there. After that, you'll hear a shot or two inside."

He put his AR-15 against the wall and unholstered his gun. He stepped to the outside door and aimed, leaving the lock hanging precariously from the wood, and he asked Steven to make sure the door opened in case they needed a quick exit.

He returned to the inside bolted one. The first shot knocked the handle off but did not dismantle the deadbolt. He hit it again. Pushing the door open, they both heard voices shouting from the room they had opened. Clive realized they were at the top of a staircase. The room below was dark.

"Don't shoot us," a man's voice hollered. "We're captives. We're not armed."

"There's a light switch at the top of the stairs," another voice yelled.

Clive cautiously crawled through the space between the two lowest bars. He straightened up and reached around the doorframe to grab his AR-15.

Clive flipped the light switch, lighting up a large basement. Holding his automatic weapon ready, he saw two men sitting on hospital beds. They held their arms up so he could see they did not have weapons. A third one was lying on a bed. The basement appeared to be something of a clinic. Could the alleged spies be hiding here? Were they using the captives as hostages?

Crawling through the same space his colleague had used, Steven stepped up behind Clive. They proceeded slowly down the steps, weapons at the ready.

"You're not in any danger from us," one of them said. "Just watch out for the kidnappers when they return."

Clive assessed the room before going all the way down. Could this be a trap? Could the Cubans be hiding and waiting to knock them off? The first bed was in the middle of the room and the other two were along the far wall. He approached the one in the middle of the room.

"I'm Eduardo Duarte," a man sitting on the bed along the wall said. "That's Macario, my patient."

Clive glanced at the man in the first bed and saw that in fact, he looked as if there was a good reason for him to be in a hospital bed. His leg seemed badly injured. There was an overbed table with medicine on it. He was convinced the man was in bad shape. He moved to Eduardo's side.

"Who sent you?" Eduardo asked.

"Your wife, her boss, and her brother," Clive replied.

"Is Nikki okay?" Eduardo asked anxiously.

"She's fine. She's been working hard to find you."

"Her brother? He's alive?" Eduardo asked. "That can't be. He was killed. I saw it happen."

"Andy Garcia?" the hoarse voice of the second man along the wall interrupted. "The kidnappers shot him dead."

"He's very much alive," Clive said. "I had breakfast with him this morning. Both Nikki and her brother are doing fine."

"I saw Andy fall when the kidnappers opened fire on us," Eduardo said. "They said he was dead. Are you sure he's alive?"

"Absolutely," Clive assured him. "He'd passed out and they left him for dead."

"Thank God," the third man said. "I'm Sammy. We need to get the hell out of here before the Cubans return."

"We need to hurry," Eduardo said. "The men have been gone for quite a while." He told them he needed five minutes to prepare his patient to leave.

Clive nodded his okay.

"We'll get you out of here and take you to a real clinic where they can set those bones," Eduardo said.

Sammy glared at Eduardo's patient.

Clive watched as Eduardo took the patient's vital signs, handed him a pill and a cup of water, and brought a bedpan for him. He admired the doctor's calm as he worked with the injured man.

# SEVENTY-TWO

## CLIVE

Clive's earbuds sounded, taking his attention away from the doctor and the patient. One of the men outside reported they could hear a helicopter. He had verified that neither one of their pilots was in the air.

"I was just informed a helicopter is flying close by. Let's get back upstairs. Now."

Eduardo said he and Sammy could help them upstairs.

The distinct sound of the rotors made the hair on Clive's neck bristle. "What are we going to do about him?" he asked, motioning toward Macario with his head.

Eduardo suggested leaving him in the clinic, out of danger.

"That's best," Macario said. "Once you establish control and arrest Bembe and his men, come back for me."

Turning to Sammy and Eduardo, Clive asked if they could use guns. They nodded. He handed his pistol and a fresh magazine to Eduardo.

Steven passed his holster and loaded gun to Sammy.

They hurried upstairs. Clive's earpiece sounded again. The chopper was headed toward the ranch. It appeared that it might land four hundred meters from the barn. Clive ordered the men to take cover inside the barn.

The chattering of the craft increased, as if the rotors were out of balance. The aircraft was much closer now. Clive ran to the kitchen window and watched as it dipped behind a small hill as if it were going to touch down. Had those in the craft seen the men behind the barn? Were they preparing to attack the house and barn on foot? Staring at the hill, he almost expected to see a small army rush to the top, but nothing appeared.

The other three men were right behind him, gawking at the helicopter's maneuvers as it rose again and headed toward the barn.

He headed to the door but stopped short before stepping out. "We'd be easy targets," Clive said. "Let's go out the front room onto the deck under the veranda."

The veranda did provide some cover, but they were on the wrong side of the house to help behind the barn. They edged up to the corner of the house, where the veranda ended.

A man strapped to a rope leaned out onto an air step through the open chopper door. He held an automatic weapon. The helicopter disappeared behind the barn.

Clive shouted. "Steven, take aim when it comes this way."

Several bursts of automatic fire ripped through the air.

After a few seconds, the helicopter sounded closer. They looked up, but the slanted veranda ceiling prevented them from seeing it. Bullets sprayed the ground in front of the wooden deck where they stood. The chopper circled, and two more barrages of bullets rang out.

Clive ordered Sammy and Eduardo back inside so he and Steven could aim at the man shooting from the air step. "Stay in the kitchen," he barked. "And hold your fire unless I tell you otherwise."

The chopper came around the front again. He signaled Steven to follow him. Clive crouched in the doorway and took aim as the aircraft turned the corner of the house. Steven, standing behind Clive, took advantage of his semi-protected stance to shoot upward, smooth and fast, as the plane passed. Neither man hit his target.

More bullets hit the ground in front of them. Steven quickly retreated inside. Clive dived into the kitchen.

"They know where we are," Clive shouted. "Upstairs. They'll think there are more of us."

They raced up the staircase, Clive in the lead. He dashed into a bedroom facing the barn. He smashed the glass out of the window with a chair and ordered Steven to do the same in a bedroom across the hall. The helicopter approached. Clive aimed and pulled the trigger. His bullets fell short. The aircraft passed too quickly. He rushed to the other room to see the man lose his footing on the air step. The man and his weapon both struck the veranda roof before falling to the ground.

Clive's earpiece came alive. "Man down. Man down."

"What?" he asked his operative behind the barn. "How can we have a man down? Who is it?"

"Three men surprised us from behind. We were waiting for the helicopter, but these guys sneaked up on us from the ground. Frank and Matt were under a tree, and I was in the barn using a window to blast the chopper when it came by. There was gunfire and I saw Matt go down. That's when I saw the assholes. Two of them are down. I shot them. Frank hit the third one, but he managed to run before either one of us could take him out."

"Do you think there are more of them on foot?"

"Besides the one who ran? I don't think there are any others. The chopper must have let them out when it dipped behind the hill."

# SEVENTY-THREE

## EDUARDO

The helicopter hovered over the hill and appeared once more as if it were going to land. Before long, it rose and flew away from the ranch. Eduardo stood by until Clive confirmed with his operative in the barn that the helicopter seemed to be leaving.

Clive instructed both helicopter pilots to follow the one that had taken off. "They're armed, so keep a safe distance. I'll call the local authorities and the FBI to apprehend them once they land or run out of fuel. Keep me informed of their whereabouts."

"I'm getting supplies from the basement to take care of the fallen man," Eduardo said.

Clive nodded his approval.

Eduardo dashed down the stairs into the clinic. Throwing supplies into a plastic bag, he told Macario what had happened. "We should be okay now. The helicopter flew away after they shot the sniper."

"Leave. Leave now," Macario cried out hoarsely. "This house is booby trapped. They'll blow it up."

"I'm not leaving without you." Eduardo placed the bag in Macario's good hand. "Get on my back."

Macario screamed in pain as Eduardo tried to bring him upright. "Go, go, go. I can't make it."

Eduardo yanked the injured man up and forced Macario onto his back. "Hold on."

The man's good arm clasped tightly across Eduardo's chest. The doctor grabbed Macario's good leg to keep him on his back as he headed for the stairs. He started to slip off and Eduardo had no choice but to hold the bad leg as well. The splint fell off. Contrary to what he expected, he felt Macario's body relax. Had the patient died?

Gasping for air by the time he reached the ground floor, Eduardo shouted for the men to get outside. "The house is booby trapped."

Sammy came to help carry Macario and he held him by the shoulders, leaving Eduardo to deal with the man's lower torso and legs, especially the badly damaged one. He was surprised at Sammy's help but relieved to get it.

Clive ran from upstairs. He was talking to Daniel on the wireless and ended the call as he dashed into the kitchen. Steven hurried into the kitchen as well. In the distance, a helicopter could be heard.

"Evacuate. Hurry!" Clive yelled.

"Head for the barn," Macario cried feebly. "They'll blow this place up."

Eduardo repeated Macario's words loud enough for everyone to hear.

Clive glanced back at the doctor. He stumbled through the kitchen door and almost knocked Steven to the ground. Recovering their balance, they bolted across the yard to take cover in the barn.

Sammy and Eduardo struggled to carry the injured man. Outside, Eduardo glanced toward the sky. The helicopter would be above them in no time. With a burst of adrenaline, he pushed Macario's good leg forward, forcing Sammy, who was running backward, to move faster.

The helicopter banked away from the house. A deafening explosion behind them knocked the three men into the ditch surrounding the barn and a fireball rolled over them.

# SEVENTY-FOUR

## NIKKI

Nikki sat in the spacious lobby of the elegant Broadmoor in Colorado Springs wishing she could use the gym to get rid of her nervous energy. Exercising at the hotel was not a good idea, though. She had no change of clothes.

Maybe she should buy an outfit, but the boutiques at the hotel were horribly expensive. Besides, she was in no mood to shop. Instead, she sat on a comfortable sofa listening to her stomach grumble. Her always healthy appetite turned voracious whenever her nerves were out of control. Agent Apollo had escorted her, after they had arrived, to The Grille restaurant at the golf club. She had ordered a hamburger, fries, and a twelve-ounce chocolate milkshake. The agent had taken a chicken salad sandwich with a cup of coffee.

Two hours later, she was hungry again. Instead of visiting one of the hotel's restaurants, she popped a piece of gum into her mouth. She had tried breathing, walking in the lobby, and meditating to pass the time. None of it worked. Her anxiety would not let up.

She walked to a gift shop in the lobby, not far from the spot Agent Apollo was standing. A display of chocolate candies caught her attention, and she bought a box of truffles for Eduardo. She had paid for the gift-wrapped box and was stepping back into the hall when Agent

Apollo's phone rang. He spoke softly but looked in her direction. She felt uneasy.

Nikki's phone rang. It was Floyd. She froze, almost unable to answer, thinking he would convey bad news.

"I need you to accompany Agent Apollo on a short ride to Cheyenne Mountain—"

"Eduardo's there?" she asked, unable to contain her excitement.

"Not quite," Floyd said. "I've loaned you to the FBI. They may need your help with some Spanish."

"Floyd, what's up? You know I can't work for the FBI."

"In this case you can. Agent Apollo will explain on the way over."

She ended the call and picked up her fedora from the sofa. Agent Apollo walked with her to the parking lot.

During the twenty-minute drive, the agent explained that they needed her to help the FBI come up with a message that would pass as Cuban Spanish.

"Is that all?"

"To begin with. We may need you for more than one message."

Apollo spoke only to convey information. They were silent until they reached the first of two security checkpoints.

# SEVENTY-FIVE

## CLIVE

The foundations of the barn shook as if a powerful earthquake had rolled through. Clive and the other operatives felt the heat and pressure from the explosion. He edged toward the extra-wide doorway and peered through it to see Eduardo, Sammy, and the injured man curled up in the ditch. He stepped outside on a cement driveway over the ditch. It was wide enough to accommodate a helicopter being moved inside the barn.

Clive heard a voice on his wireless. Daniel had seen the explosion from the air when he was following the spies' helicopter. He was checking on his colleagues.

"Too early to tell," Clive answered, "but you come on in. Stay close and I'll call you. We have casualties for sure. And the fire is still raging." He asked Daniel to call for a medevac helicopter and alert the two closest fire stations.

He ordered Stan to tail the spies with his helicopter. The FBI would send another one to intercept them. They had Stan's call sign so the two chopper crews could coordinate.

Then he called his office. He asked them to make sure the FBI arrested the spies whenever their helicopter landed—or crashed.

# SEVENTY-SIX

## EDUARDO

In the ditch, Eduardo slowly sat up and ran his hand over the back of his aching head. His ears were ringing from the blast. He saw Sammy but could not hear him as he wrestled his legs out from under Macario, who lay unmoving across him.

Eduardo glanced toward the house. It was burning. He wanted to move and take his patient into the barn. He struggled to get up. He should at least crawl over and make sure that Macario was still alive.

He put pressure on his ears to get them cleared up. It helped a little. He inched toward his patient and checked his pulse. Macario was alive, though he appeared to be unconscious.

Eduardo saw Clive standing nearby.

"We've lost the evidence," Eduardo said, coughing. His voice echoed in his head and smoke burned his nostrils. "We may not be able to prove much."

"The physical evidence may be gone. But they incinerated their own records. That warrants a full-blown investigation," Clive said.

"It's not a full-scale job yet?" Eduardo frowned. The smoke made him cough again. "What does it take to get the FBI and the CIA to act?"

# SEVENTY-SEVEN

## NIKKI

Nikki was surprised that the tunnel into the North American Aerospace Defense Command was wide open for them to enter. At the first blast door, she met three people in the rock-walled foyer of NORAD's bunker facility. This was as far as she could go. She would not be allowed beyond the second blast door. Normally she would be fascinated at being in a place storing top-level secrets, and the electronic components built into the blast doors to protect those secrets would merit closer observation.

She'd googled the bunker on the way over and discovered that these doors, twenty-three tons each, were on a secondary tunnel protecting the working facilities. Even through the open blast doors, she could only see concrete floors and the naked rock of the tunnel. The next foyer, between the two sets of doors, was slightly better with plain, off-white walls. She thought a chair or two might make the space more inviting, but then guests were rarely in this place.

A tall, lean man introduced himself as Cougar. Of course, that was not his real name. He probably used it today for her benefit. He handed her a slip of paper with a couple of sentences and a clipboard with paper and pen attached.

"Translate this message into Cuban Spanish," Cougar said. He was dressed, as were the other two, in Air Force camouflage uniforms.

She glanced at the paper.

Test flight F-53-521 planned from CA in 5 days from today. Confirm receipt.

The lines made little sense to Nikki, but given the seriousness of the operation, she could not take it lightly.

Prueba del vuelo F-53-521 está planificado de CA dentro de 5 días de hoy.
Mandar acuse de recibo.

She handed the clipboard back with her handwritten translation. Guessing that her trip to Cuba was what made her a language expert in their eyes, she hoped whoever received it viewed it as Cuban Spanish.

Cougar looked at it and nodded. "Thank you. Please wait a few minutes. I'll be back."

The other two airmen stayed with her and Agent Apollo in the empty foyer. A few minutes later, Cougar returned. He thanked them and told them they could leave.

On the scenic return drive to the Broadmoor, Nikki's phone rang. Her heart palpitated again when she saw it was Floyd.

"I have good news," Floyd said. There was a lot of interference on the line, and she labored to hear him. "Eduardo has been rescued and, other than a few injuries, I'm told he's okay."

Nikki was overjoyed and emotional. "Thank God. Thank you, Floyd."

"All I can tell you is that Eduardo needs to be checked by a doctor. Air ambulances are heading in to pick him and the others up. It'll be a couple of hours before you can see him."

"Are you sure he's okay?" she asked, anxiety cracking her voice. "Please tell me what happened."

Floyd told her he lacked details, but there had been gunfire and the spies had blown up the control center to destroy evidence. By the time the house went up in flames, everyone had evacuated, although there were injuries.

"Where will they take Eduardo?" she asked.

"The hospital in Colorado Springs."

# SEVENTY-EIGHT

## EDUARDO

Eduardo rubbed his temples. Pain had ripped through his head after the blast. Now it subsided into a dull ache. Before stepping away, Clive told him to take his time getting up.

Eduardo recruited Sammy to help him move Macario inside the barn, away from the smoke fumes. He was afraid his patient might go into shock.

They laid him on flattened cardboard packaging on the concrete floor, making him as comfortable as possible under the circumstances. Eduardo pulled off his fire-singed shirt and placed it under Macario's head. He spoke softly, providing assurances to the half-conscious man, as he checked his pulse.

Macario looked up and half-smiled as if in gratitude.

Eduardo saw boxes nearby containing bottled spring water and asked Sammy to grab one and give small sips to the patient. "I'll be back after I check on the injured man from our team."

Clive caught up with him outside. The two men walked to the far side of the barn to check on Matt, the man who had been shot. Eduardo took his pulse at the carotid artery. He looked at Clive and shook his head. "He's gone. I'm sorry."

Clive told Eduardo he had to take a call on his wireless earpiece.

Eduardo glanced around and signaled he would check on the two fallen men from the spy group.

When the call ended, Clive caught up with him. "That was Daniel. I told him to bring his chopper in for whatever we might need. The air ambulance should be here in less than half an hour."

Eduardo stood after checking the carotid arteries of both men. He confirmed they had been killed. They took the two Cuban corpses, one at a time, and placed them near the barn. Next they carried Matt's body closer to the barn, away from the Cubans, out of respect.

Daniel landed the helicopter and joined Eduardo and Clive.

"I'll take the bodies back in our helicopter," Clive said. "That will leave the medevac to take care of Eduardo, Sammy, and Macario. Steven and my other three guys can ride with us."

Eduardo checked on his patient. There was not much he could do until the EMT team arrived. "We're damned lucky to be alive," he said. "That ditch saved us."

The medevac helicopter arrived. Eduardo greeted the pilot and showed the medical team where Macario was still clinging to life inside the barn.

He watched closely as the EMTs placed Macario on a stretcher and carried him to the air ambulance. After they secured the stretcher inside the helicopter, Eduardo told Clive he hoped to see him at the hospital in Colorado Springs.

"You bet. I'll be there shortly," Clive assured him. He held up his hand signaling for Eduardo to wait. He adjusted his wireless earpiece and appeared to be listening. After a few seconds, he thanked Stan. He updated Eduardo that an FBI helicopter pilot had contacted Stan reporting that they were following the aircraft of interest. "You'd better leave. Nikki will be waiting for you."

Eduardo nodded and clamped his lips to hold in his emotions. Using a grab bar, he pulled himself into the chopper. He was reluctant to hand over care of his patient to the EMTs and positioned himself to supervise how they handled his injured leg. He was glad Macario would finally receive the care he needed.

One of the EMTs placed a blood pressure cuff on Eduardo and explained the medical helicopter would take them to the hospital in

Colorado Springs. He assured him that surgeons would probably operate on Macario's compound fracture and treat his infected leg. The medic told Eduardo that it was amazing the injured man was in as good a shape as he was, given the trauma he had gone through.

When the EMT completed the blood pressure, pulse, and oxygen check on Eduardo, he moved to Sammy.

Notwithstanding his headache, Eduardo was certain the ditch had saved their lives from the fireball that rolled over them when the spies had blown up the house. The odor of the burning house still filled his nostrils.

As soon as he buckled himself in, Eduardo asked one of the EMTs if he could borrow a phone.

The pilot handed him his phone and prepared the helicopter for takeoff.

He dialed Nikki. She did not answer. He was anxious to see her at the hospital, he said in the message. More importantly, he wanted to tell her he loved her. That would wait until he saw her, when he could throw his arms around her and hold her tight.

Sirens drowned out the noise of the rotors as they started turning. A fire engine raced over the dirt road, with a second one close behind. Eduardo realized with relief that he could also hear the swishing of the rotors as they moved overhead. The frequency increased until the chopper lifted off. He looked out over the scene below. Firefighters were setting up the hoses to douse water on the flames dancing skyward through the roof of the house.

The flight seemed interminable. Eduardo was so eager to see Nikki that he could hardly stand it. Eventually, the helicopter landed at the helipad at UCHealth Memorial Central Hospital. The medics lowered Macario out on the stretcher and rolled him in. Eduardo and Sammy were asked to get onto stretchers that hospital personnel had brought out. Blankets were spread over them. Eduardo was happy for the comfort of a warm blanket.

At the emergency room, Nikki rushed over as Eduardo's stretcher was rolled in. The EMT asked her to step back.

"He's my husband," Nikki said, not budging.

"You can see him as soon as we get him admitted and taken to a room."

She removed her hat to kiss Eduardo's forehead. "I'll see you soon, my love."

He reached for her hand and squeezed it. "I'm fine. They'll release me in an hour or two."

Nikki placed the gift-wrapped chocolates on Eduardo's stretcher.

The EMT handed it back to her. "Give it to him once he's admitted. And don't plan any outings yet. They may keep him overnight for observation." He asked Nikki to stay in the waiting room until the nursing staff called her.

# SEVENTY-NINE

## NIKKI

Nikki walked past the nurses' station in the waiting room. A middle-aged man in a lightweight jacket was inquiring about his uncle Macario, who had just been admitted with bad injuries.

What were the chances a man, with a Cuban accent, would inquire about a patient with injuries like the ones Floyd had explained to her that Eduardo had been treating? This man was here to harm Macario. Nikki was sure of it.

She stepped away, dialed Clive, and explained what she'd overheard. "Send someone over right now. Plainclothes preferably. Meanwhile, I'll follow this guy."

Clive described Macario to make sure Nikki did not pull her gun on an innocent family.

Nikki anticipated the man's steps and was waiting with an open elevator door. Her purse, with the baby Glock inside, was casually flung over her shoulder and her hat was cocked to one side. She asked him in a very British accent what floor he needed.

The man thanked her as he got off on the third floor. She carried the gift-wrapped box as if she were going to deliver a royal gift to someone on the same floor.

He walked slowly down the hall. Nikki stopped to use her phone. She updated Clive about the floor they were on and ended the call. She picked up speed until she saw what room the man had gone into.

She passed the room slowly. A couple of nurses were caring for the patient. It was curious, she thought, that Clive had not ordered police protection for him. At that point, one of the nurses stepped into the hall and Nikki inquired about him.

"We're stabilizing him before surgery," one nurse said. "They won't operate until tomorrow morning."

The second nurse left the room, leaving the unknown man alone with Macario.

Nikki put her hand on the baby Glock as she moved in to have another look. The man got closer to Macario and took something from inside his coat.

A handgun.

He tucked it into Macario's neck and whispered something in his ear.

Nikki pulled her baby Glock. In doing so, she dropped the chocolates.

The shooter turned without letting up on Macario's throat.

Nikki tightened her grip on the baby Glock. She noted his expression. He looked angry. Maybe for not considering the woman in the elevator as a threat. Now she was pointing a gun at him.

"Put it down," she ordered.

The man laughed. He had a crooked mouth, as if it had deformed after years of clamping a cigar between his lips.

"A woman never tells me what to do," he said, cocking the gun he held against Macario's neck.

Two people rushed into the room.

"You heard her," a heavyset woman said. "Put your gun on the bedstand."

"Now! before I shoot you," the second woman said gruffly.

He did as they asked. The second woman stepped in to handcuff him. The heavyset one took the revolver.

"You're outfoxed," the heavyset one said. "By females, no less."

Two uniformed police officers arrived and arrested the handcuffed man.

"Great job," the second plainclothes woman said to Nikki. "If you ever want a job as a special agent, let us know. Clive told me you'd be a good addition to our office or at the CIA." She also told Nikki she could return to the ER. They would stay in Macario's room to keep him safe.

Nikki flew back to the waiting room. She could hardly wait to see Eduardo.

# EIGHTY

## NIKKI

Nikki fidgeted in the waiting room. Finally, she called Floyd. No answer. She left a message that she'd just helped nab another Cuban asset.

At last, the nurse escorted Nikki to Eduardo's room.

Nikki kissed him and hugged him gently. He pulled her close.

She told him about dropping the chocolate truffles upstairs in Macario's room. He was about to ask something when the emergency room doctor, a short man wearing a white gown two sizes too big, stepped in. He examined Eduardo and ordered a CT scan of the skull and x-rays of the torso. When he saw burn lesions on his back and neck, he put in a call for a burn specialist to evaluate them. He also recommended seeing an audiologist soon after getting released.

"From what I've been told, you're a very lucky guy," the doctor said.

Eduardo grabbed Nikki's hand and kissed it. "I certainly am," he said, looking at his wife.

Nikki went with him when Eduardo was taken for the scan and x-rays. Shortly after they returned to the room, the burn specialist and a petite nurse with spiked blond hair came in.

The doctor decided that the burns were not severe enough to

require intervention. He prescribed an ointment and the nurse said she would apply it before he slept that night.

It was almost nine p.m. when the nurse applied the ointment and bandaged the burn areas. She told him to call if he needed anything during the night. She closed the door.

No sooner had they left than Nikki told Eduardo she was going to climb in bed with him.

"Are you sure this is a good idea?" he asked. "We're in a hospital room, not a hotel."

"We'll be fine," she said, slipping her blouse off and tossing it on the foot of the bed. She stood in her sexy black bra in the dim light and unzipped her pants. "The nurse won't make another round until midnight, and I need to snuggle up to you. I promise to be careful with your burns. Besides, they're bandaged."

A knock on the door startled Nikki. She zipped her pants and hurriedly pulled her blouse back over her head. She went to the door, hand combing her hair, expecting to see an aide or a doctor. Instead, it was Floyd.

"May I come in?"

"Of course! I didn't know you were flying in. This is great!"

"How's Eduardo?"

"See for yourself." Nikki extended her arm toward Eduardo in a sweeping motion.

"Are the doctors taking good care of you?" Floyd asked with a wide grin. He placed a shopping bag at the foot of the bed. "A change of clothes. I understand your last set got slightly burned."

Eduardo laughed and clasped Floyd's hands.

"I know it's late, but I came here directly from the airport. I wanted to make certain you're in good hands. Clive called to fill me in, and I've invited him to join us for a few minutes."

"When we talked earlier I didn't know you were in flight," Nikki said.

"That's why our connection had all that interference. I'm glad you didn't guess I was flying in. I wanted to surprise you," Floyd said.

# EIGHTY-ONE

## NIKKI

"It took eleven seconds to get your translated message to the International Space Station," Floyd said.

"Whoa, you're losing me. What do you mean by the International Space Station?" Nikki asked. "Surely you don't mean that my translation went to the ISS."

"I do indeed mean that, and it was good timing. The planets were aligned such that transmission was quick," Floyd said. "Receipt was confirmed in no time too."

"You're messing with me. It *must* take more than eleven seconds to get a message to the ISS."

Floyd explained that the translated message had been sent to a receiver at NASA using special coding that directed it to NASA's SCaN program. From there, it was automatically sent through a private communication line for one of the astronauts by employing a NASA satellite. "I wasn't told, but I assume it was the Russian astronaut."

"Astronauts have private lines up there?" Nikki asked, astonished.

"Yep, each one," Floyd said. "They spend months up there, you know. They have to provide a way for family members to reach them."

"Wow, I had no idea. I still don't get why a message was sent up there."

"Something to do with the info being received and retransmitted on the equipment that Eduardo photographed. NORAD used the message to verify that secret data was being stolen and sent to space where an astronaut in collaboration with the Chinese would observe and confirm testing of our defense system."

"So, the stingrays were sending info to outer space," Eduardo said. "Andy will love that. Did the equipment use quantum technology?"

"Don't know," Floyd said. "Some kind of echo technology. When the info came to Cheyenne Mountain, the Cubans would capture it and transmit it to their destination without leaving a trace. The US and Canada couldn't detect it because it's like a message wrapped within a message."

"Too much information," Nikki said, brushing her hair away from her forehead. "All I need are the basics."

"Since it's impossible to detect without someone reporting it," Floyd said, "that's where Eduardo's photo convinced the FBI and CIA that something was happening."

"Even with the picture, the agencies took their time," Eduardo said. "They wanted more proof before they fully committed."

"You got it," Floyd said, glancing at his watch. "Clive's arranged for his helicopter to pick up Andy and his family early tomorrow morning. They'll fly to the airport here and when you're released, we'll join them and fly back to the rental property."

"What about Sammy?" Eduardo asked. "Will there be room for him?"

There was a knock on the door.

Floyd answered and found Clive standing in the hall.

"Come on in."

"How's our superhero doing?" Clive asked Eduardo.

"Thanks," Eduardo said, smiling at Nikki, "the only superhero around here is my wife."

"You saved my husband," Nikki said in a shaky voice. "We owe you so much."

Clive shook his head. "It's the other way around. Eduardo's photo alerted us that important intel that compromised our national security was diverted to agencies in foreign countries."

Floyd nodded.

Turning to face Nikki, Clive told her that if they had not pursued the Cuban kidnappers, the group would still be spying on behalf of the MSS and stealing important data.

"The spies have been captured?" Eduardo asked.

"That's right. We now have eight of them in custody, including the one Nikki helped us catch right here in the hospital."

"You caught one here?" Eduardo asked, sitting up straight. "You're not talking about Macario, are you?"

"No, he's one floor above. Relaxing tonight. He'll have surgery tomorrow," Clive explained. "And the deceased spies, two from the control center and the one from the safe house, are in the morgue. We think that accounts for all of them."

Nikki wanted to know if her brother and his family would be safe at the ranch house in the Taos Ski Valley. "What if there are other mercenaries on the loose? They know the location and could return to harm them."

"Wait a minute, I'm confused," Eduardo said. His face became flushed. "They came after you at the rental property?"

Nikki nodded. "I forgot to mention it."

"How are Andy and his family?"

"Everyone's fine," Nikki said.

"It's complicated," Floyd said. He explained that Nikki and her brother's family escaped the Taos ranch house just in time and Clive provided a safehouse in Colorado. The mercenaries located them in that one too. Clive took them to his house near the town of Cortes. Andy and his family were there now.

"I wouldn't trust that you have all the spies in custody," Nikki said.

"We'll know after we interrogate them," Clive said.

Eduardo asked about Macario. He wanted to see him before leaving the hospital.

"That can be arranged. We'll question him as soon as the doctor clears it. All I know at this point is what you've told us, that he has important data about the intel gathering operation the MSS was conducting here."

"And Sammy?" Eduardo asked, glancing at Nikki.

"Like you, he's under observation for the night," Clive responded, looking away.

The door to the room swung open. A plump, round-faced nurse wearing a grim expression stepped in. "Party's over. It's ten p.m. My patient needs his rest."

Floyd and Clive slouched and looked a bit sheepish.

"It's important for my husband to see his friends," Nikki offered as an excuse.

"I don't know how you got past the nurses' station. Visiting hours ended at seven. You must all leave. Now," the nurse said emphatically.

"I'm his wife. I'm sleeping on the couch." Nikki pointed to the bedding piled on it.

The nurse followed the two visitors out of the room.

"I don't think we'll have privacy until you're out of here. I'll just crawl into the sleeper couch," Nikki said, giving Eduardo a good night kiss.

# EIGHTY-TWO
## EDUARDO

At five o'clock in the morning, the plump nurse from the night before checked Eduardo's vital signs. When she finished, she told him the doctor had released him and he could get dressed. She handed Nikki a bag of bandages and a tube of silver sulfadiazine cream.

"Apply the ointment twice a day after cleaning the burns. Then cover them with bandages," she said. "Do it for at least ten days."

Eduardo asked if Sammy Amaya was also being released.

The nurse looked at him with an expression of distant distaste. "Why do you ask?"

"He could catch a ride with us back to his house."

"He's no longer here," she said.

"What? He's checked out already?" Nikki asked in surprise.

The nurse frowned. "No, he disappeared in the middle of the night."

"You mean he left without notifying anyone?" Eduardo asked. "Why would he do that?"

The nurse shrugged. "Maybe somebody's after him."

Nikki gave her husband a look. He needed no telepathy to get the message. *I told you he was hiding something.*

# EIGHTY-THREE

## EDUARDO

Eduardo and Nikki greeted a police officer outside of Macario's room. A nurse told them she gave him medication to relax before surgery. Macario was hooked up to all the monitoring equipment that Eduardo would have wanted at the clinic. Although he sounded groggy, Macario smiled as he spoke.

"You're looking great!" Eduardo said. "You'll be out of here in no time."

Macario thanked him for the special care. He asked about Bembe and his team of spies.

"They've been apprehended. That's all we know," Nikki said.

With his good hand, Macario grabbed hers and squeezed it tight. "Thank you, my dear, for saving me."

"Not me. Eduardo's the one who rescued you," she said.

"You saved me yesterday. Fausto, my former comrade, would have killed me."

"Fausto? Here?" Eduardo asked. Turning to Nikki, he beamed. "That's a real coup! That's the guy with the yellow pickup. The tag number that I sent from Cheyenne Mountain. Remember? Give Clive the tag number."

Nikki called Charlotte to get the license plate information. Her phone had been demolished, so she no longer had the photo. Charlotte texted the data, and she forwarded it to Clive.

She handed her burner to Eduardo with Clive's response: the police discovered the truck in the parking lot after Nikki helped to get Fausto arrested in Macario's room.

"It seems we're getting the Cubans accounted for," Eduardo told Macario. "You'll be called as a witness against Bembe and his friends. You're the one to know if they've all been caught. That should help your cause."

In a whisper, Macario confirmed that Clive already had the names of all the DI agents and handlers. "Just in case I don't make it through the surgery."

Nikki told him he would survive just fine. "You've had a great doctor taking care of you. You can't disappoint him now."

Macario cleared his throat. "Sammy's a good man. It's so sad about his family. I've always felt guilty about it. Especially about his boys."

"Guilt is a terrible feeling," Eduardo said. "It seemed you two ended it on a good note yesterday. Sammy seems to have forgiven you."

"I was the one who found him, the escaped former DI agent, living in Mexico City. A man was sent in to kill him. Ana, his wife, tried to defend herself and the twin boys. The assassin killed her in self-defense. He didn't need to harm those boys. But he did. Then he waited for Carlos—that was Sammy's name back then."

Macario paused. Eduardo thought that was the end of the conversation and he gave him a Security Source card in case he ever needed to contact them.

"Give the card to the nurse to place with your personal items," Nikki added.

"The assassin was in the house when Sammy returned and discovered his family had been killed," Macario said, glancing at the card. "The assassin communicated to us that Ana had wounded him. He died too. Whether he died of the wounds Ana inflicted, or if Sammy killed him, I'll probably never know. By the time we found out about the failure of the mission, Sammy had left the country. In tracking him, I later discovered the CIA had extracted him from Mexico City by helicopter."

Eduardo swallowed hard. He wasn't insensitive to the situation, nor did he want to display curiosity about Sammy's past life. "Until yesterday, you and Sammy seemed to be strangers."

"I knew who Sammy was. He was never aware of my existence until we took his mules. Even then, he didn't know what I'd done. Once he left Mexico, it took me a little more than nine years to locate him again."

"How did you find him?"

"Looking at drum purchases done either in cash or using cashier's checks. He had a bass drum delivered last week."

"Ingenious," Eduardo said.

"I'd been fed up with the DI for years. They kept me on Sammy's trail. They didn't know I was determined to help him escape. I admired Sammy so much for leaving Cuba's intelligence system. Of course, I was going to leave too. Contact the CIA for witness protection. But the way it played out, I got hurt."

"Sammy could have killed you yesterday, you know."

"Yes," Macario said. "And he had every right."

The nurse came back and said they were ready to wheel Macario into the operating room.

In the hallway, Eduardo told Nikki that Sammy had opened up about his past life. "But he didn't mention the assassin in his house, the one who killed his wife and their children. Maybe Sammy killed him and that's why he forgave Macario."

"For whatever reason, he might have thought it was too painful to bring up. Or the trauma made him forget it."

"Guess now I'll never know," he said.

Nikki said she could see why her husband had taken such a liking to Macario. "I hope he gets into witness protection."

"Speaking of other people, there's something I want to ask you."

Nikki turned to face her husband, as if waiting for him to explain.

"It's about Keiko. Our Japanese housekeeper that took such good care of my mom and me."

"Is she okay?" Nikki asked.

Eduardo nodded.

"Why don't we bring her to Miami to live with us?" Nikki asked. "We don't go to Colombia as often as we thought we would."

"You're amazing." Eduardo kissed Nikki on the lips. "That's exactly what I was going to ask you."

# EIGHTY-FOUR

## NIKKI

Everyone was silent as Floyd drove Nikki, Eduardo, and Clive to the airport in Colorado Springs. Clive would fly with them to the rental property in the Taos Ski Valley. Daniel, the pilot, was on standby. He would take them back as a courtesy for uncovering the spy group.

Nikki knew Andy and his family would meet them at the airport. She also suspected that Clive had not yet considered the part of the case involving Andy to be closed. That could be the reason he was flying them to the rental property. Perhaps Andy was guilty of wrongdoing after all.

Clive mentioned to Eduardo that the police had found a stash of important documents in the clinic of the farmhouse, hidden in a closet under the stairwell. "They turned it over to Steven, my right-hand guy, and he thinks it's a goldmine of evidence."

"I thought all the evidence had burned with the house," Eduardo said.

"The basement was mostly spared."

Eduardo high-fived Clive. He winced as he brushed against the seat. The pain in his back reminded him it was burned.

At the airport, Floyd met them. Neptune wagged his tail. Andy glanced around and asked why Sammy was not with them.

"He disappeared in the middle of the night," Nikki said.

"Disappeared?" Andy asked, alarmed. "What does that mean?"

"For whatever reason, he picked up in the middle of the night and left without checking out," Floyd said, taking a small suitcase from the rental car's trunk and passing it to the pilot. "I'll return the car and be back in ten minutes."

Andy climbed into the back of the helicopter. He could not suppress his tears and probably wanted to be left alone. Cindy pulled herself up while Daniel held Olivia. She took a seat in the middle row, in front of Andy.

"He's dead. I know it," Andy whispered.

"Sammy isn't dead," Nikki said over her shoulder to her brother as she settled into the seat next to the door in the middle row. She placed her purse in the small of her back, against the seat, to make sure her baby Glock was safe.

The pilot handed Olivia to Nikki. She hugged her niece while Cindy snapped the seatbelt into place. Cindy held her arms out and Olivia went to her mother.

Nikki felt sorry for Andy. He was so close to Sammy. His sorrow reminded her of how she'd felt after her son Robbie's death. Her brother had not offered much emotional support when she needed it. She still felt a twinge of anger and hurt from all those years ago, but she could empathize.

From what Eduardo had told her, Sammy had shown total and complete hatred toward Macario, the man who had found them in Mexico City. The same man who had sent an assassin to kill Sammy. Instead, Sammy survived. His wife and twin sons had been killed. Yet Sammy had not taken his chance to avenge them by killing Macario. Apparently he had forgiven the man. He couldn't be such a bad guy, after all, she reasoned.

"He could be dead," Andy emphasized. "If the Cubans have taken him."

"I can assure you Sammy's safe and very much alive." Clive lifted the German shepherd into the back seat of the helicopter. He adjusted his sunglasses before climbing into the front, next to the pilot.

"How do you know?" Andy asked.

Clive turned and looked straight into Andy's eyes. "Just take my word for it."

Eduardo strapped himself in the seat between Nikki and Cindy.

Floyd was the last one to board. He nudged Neptune over a bit and took a seat in the back row with Andy. The German shepherd put his head on Andy's lap.

Once they were all settled, Daniel strapped himself in. Soon they were airborne.

Nikki made a mental note to check out flight school once she and Eduardo were back in Florida.

# EIGHTY-FIVE

## NIKKI

Olivia's cries startled Nikki out of a dream. She had been taking flying lessons. The pilot brought the helicopter down in the front yard of the rental house. When the rotors stopped, Clive and Floyd disembarked and strode toward the house with their guns out.

"Do they expect trouble?" she asked, taking her headset off.

Eduardo reached for her hand. "Everything's fine. They're just being cautious."

The two men went inside the house, returned to the yard, checked the barn, and sauntered back to the chopper.

"Looks safe," Floyd said. "A few thirsty animals in the barn will be happy to see you."

Clive told everyone he needed to speak with them as soon as they got out of the chopper. After that, Andy could check on his lab animals.

Cindy asked if she could be excused. Olivia needed a nap and she wanted to make a pot of coffee for everyone.

Clive took an envelope from his pocket and handed it to Andy. "Your friend was extracted from the hospital for his own safety. Although we believe we've caught all the MSS spies that could cause him harm, we're not certain yet. Sammy will get a new identity and start a new life."

Andy looked aghast.

"Don't fret. He'll be back someday. Told me you're like a brother to him. Said he'll tag bears and help with your research. In the meantime, he asks you and Cindy to get the mules off the Colorado Plains. They were left about fifteen miles from where the Cubans abandoned the trucks and trailers. These are registered to the LLC, so they belong to you. The ranch is for you and your family to use as you see fit. He explained it all in the letter."

Andy shook his head. "Hey, Sis, did you hear that? The CIA is taking care of Sammy."

"Why didn't you tell me he was CIA?" Nikki asked, turning away from her brother to keep her anger from showing.

"I couldn't," Andy whispered. "I had to keep my brother's secret." He walked toward the barn, leaving the others behind.

Eduardo turned to Clive. "I don't get it. After we escaped through the tunnel, Sammy confessed that he'd worked at Los Alamos and had spied there for the Cuban government. Told me that at one point, he regretted it and asked the CIA if he could serve them as a double agent. They'd said no and he went to Mexico where he hid out until a group of Cubans caught up with him. Macario included, obviously. He told me they'd murdered his wife and twin boys."

"There's a lot of truth to what he told you," Clive said, rubbing his hands together, "but he was a double agent from the start. He gave you the version of his history that he thought prudent. To keep you safe in case the spies interrogated you."

"Why didn't he tell me the full truth?"

"Like I said, to keep you safe," Clive said. "I can't reveal too much more but when he accepted a job at Los Alamos, a Cuban spotter passed Sammy's information to a Cuban intelligence officer who approached him with an offer. Sammy, not his name then, went straight to the CIA and told them about the deal the DI offered him. Said he could become a double agent, working for his own country, or he would leave the job at Los Alamos to get rid of Cuban recruitment officers. He would not deal in treason."

"Why did he go to Mexico?" Eduardo asked. "He told me that's where his family was killed."

"We sent him there because the Cubans suspected he was giving them disinformation. He met Ana, they married, and after a few years in his new life, they found him. He was known then as Carlos Torres. They killed his family, but we extracted him before they could grab him."

"Wait a minute," Eduardo said. "He told me he'd met a woman in Santa Fe and that's why he went to Mexico."

"That was part of the background story. He met Ana in Mexico City, and they had twin boys."

"And he came back here?" Nikki asked in an incredulous tone. "Wasn't that dangerous?"

"Yes and no. He'd had another identity change. A complete overhaul, I would call it. He did not look or sound like the same man. He's done that twice now and I'm afraid he's going to do it again. He's caught several foreign spies, handlers, and given us good intel. It's no coincidence that he was kidnapped. I'm sorry you got caught up in it."

Nikki thought it all made sense now. The only issue that still troubled her was that Andy had tried to rescue Sammy. Even when he knew Sammy was an operative or had been one. When would her brother learn to take care of his own family?

Clive explained that Andy and his family would receive protection until it was determined they were safe.

"Must they relocate?" Nikki asked.

"We don't think so, but time will tell."

Nikki headed to the barn. To talk with her brother. Just the two of them. The rest of the group, including the pilot, went to the house.

She found Andy reading Sammy's letter. Giving him space, she stood at the doorway and glanced at the shadow she cast on the earthen floor.

"I'll be managing the mule farm," Andy said, walking toward her.

"What about the lab animals?"

"Cindy and I can take care of everything. The current grant for the bear project will end in another year and a half. That gives me two seasons and I might hire someone to help me."

Andy's eyes met Nikki's.

"I'm not good with words," he said, "but I'm sorry."

She looked perplexed. "Eduardo survived."

"I mean about Robbie. When he died. I couldn't deal with his death. It was such a shock. The only way I could cope was by ignoring it. Then I caused Eduardo's abduction. That was my fault. I was impetuous and irresponsible. I acted against Sammy's wishes. He told me that if anything happened to him, to let it be. Told me not to get involved."

Nikki looked up at him. "I felt you didn't understand my pain."

Andy hugged her. "I did feel it, but I couldn't express it."

He asked her to help him feed and water the lab animals. They spent the next half hour tending to the cages and making sure the 'roo rats and chipmunks were behaving normally.

"I'll call my veterinarian to check on these guys. I'll also clean the cages tomorrow," Andy said, "but for now let's join Cindy and everyone in the house."

"Good idea," Nikki said. "Life needs to return to normal."

# EIGHTY-SIX

## NIKKI

"The lab animals are doing well despite being on their own for three days," Nikki announced.

She and Andy joined the others in the kitchen. She took her fedora off and set it on a hat rack near the door.

"Never dreamed when we flew out here we'd encounter a fire raging in the wilderness. A fire that set off such a series of events. Evacuation, stolen mules, kidnapped people, mercenary spies, the CIA, the FBI. Not the kind of vacation we wanted. I never lost hope, but I did lose a lot of sleep."

She nuzzled Eduardo. He put his arm around her waist, brushed strands of hair off her face, and kissed her lightly. "You're going to lose sleep tonight too," he whispered in her ear as he squeezed her tightly.

"I'm feeling optimistic again," she said, smiling at her husband.

Across the room, Andy handed Sammy's letter to Cindy. She read it aloud.

Dear Cindy, Andy, and Olivia,

You are family to me and I'm sorry that the duties of my

primary job have interfered with my ability to live near you, but I remain a steadfast member of this family unit.

The ranch and greenhouse, my beloved drums and mules are yours to do with as you choose. I know Neptune will be happy with you. If you go to that special drum I told you about, Andy, you will find a bag of seeds, part of the yield from the farm, and you will need to plant them to grow feed for the mules. Please, Brother, go there ASAP.

I hope Nikki and Eduardo will forgive me for all the trouble that came their way because of me. Someday I'll make good on my promise to take them to the hermit's cave.

Don't look for me. I will find you when the time is right. Whisper in the bears' ears that I will return to help with the study. I truly believe the future of humankind in space depends on the ability to hibernate across the cosmos.

I love you all,

Sammy


Cindy wiped her eyes. "I shouldn't be sad. Sammy would not want that." She folded and pocketed the letter. She asked the group to help themselves to coffee and cookies.

They sat around the kitchen table. Sammy was the topic of conversation.

Nikki, still trying to fill in the gaps on Sammy's life, asked her brother what Sammy really was doing on those trips to Spain.

"Oh, he never traveled overseas," Andy said. "He had no passport."

"What about a driver's license?" she asked.

"That's in the name of Adolfo Sanchez, but he tried not to use it."

Eduardo wanted to know what Sammy did when he was away under the guise of being in Spain.

"That I don't know. Meeting with people, handing over information, work, whatever."

Eduardo looked askance at his brother-in-law. "Come on, I think you can tell us. After all, he's not in danger right now."

"I don't know. Seriously. Even I don't know everything about Sammy. I think Sammy keeps secrets from himself too."

Floyd, changing the topic, grilled Andy and Cindy about the study of hibernation in the lab animals and the bears. Andy turned his computer on and pulled up photos of bears hibernating in caves. He also checked on the fire that was still raging through the Pecos Wilderness and had spread to the Carson National Forest. It was now the largest fire in New Mexico's history.

"Looks like we'll stay at the rental property for another month," Andy said. "The good news is that Peñasco is holding on. They've built a shelter for people who've lost their homes in the Mora Valley."

Nikki knew that her brother had provided a donation for the shelter the morning that deputy had stopped by the house. That morning she thought he might arrest Andy for possession of Sammy's pickup. But the truck was most likely registered to the limited liability corporation, and the LLC was in her brother's name. Andy had owned that pickup all along.

Cindy was animated as she explained a slideshow of female bears and their cubs to Floyd. "They have implanted chips. I hope Andy will be able to find them this winter. The fires may force them to move too far away."

Floyd seemed enthralled with the slideshows.

Neptune laid down between Cindy and Floyd. With Olivia asleep in the other room, the German shepherd must have felt lonely without anyone to give him attention.

"Too bad it's the wrong season." Floyd chewed on a toothpick and scratched Neptune's head. "I'd love to trek into the caves and help for a couple of days."

"I doubt Milena would like you doing that," Nikki said.

Floyd agreed that his wife would not want him that close to wild bears.

"Is there anything we can do to help while we're still here?" Eduardo asked.

Andy suggested they take their vacation since he and Cindy could handle everything at the rented ranch.

"As an alternative to seeing bears in caves," Nikki gushed to Floyd, "why don't you join Eduardo and me in Chaco Canyon. We have five days before Eduardo needs to be at work in Florida."

Eduardo interrupted Nikki.

"After talking with Sammy," he said, "I'd rather see Los Alamos. Plus, the scenery is supposed to be spectacular there and in nearby Ghost Ranch."

Nikki's eyes lit up. She touched her world tree pendant. "Ghost Ranch? Isn't that where Georgia O'Keeffe painted? Let's go. Floyd, why don't you join us?"

"How about coming out with me to catch the mules?" Andy asked, offering yet another choice.

"On the Colorado prairie? Are you serious?" Floyd asked.

"Absolutely. I can use some good help." Andy glanced at his wife. "Do you want to go mule catching?"

Cindy begged off by saying someone had to take care of the lab animals. "Besides, Olivia would be difficult to handle on the prairie."

"Does anyone else want the adventure of catching wild mules?" Andy laughed. "Out on the prairie, they'll become feral in no time."

"Sounds like fun, but I have another job I'm committed to," Clive said. "Whoever wants to go, the chopper can drop you off at the trailers. You can unhitch one of the trucks and drive around until you catch a mule or two."

Floyd looked as if he were thinking as he chewed on the toothpick. "We can ride the first couple of mules out to gather the rest," he said. "Then we can herd them all to the trailers."

"Or the trailers can come to the mules," Andy said.

"That'd take the fun out of it," Floyd said.

"Who's in?" Andy asked.

Floyd chewed on the toothpick for a few seconds longer and nodded slowly. "I'll do it."

# EIGHTY-SEVEN

## CLIVE

"Before you start anything on the prairie, you should pick up those seeds," Clive said to Andy.

"The mule farm is near Peñasco. That can wait."

"The helicopter's available. Let's leave right now and we'll return here before we search for the mules." Clive took his aviator glasses from his shirt pocket and put them on. "Let's do it."

Cindy said a late lunch would be ready when they returned from Sammy's farm, and it gave her time to prepare food and drink for the prairie crew to take with them. She would get the sleeping bags out too. She asked for Neptune to stay with her and Olivia. His wound was getting better, but they had to avoid infection. Alicia, her friend in Taos, could stay with her. Just to make sure her sleepwalking did not cause an issue while Andy was away.

"You'll need this if you're to catch mules on the prairie," Andy said. He handed Floyd a cowboy hat.

Clive asked if anyone else wanted to go. Daniel was the first to rise, but whether he wanted to go or not, he was the pilot. He was committed.

Nikki, Eduardo, Andy, and Floyd stood. Nikki grabbed her fedora on the way out.

"Where's yours?" she asked Eduardo.

"Lost it on the prairie."

"Maybe we'll find it."

"I'd rather have a new one."

Clive, right behind them, offered a front seat view to Eduardo.

"I'd like that," he said, taking the seat next to Daniel.

They arrived at Sammy's cabin in no time and climbed out of the chopper. Andy took them straight to Sammy's soundproof music room. He pointed to the hand drum in the corner. A Native American one with rawhide on both sides and a two-tone buffalo emblem on the log-like wooden frame.

Clive picked it up and examined it. He shook it but there was no sound.

"To play it, you tap on the rawhide," Andy said.

"I'm trying to see if the seeds are inside." Clive handed the drum to Andy. "Why don't you open it up?"

Andy turned it over a couple of times. He pulled on a rawhide sinew cord. It unraveled like pulling a loose string on an item of clothing. Lifting the dry drumhead, he and Clive saw a brown paper bag on the inside of the hollow log frame.

He pulled the paper bag, but it did not budge. Pulling harder, it broke loose. Hundred-dollar bills fell out, like confetti, covering the floor.

Clive laughed. "Best damned seeds I've ever seen. Did you know what you were going to find?"

Andy shook his head. "Seeds for the greenhouse, not money."

Clive studied his expression. "How much do you suppose is here?"

Andy shrugged. "No clue."

Clive picked a few up and checked for the 3-D blue line to make sure the bills were authentic. They were.

"Do you want to take them to the bank to verify it's not stolen cash?" Nikki asked.

"That's difficult to do on this amount. If it were millions, yes."

"How much is here, do you think?" she asked.

"Somewhere between eighty and one hundred thousand," Clive said.

Andy put little stacks of bills on a side table and stretched out the paper that still had a few bills tucked in it. "Says here that it should roughly be one hundred thousand."

"Not bad seed money," Clive said.

"I'll use what I need to run the mule farm, but it's Sammy's money. He earned it from the mules. And I'll keep good books. That way, when he returns, he'll know where it was spent. With luck, I should increase the value of the farm operation in the next few years. As long as people are interested in buying good mules."

"Are you going to keep it all in cash?" Nikki asked, looking at the pile of bills.

"Naw, too dangerous. I'll slowly deposit it as I have transactions." Andy turned to Clive. "Unless you need to take the money because you think it's illegal. In that case, you can have it."

"I've known Sammy longer than you have. I've found him to be an honest guy. Keep the money for running the farm."

"If we're through here," Nikki said, cocking her hat to one side, "let's get on with the wild mule adventure."

# A NOTE FROM KATHRYN

Thank you for reading *Rage in the Wilderness*, the fifth novel in the **Nikki Garcia Mystery Series**. If you enjoyed it, I'd very much appreciate a review on Amazon, BookBub, and Goodreads so that other readers may also find Nikki's adventures.

**Amazon:**
https://www.amazon.com/dp/B0CRTH1Q47?maas=maas_adg_A284B3E8DEA2CFC118E-F79A3EC5E68E7_afap_abs&ref_=aa_maas&tag=maas

**BookBub:**
https://www.bookbub.com/profile/kathryn-lane

**Goodreads:**
https://www.goodreads.com/author/show/15096935.Kathryn_Lane?clear_facebook_session=true

**Newsletter:**
If you'd like to learn about my new releases, sales, and giveaways,

A NOTE FROM KATHRYN

please sign up for my newsletter at https://www.kathryn-lane.com.
Email: KathrynLaneAuthor@gmail.com

**Follow me on social media:**
Instagram: https://www.instagram.com/kathrynlaneauthor/
Facebook: https://www.facebook.com/kathrynlanewriter/
X (formerly Twitter): https://twitter.com/KathrynLane13

Happy reading,
**Kathryn Lane**

ALSO BY KATHRYN LANE

**The Nikki Garcia Mystery Series**
*Waking Up in Medellin*
*Danger in the Coyote Zone*
*Revenge in Barcelona*
*Missing in Miami*
*Rage in the Wilderness*

**Audiobook:** *Waking Up in Medellin*
**Box Set:** *The Nikki Garcia Mystery Series: Box Set*
**Translated into Spanish:** *Despertando en Medellín*

**Other Books by Kathryn Lane**
*Stolen Diary*
*Backyard Volcano and Other Mysteries of the Heart*

# AWARDS AND PRAISE FOR KATHRYN'S BOOKS

### WAKING UP IN MEDELLIN (A NIKKI GARCIA THRILLER)

***Waking Up in Medellin*** was named "Best Fiction Book of the Year—2017" by the Killer Nashville International Mystery Writers' Conference and won Killer Nashville's "Best Fiction—Adult Suspense—2017." It was also a finalist for the Roné Award.

### DANGER IN THE COYOTE ZONE (A NIKKI GARCIA MYSTERY)

***Danger in the Coyote Zone*** won first place in the 2018 Action/Adventure Category of the Latino Books into Movies Award. It was named a finalist in both the 2018 Book Excellence Awards and the thriller category at the 2018 Killer Nashville International Mystery Writers' Conference.

### REVENGE IN BARCELONA (A NIKKI GARCIA MYSTERY)

***Revenge in Barcelona*** won first place in the Latino Books into Movies—Latino themed TV series category 2020 and a silver medal in the Reader Views Literary Awards mystery category 2020. It was a finalist in the Eric Hoffer 2020 Book Awards, the Silver Falchion in suspense by Killer Nashville, the suspense category by Next Generation Book Awards, and the 2020

International Latino Book Awards. It was also awarded five stars by Readers' Favorite.

## MISSING IN MIAMI (NIKKI GARCIA MYSTERY #4)

First Place
Award Winner

***Missing in Miami*** is the winner of the 2022 International Latino Book Awards, Best eBook Fiction. It received honorable mention in the 2022 International Latino Book Awards for best novel, mystery. It was noted as a distinguished favorite in the mystery category of the NYC Big Book Award and a finalist in Readers' Favorite, fiction-mystery-general.

## STOLEN DIARY (A COMING-OF-AGE MYSTERY)

***Stolen Diary*** is the winner of the 2023 National Association of Independent Writers and Editors Book Awards Contest in the Genre Book category, and the winner of the 2023 National Indie Excellence Award for general fiction.

## BACKYARD VOLCANO AND OTHER MYSTERIES OF THE HEART (SHORT STORY COLLECTION)

***Backyard Volcano and Other Mysteries of the Heart*** was named "Best Short Story Collection—2018" by the Killer Nashville International Mystery Writers' Conference.

# ACKNOWLEDGEMENTS

I am indebted to countless individuals, many of them from book clubs I visit, who ask for more Nikki Garcia adventures and sequels to Jasmin's story and suggest future locations to set them in. Their enthusiasm for my work motivates me to continue writing. The list runs too long to include them all. Those who contributed directly to *Rage in the Wilderness* are listed here.

My incredible husband, Bob Hurt, not only supports my writing but also participates in many of my writing activities. Coincidentally, he happens to be my most enthusiastic fan.

I am deeply indebted to James M. Olson, professor of the practice emeritus at Texas A&M University's Bush School of Government and Public Service, and former chief of counterintelligence at the CIA, who generously discussed various aspects of espionage and suggested topics for my research.

I am grateful to Robert Moore (nobob3200) for sharing his expertise on information gathering, including the interception of electronic signals.

I thank Amber and Richard Kingbury, who graciously taught me a lot about mules during a one-day demonstration using their own gorgeous herd. They made a mule lover out of me!

Thanks to Michael Savana, who provided information on Cheyenne Mountain and its surroundings to help me describe the location.

Cheers and appreciation to Sharon Sorensen, who set up research meetings for me with experts in the intelligence field that added fresh insights to my online research.

I owe gratitude to Billy "Drummer Boy" Mangus for the information he shared with me about percussion drums.

I am deeply indebted to my expert readers, Pattie Hogan, David R. Stafseth, and Jorge Lane Terrazas, for their hard work in reviewing the manuscript and the feedback they offered.

Dr. Lowell Mick White, who generously guided my early efforts to write, please accept my deepest gratitude.

To my Houston Writers' Group—thank you.

Special thanks to my editor, Sandra A. Spicher. And thanks to Tim Barber for the cover design, Danielle Hartman Acee for the book interior, and Maureen Donelan for the logo of Tortuga Publishing, LLC.

And to my readers, friends, and fans—I could not do it without you!

***Kathryn Lane***
February 8, 2024

# ABOUT THE AUTHOR

Kathryn Lane is the award-winning author of the *Nikki Garcia Mystery Series* and *Stolen Diary* and short stories.

In her writing, she draws deeply from her experiences growing up in a small town in northern Mexico as well as her work and travel in over ninety countries around the globe during her career in international finance with Johnson & Johnson.

Kathryn and her husband, Bob Hurt, split their time between Texas and northern New Mexico, where the mountain scenery inspires her to write.

Kathryn's Website
Kathryn-lane.com

amazon.com/-/e/B01D0J1YES
bookbub.com/authors/kathryn-lane
goodreads.com/kathrynlane
facebook.com/kathrynlanewriter

Made in the USA
Middletown, DE
24 April 2024

53446588R00165